Thirteen Stories by Eudora Welty

By Eudora Welty

THIRTEEN STORIES

Selected and with an Introduction by Ruth M. Vande Kieft

BY EUDORA WELTY

A Harvest/HBJ Book
Harcourt Brace Jovanovich, Publishers
San Diego   New York   London

Contents

v

Thirteen Stories by Eudora Welty

Introduction

This volume contains a selection of representative and enduring stories written by Eudora Welty over a period of some twenty-five years.

Miss Welty's training in her craft was the sort described by Robert Frost as taking place "cavalierly and as it happens in and out of books." Her father, originally from Ohio, was president of a Southern insurance company, and her mother was a West Virginian of Virginia stock; they were kindly and understanding parents. A sensitive and imaginative girl, she grew up in a free and easy way in Jackson, Mississippi, attending the public schools, reading omnivorously, fancying for a number of years that she wanted to be a painter. Following her graduation from Central High School in Jackson, she spent two years at Mississippi State College for Women, in Columbus, and another two at the University of Wisconsin, where as an English major she began a more concentrated study of literature. After having received a Bachelor of Arts degree in 1929, she enrolled in the School of Business at Columbia University in order to study advertising. But the Depression had begun; she was unable to find suitable employment, and soon returned to Mississippi. For the next nine years she worked at various jobs in advertising and publicity, as well as at her own writing. Her first full-time job was with the Works Progress Administration; as a publicity assistant, she traveled all over Mississippi, writing newspaper copy, taking photographs, observing, talking to all sorts of people, and so acquiring material for many of her stories.

She offered to various New York publishers a group of unposed photographs of Negro life, "thinking or hoping," she later said, "if they liked my pictures (which I thought were fine) they might be inclined to take my stories (which I felt very dubious about, but I *wondered* about them—they being what I cared about), but they weren't decoyed. Once a year for three or four years I carried around the two bundles under my arm on my two weeks' trip to New York, and carried them home again—not much downcast, perhaps because all the time I simply loved writing, and was going to do it anyway."

She had already been successful, however, in getting her work into magazines. Her first story appeared in a "little magazine" named *Manuscript* in 1936, and within three years Robert Penn Warren and Cleanth Brooks, editors of the influential *Southern Review*, published six other stories, including three in the present collection: "Old Mr. Marblehall," "Petrified Man," and "The Hitch-Hikers." Soon "A Worn Path," "Why I Live at the P.O.," and "Powerhouse" appeared in *The Atlantic Monthly*. Her first collection of stories, *A Curtain of Green*, was published in 1941, with a preface by Katherine Anne Porter; a short novel, *The Robber Bridegroom*, followed in 1942, and her second collection of stories, *The Wide Net*, in 1943. *Delta Wedding*, a full-length novel, appeared in 1946; *The Golden Apples*, a book of connected stories, in 1949; *The Bride of the Innisfallen*, a miscellaneous collection, in 1955; and *The Ponder Heart*, another short novel, in 1954.

In 1942 and in 1943, Miss Welty received first prize O. Henry Memorial awards for "The Wide Net" and "Livvie"; she held two Guggenheim Fellowships, and *The Ponder Heart* won her the William Dean Howells medal awarded by the American Academy of Arts and

Letters for "the most distinguished work of American fiction during the period from 1950-1955." She was elected to the National Institute of Arts and Letters in 1952, and has been an Honorary Consultant of the Library of Congress. Although she makes public appearances, both lecturing and reading her stories, and now and again contributes her perceptive criticism to various magazines and reviews, she is generally out of the public eye, warmly admired by her friends, quietly dedicated to the practice of her art.

The dominant characteristics of Miss Welty's fiction are the lyrical impulse that provides its inciting force and unity, the emphasis on place that gives it focus, and the scope and experimentation that lend it variety.

In an essay called "How I Write," she has supplied her own answer to the question, "Where do the stories come from?" The source is the lyrical impulse—"the impulse to praise, to love, to call up, to prophesy." It is "the outside signal that has startled or moved the creative mind to complicity and brought the story to active being: the irresistible, the magnetic, the alarming (pleasurable or disturbing), the overwhelming person, place, or thing." Her stories may be viewed, then, as celebrations of so many pieces of life with "the mysteries rushing unsubmissively through them by the minute": life not so much analyzed and interpreted as rendered and wondered at, perhaps because what is shown is extraordinary, perhaps because it is simply ordinary.

There is no end, she seems to show us—now hilariously and now gravely—to the surprises and horrors in life. Children, like those in "Moon Lake," are always stumbling on them: it is because Miss Welty has retained something of the child's fresh and ingenuous view that impressions of beauty and pain are made so indelibly through her stories. Among these stories the reader will find some of her extraordinary, monolithic characters: Powerhouse, master of fantasy conveyed through music; Phoenix, with her eternally young and faithful old Heart; Lorenzo Dow, Murrell, and Audubon, each driven by his own vision, each with his burning mission. And then there are the ordinary ones: Mr.

Marblehall, quietly making war with public indifference by conjuring up his own shocking double life; Livvie, too young to remain queen in Solomon's palace, tending the old man's wintry retirement; William Wallace, who must recover his wife by encountering the mysteries of life and birth in the depths of the Pearl River; and that whole collection of perfectly ordinary women who turn into Medusas before our eyes in Leota's beauty parlor. The universe is dazzling and fearful, and people are remarkable. The next hitchhiker you pick up may murder his fellow in your car; the "outcast Indian Maiden," whose savagery you exposed to a credulous public, may turn out to be an innocent and uncomprehending little clubfooted Negro, and leave you with an unhealed heart and a heavy burden of guilt; and the wonderful man from Connemara is bound to pop up like a Jack-in-the-box with his explosive *"Oh* my God!" about some small thing or other.

All these are human concerns for celebration by a lyricist in prose. So also is each sensuous detail of the natural world, the breath and texture of atmosphere, the color and perfume of flowers and foliage, the brightness or dimness of weather, the slow changes of the seasons and years and times of life, and the folk rituals that mark those changes. The crises produced by the unpredictable event, the outrageous act, the accident, the chance meeting, the sudden tragedy are counterpointed in Miss Welty's fiction by the larger, steadying rhythms of nature and human feeling. We may gasp in terror or delight, but then we go on breathing just the same.

Feeling, the lyrical impulse, is the presiding angel who, according to Miss Welty, "carries the crown" for the writer of fiction; place, or setting, however, she calls one of fiction's most important "lesser angels." It is clearly a guardian of her own art. In an essay called "Place in Fiction," she has argued convincingly for its significance. She demonstrates how place provides not only a region or setting for a story, but also a means of fixing it to what is known, recognizable, concrete in the everyday world. Feelings and associations attach themselves to places, which have a more lasting identity than individual human beings. "Place in fiction," she says, "is the named, identified, concrete, exact and exacting, and therefore credible, gathering-spot of all that has been felt, is about to be experienced. . . ." It serves to focus the vision of the writer, to assist him in convincing the reader that the fictional lie is the world's reality, to aid him in capturing and disclosing the more subtle and elusive of human thoughts and feelings that need pinning down. Place is like the "steadily visible" surface, the carefully painted scene on the outside of the old china night light, which alight becomes excitingly "the combination of internal and external, glowing at the imagination as one." Such a use of place for Miss Welty does not result in merely "regional" fiction, for the regional, though everywhere present, is to be transcended: the whole concept of local color would have been alien to Cervantes, Jane Austen, Emily Brontë, Turgenev, or the writers of the Old Testament, who simply wrote of what they knew. "It seems plain," she concludes, "that the art that speaks most clearly, explicitly, directly, and passionately from its place of origin will remain the longest understood. It is through place that we put out roots, wherever birth, chance, fate, or our traveling selves set us down; but where those roots reach toward . . . is the deep and running vein, eternal and consistent and everywhere purely itself —that feeds and is fed by the human understanding."

Miss Welty's own place is, of course, Mississippi—its towns and countryside, its red clay farms and hills, its pine forests, lakes, rivers, and Delta bottoms. Pre-eminently, in the stories of this collection, it is the Natchez Trace, a path originally carved out of the wilderness by animals, later followed by Indians, and then literally deepened into the forest bed as it was traveled by rivermen making their way home after coming down the Mississippi, by traders, pioneers, settlers, mail carriers, cutting northeast upward from Natchez toward Nashville, Tennessee. It is on this ancient Trace, in pioneer times, that we find evangelist Lorenzo Dow riding his horse at top speed to encounter two other actual historical characters, the outlaw James Murrell and the naturalist John James Audubon, the three converging on the wilderness floor for their "still moment" of private revelation—Miss Welty's purely imaginary addition to an actuality already mysterious and legendary. It is away up on the old abandoned Trace that Solomon carries Livvie to his "nice house" in the country; it is the Trace that William Wallace and his entourage follow, on their way to the Pearl River, in "The Wide Net"; it is from back off the Trace that Phoenix makes her "worn path," and her destination is Natchez, the "little party-giving town" where Old Mr. Marblehall is leading his fantastic double life.

Whether or not they are fictional, Miss Welty's place names always sound right: that is, both probable and improbable, according to the vagaries of history and humanity. And this is symptomatic of the larger and more important rightness that derives from the happy fusion of imaginative vision and actuality of place in her fiction. Place has given the social accuracy, including its comic vitality, to those of her stories that present Southern towns and clans, such as "Lily Daw and the Three Ladies" and "The Wide Net." She has described certain of her stories, such as "Petrified Man" and "Why I Live at the P.O.," as having been written "by ear." That acutely tuned ear has caught the speech of a way of life, of a set of shared and yet subtly various social traditions, prejudices, interests, problems, human reactions, as well as private foibles and idiosyncrasies, flashes of sheer oddness, perversity, or humor, which continually surprise us by their freshness and convince us by their fidelity. The dialogue in many of the stories begs to be read aloud. The rhythms and idioms, and a rhetoric at once plain and fancy, economical and elaborate, bend the most recalcitrant accents and intonations to a gossipy Southern loquaciousness that is at the same time dreadful, funny, and touching.

The last story in this collection, which is set in Ireland, demonstrates again the importance of place to Miss Welty's fiction. It does so in that a specific locality (one among others in which her "traveling self" set her down) helps to define the thoughts and reactions of a young American wife who is temporarily running away from her husband in London, because of a strange and elusive "trouble" with him. Everything that she sees and experiences on her trip to Ireland and on her ramblings through glorious, fresh, wildly funny, dazzlingly lovely Cork (so it registers for her) explains both to us and to her what her "trouble" has been with her husband: something like an excess of hope, joy, and wonder at the glory and mystery of human life, epitomized in her vision of the young bride. Subtle emotions are still conveyed to a large extent by a place and the people belonging to it, though the place happens to be Ireland, not Mississippi.

A remarkable fact about these stories is that in their subjects, themes, tone, form, and technique, they do not easily lend themselves to generalizations. Speaking of stories by other writers, Miss Welty says that a reader should regard each one as an entity, a "little world in space, just as we can isolate one star in the sky by a concentrated vision." Readers of her own stories will differ about which stars are of greater and which of lesser magnitude, but they are bound to find the range wide, from a vigorous levity to the terror of hallucination or the sweet pain of the heart's secrets. Each reader will find some constellations of his own. He may notice, for one thing, that though the stories as a whole include various sorts of comedy, tragedy, satire, and fantasy, most characteristically these elements are blended within individual stories. No reader, one hopes, will allow his pleasure in the delicious comedy of "Lily Daw and the Three Ladies" and "Why I Live at the P.O." to be diminished by somber reflections on feeble-mindedness and paranoia. But "Petrified Man," though grotesquely funny in its scenes, characterizations, and dialogue, is actually a caustic satire on woman's inhumanity to man and the vulgarity and perversity of a certain kind of city life. "Moon Lake," "The Hitch-Hikers," "The Wide Net," "The Worn Path," "Powerhouse" have their elements of pathos, and threaten, at various stages, to turn into tragedy. Yet the interplay of light and shadow is continuous; the weather shifts; the tone modulates, slowly or swiftly; and nothing is exactly as we expected it to be, except that in our bones we feel that it is very much like life—full of the fluctuations we are born to in an odd, painful, and exciting universe, in which dreams are always colliding with reality or embroidering it; the grotesque lies close to the lovely; and comedy always borders on tragedy or pathos. Powerhouse instinctively knows this when he picks something awful out of the air ("I got a telegram my wife is dead"), teases and plays with it ("Truth is something worse, I ain't said what yet. It's something hasn't come to me, but I ain't saying it won't. And when it does, then want me to tell you?"), masters it, puts it *in the world*, in his fantastic art. And so does his creator.

Miss Welty's central and universal concern is the mystery of the inner life. "Relationship *is* a pervading and changing mystery," she has said; "it is not words that make it so in life, but words have to make it so in a story. Brutal or lovely, the mystery waits for people wherever they go, whatever extreme they run to." "Mystery" here suggests the enigma of man's being, and his relation to the universe; it suggests also what is concealed, secret, inviolable in human beings, putting up the barriers, making our meaning and identity puzzling to ourselves. This particular theme is explored beautifully and poignantly in the story "A Still Moment," in which evangelist, murderer, and naturalist share a common and yet disparate revelation of nature, looking at a snowy heron. Lorenzo's shattering illumination, that "God had . . . given Love first and then Separateness, as though it did not matter to Him which came first," sums up the yearning love of human beings, their desire for response and understanding, and the fundamental solitude experienced by many of the characters in these stories. They are poised alone; no other creature can fathom their hidden selves. Tom Harris of "The Hitch-Hikers" is one of these puzzled and lonely men, a generous sort, but rootless. His life is full of giving yet empty of permanent commitment; his love is freely floating yet weary, desolate. Moral loneliness, the burden of an inexpiable guilt that no one will recognize, afflicts Steve in "Keela, the Outcast Indian Maiden." Mr. Marblehall's is the loneliness of being ignored, and Livvie's the loneliness of physical and emotional isolation from the world in which she naturally belongs. Livvie returns to life (the original title of that story was "Livvie Is Back"), and Old Phoenix is never for a moment really lost, even though her senses are dimmed with age and memory betrays her briefly when she reaches the end of her worn path. But not everyone is so harmonious as Phoenix, so lucky as Livvie.

Although Miss Welty's theme is the pervading and changing mystery of human relationships, her technique is adapted to the tone and the disclosures of each individual story. In her projection of the constant interplay between the inner world of feelings and dreams and fantasies and the external world of event and social reality, she has employed a variety of fictional points of view. In many instances she penetrates the minds and feelings of her characters intuitively. Young Nina in "Moon Lake" reflects that "it's only interesting, only worthy, to try for the fiercest secrets. To slip into them all—to change. To change for a moment into Gertrude, into Mrs. Gruenwald, into Twosie—into a boy. To *have been* an orphan." Just so, as narrator, Miss Welty changes into a host of characters, most of them possessed of a psychological depth and complexity that seem to be independent of rational intelligence. Sometimes the narrator turns herself over completely to the speaker, as in the monologue of "Why I Live at the P.O."; sometimes her method is largely dramatic—a few scenes swiftly drawn, stage directions and dialogue—as in "Petrified Man," "Lily Daw and the Three Ladies," and "Keela, the Outcast Indian Maiden." In "Powerhouse" she assumes the implicitly collective point of view of the jazz musician's fascinated audience, abandons herself to the fantasy observed and created, and sweeps us along through an approximation, in prose, of the form and moods of the music that is being played. Sometimes she begins her stories as observer, with straightforward exposition and close description; then, because we already know so much from the outside, we

scarcely notice when she slips into the mind of a character, or as quietly slips out again, in a graceful and natural alternation of scene and summary, interior monologue and dialogue, fact and fantasy. The transitions are
unobtrusive because the style, the figures of speech, and
the rhythms are usually of a piece with the rich sim-
plicity of the characters. Motive is frequently suggested
by way of metaphor—abundant, deft, sparkling. Folk
expressions appear frequently.

Style is one of the greatest sources of delight in these
stories. Light and pure as air, searching, hovering, elusive, it has also a freshness and vigor that provide the
substance, the matter-of-fact quality of the atmosphere
we breathe. Miss Welty's pleasure in variety and experimentation is apparent from the contrast between the
artless clairvoyance of such early stories as "The Worn
Path" and "Livvie" and the subtle impressionism of a
much later story, "The Bride of the Innisfallen."
Whether her style is direct or oblique, simple or com-
plex, always she delights us with a fresh performance, a
new creation.

Symbol and myth also have their uses in these stories.
In a symbol, as Carlyle said, "there is concealment and
yet revelation"; thus Miss Welty's fiction naturally in-
cludes symbols, because they embody and enhance the
mysteries she seeks out. Yet no detail of action, charac-
terization, or name is distorted or denatured for the
sake of a symbolic point; symbols appear unobtrusively
because they are born into the material. In her work
symbols function quietly, contributing to the form and
the poetic density of the stories, deepening and enrich-
ing their surface meanings.

Miss Welty is as wary of symbol-hunting as she is of
schematization. "The analyst," she mildly protests,
"should the story come under his eye, may miss this
gentle shock and this pleasure too, for he's picked up
the story at once by its heels (as if it had swallowed a
button), and is examining the writing as his own process in reverse, as though a story (or any system of
feeling) could be accessible for being upside down."
Not that she is opposed to analysis; she seems only to

be asking that the stories be met with the openness, the sense of urgency and adventure, with which they were created.

In short, reading a story by Eudora Welty is not like rowing across a lake, with your destination on the other side dimly or clearly perceived. It is more like climbing into a small, well-designed craft, cutting your moorings, and then abandoning yourself to a trip down a changing stream to an unknown point. You have no notion what will happen, but you soon discover that someone with great skill is steering and guiding the craft, determining the pace according to or perhaps despite the current. She seems to say, "Watch, be alert, trust me." The stream rushes and changes; now you are hurtled through foaming rapids and bump against a rock; now you are brushed in the face by an overhanging bough; now you open onto a luminous pool, where the boat dallies and you gaze into quiet depths in which strange hidden life is drifting down under, and maybe, half dreaming, you see your own pensive face reflected on the surface; then you are off again and away. Everywhere there are fearful and pleasing events to shock and surprise; shy, elusive creatures to be detected behind the curtain of green; fascinating details to be seen up, down, and all about. When you reach your destination, *that* may seem, finally, the culmination of your trip; but sometimes you will want to look back and ask, "Where are we now, and what am I to think?" The helmsman, who has never been visible *as a person*, may never answer; and only then you may reflect that the significance of the journey was in the process, and that the parts of the process together make the experience a whole.

If the author of these stories seems to say "trust me," it is for other and perhaps better reasons than craftsmanship, than skill in guiding the reader through the delights and hazards of life by the techniques of fiction. Fundamentally, it is the heart and mind of this writer that are to be trusted. She is more than one of art's faithful disciples: she is one of life's true lovers. Her vision is compassionate, humorous, intelligent, full of a loving detachment, full of poised awareness of and sympathy for her characters. She has a profound respect for their reality *as persons*. They are not manipulated by opinion, they are not roundly judged. They are often celebrated, but rarely condemned, except, as in "Petrified Man," out of the most implicitly humane of moral visions. Starting from the lyrical impulse, taking as her materials her own place and people, and presenting them in her own highly individual style, she explores what is universal in humanity for our relish, our wonder, and our contemplation.

The Wide Net

William Wallace Jamieson's wife Hazel was going to
have a baby. But this was October, and it was six
months away, and she acted exactly as though it would
be tomorrow. When he came in the room she would not
speak to him, but would look as straight at nothing as
she could, with her eyes glowing. If he only touched her
she stuck out her tongue or ran around the table. So
one night he went out with two of the boys down the
road and stayed out all night. But that was the worst
thing yet, because when he came home in the early
morning Hazel had vanished. He went through the
house not believing his eyes, balancing with both hands
out, his yellow cowlick rising on end, and then he
turned the kitchen inside out looking for her, but it did
no good. Then when he got back to the front room he
saw she had left him a little letter, in an envelope. That
was doing something behind someone's back. He took
out the letter, pushed it open, held it out at a distance
from his eyes. . . . After one look he was scared to
read the exact words, and he crushed the whole thing in
his hand instantly, but what it had said was that she
would not put up with him after that and was going to
the river to drown herself.

"Drown herself. . . . But she's in mortal fear of the water!"

He ran out front, his face red like the red of the picked cotton field he ran over, and down in the road he gave a loud shout for Virgil Thomas, who was just going in his own house, to come out again. He could just see the edge of Virgil, he had almost got in, he had one foot inside the door.

They met half-way between the farms, under the shade-tree.

"Haven't you had enough of the night?" asked Virgil. There they were, their pants all covered with dust and dew, and they had had to carry the third man home flat between them.

"I've lost Hazel, she's vanished, she went to drown herself."

"Why, that ain't like Hazel," said Virgil.

William Wallace reached out and shook him. "You heard me. Don't you know we have to drag the river?"

"Right this minute?"

"You ain't got nothing to do till spring."

"Let me go set foot inside the house and speak to my mother and tell her a story, and I'll come back."

"This will take the wide net," said William Wallace. His eyebrows gathered, and he was talking to himself.

"How come Hazel to go and do that way?" asked Virgil as they started out.

William Wallace said, "I reckon she got lonesome."

"That don't argue—drown herself for getting lonesome. My mother gets lonesome."

"Well," said William Wallace. "It argues for Hazel."

"How long is it now since you and her was married?"

"Why, it's been a year."

"It don't seem that long to me. A year!"

"It was this time last year. It seems longer," said William Wallace, breaking a stick off a tree in surprise. They walked along, kicking at the flowers on the road's edge. "I remember the day I seen her first, and that seems a long time ago. She was coming along the road holding a little frying-size chicken from her grandma, under her arm, and she had it real quiet. I spoke to her with nice manners. We knowed each other's names, being bound to, just didn't know each other to speak to. I says, 'Where are you taking the fryer?' and she says, 'Mind your manners,' and I kept on till after while she says, 'If you want to walk me home, take littler steps.' So I didn't lose time. It was just four miles across the field and full of blackberries, and from the top of the hill there was Dover below, looking sizeable-like and clean, spread out between the two churches like that. When we got down, I says to her, 'What kind of water's in this well?' and she says, 'The best water in the world.' So I drew a bucket and took out a dipper and she drank and I drank. I didn't think it was that remarkable, but I didn't tell her."

"What happened that night?" asked Virgil.

"We ate the chicken," said William Wallace, "and it was tender. Of course that wasn't all they had. The night I was trying their table out, it sure had good things to eat from one end to the other. Her mama and papa sat at the head and foot and we was face to face with each other across it, with I remember a pat of butter between. They had real sweet butter, with a tree drawed down it, elegant-like. Her mama eats like a man. I had brought her a whole hat-ful of berries and she didn't even pass them to her husband. Hazel, she would leap up and take a pitcher of new milk and fill up the glasses. I had heard how they couldn't have a singing at the church without a fight over her."

"Oh, she's a pretty girl, all right," said Virgil. "It's a pity for the ones like her to grow old, and get like their mothers."

"Another thing will be that her mother will get wind of this and come after me," said William Wallace.

"Her mother will eat you alive," said Virgil.

"She's just been watching her chance," said William Wallace. "Why did I think I could stay out all night."

"Just something come over you."

"First it was just a carnival at Carthage, and I had to let them guess my weight . . . and after that . . ."

"It was nice to be sitting on your neck in a ditch

singing," prompted Virgil, "in the moonlight. And playing on the harmonica like you can play."

"Even if Hazel did sit home knowing I was drunk,
that wouldn't kill her," said William Wallace. "What she
knows ain't ever killed her yet. . . . She's smart, too,
for a girl," he said.

"She's a lot smarter than her cousins in Beula," said
Virgil. "And especially Edna Earle, that never did get to
be what you'd call a heavy thinker. Edna Earle could sit
and ponder all day on how the little tail of the 'C' got
through the 'L' in a Coca-Cola sign."

"Hazel *is* smart," said William Wallace. They walked
on. "You ought to see her pantry shelf, it looks like a
hundred jars when you open the door. I don't see how
she could turn around and jump in the river."

"It's a woman's trick."

"I always behaved before. Till the one night—last
night."

"Yes, but the one night," said Virgil. "And she was
waiting to take advantage."

"She jumped in the river because she was scared to
death of the water and that was to make it worse," he
said. "She remembered how I used to have to pick her
up and carry her over the oak-log bridge, how she'd
shut her eyes and make a dead-weight and hold me
round the neck, just for a little creek. I don't see how
she brought herself to jump."

"Jumped backwards," said Virgil. "Didn't look."

When they turned off, it was still early in the pink
and green fields. The fumes of morning, sweet and bitter, sprang up where they walked. The insects ticked
softly, their strength in reserve; butterflies chopped the
air, going to the east, and the birds flew carelessly and
sang by fits and starts, not the way they did in the
evening in sustained and drowsy songs.

"It's a pretty *day* for sure," said William Wallace.
"It's a pretty *day* for it."

"I don't see a sign of her ever going along here," said
Virgil.

"Well," said William Wallace. "She wouldn't have

dropped anything. I never saw a girl to leave less signs of where she's been."

"Not even a plum seed," said Virgil, kicking the grass.

In the grove it was so quiet that once William Wallace gave a jump, as if he could almost hear a sound of himself wondering where she had gone. A descent of energy came down on him in the thick of the woods and he ran at a rabbit and caught it in his hands.

"Rabbit . . . Rabbit . . ." He acted as if he wanted to take it off to himself and hold it up and talk to it. He laid a palm against its pushing heart. "Now . . . There now . . ."

"Let her go, William Wallace, let her go." Virgil, chewing on an elderberry whistle he had just made, stood at his shoulder: "What do you want with a live rabbit?"

William Wallace squatted down and set the rabbit on the ground but held it under his hand. It was a little, old, brown rabbit. It did not try to move. "See there?"

"Let her go."

"She can go if she wants to, but she don't want to."

Gently he lifted his hand. The round eye was shining at him sideways in the green gloom.

"Anybody can freeze a rabbit, that wants to," said Virgil. Suddenly he gave a far-reaching blast on the whistle, and the rabbit went in a streak. "Was you out catching cotton-tails, or was you out catching your wife?" he said, taking the turn to the open fields. "I come along to keep you on the track."

"Who'll we get, now?" They stood on top of a hill and William Wallace looked critically over the country-side. "Any of the Malones?"

"I was always scared of the Malones," said Virgil. "Too many of them."

"This is my day with the net, and they would have to watch out," said William Wallace. "I reckon some Malones, and the Doyles, will be enough. The six Doyles and their dogs, and you and me, and two little nigger boys is enough, with just a few Malones."

"That ought to be enough," said Virgil, "no matter what."

"I'll bring the Malones, and you bring the Doyles," said William Wallace, and they separated at the spring.

When William Wallace came back, with a string of Malones just showing behind him on the hilltop, he found Virgil with the two little Rippen boys waiting behind him, solemn little towheads. As soon as he walked up, Grady, the one in front, lifted his hand to signal silence and caution to his brother Brucie who began panting merrily and untrustworthily behind him.

Brucie bent readily under William Wallace's hand-pat, and gave him a dreamy look out of the tops of his round eyes, which were pure green-and-white like clover tops. William Wallace gave him a nickel. Grady hung his head; his white hair lay in a little tail in the nape of his neck.

"Let's let them come," said Virgil.

"Well, they can come then, but if we keep letting everybody come it is going to be too many," said William Wallace.

"They'll appreciate it, those little-old boys," said Virgil. Brucie held up at arm's length a long red thread with a bent pin tied on the end; and a look of helpless and intense interest gathered Grady's face like a draw-string—his eyes, one bright with a sty, shone pleadingly under his white bangs, and he snapped his jaw and tried to speak. . . . "Their papa was drowned in the Pearl River," said Virgil.

There was a shout from the gully.

"Here come all the Malones," cried William Wallace. "I asked four of them would they come, but the rest of the family invited themselves."

"Did you ever see a time when they didn't," said Virgil. "And yonder from the other direction comes the Doyles, still with biscuit crumbs on their cheeks, I bet, now it's nothing to do but eat as their mother said."

"If two little niggers would come along now, or one big nigger," said William Wallace. And the words were hardly out of his mouth when two little Negro boys came along, going somewhere, one behind the other, stepping high and gay in their overalls, as though they waded in honeydew to the waist.

"Come here, boys. What's your names?"

"Sam and Robbie Bell."

"Come along with us, we're going to drag the river."

"You hear that, Robbie Bell?" said Sam.

They smiled.

The Doyles came noiselessly, their dogs made all the fuss. The Malones, eight giants with great long black eyelashes, were already stamping the ground and pawing each other, ready to go. Everybody went up together to see Doc.

Old Doc owned the wide net. He had a house on top of the hill and he sat and looked out from a rocker on the front porch.

"Climb the hill and come in!" he began to intone across the valley. "Harvest's over . . . slipped up on everybody . . . cotton's picked, gone to the gin . . . hay cut . . . molasses made around here. . . . Big explosion's over, supervisors elected, some pleased, some not. . . . We're hearing talk of war!"

When they got closer, he was saying, "Many's been saved at revival, twenty-two last Sunday including a Doyle, ought to counted two. Hope they'll be a blessing to Dover community besides a shining star in Heaven. Now what?" he asked, for they had arrived and stood gathered in front of the steps.

"If nobody is using your wide net, could we use it?" asked William Wallace.

"You just used it a month ago," said Doc. "It ain't your turn."

Virgil jogged William Wallace's arm and cleared his throat. "This time is kind of special," he said. "We got reason to think William Wallace's wife Hazel is in the river, drowned."

"What reason have you got to think she's in the river drowned?" asked Doc. He took out his old pipe. "I'm asking the husband."

"Because she's not in the house," said William Wallace.

"Vanished?" and he knocked out the pipe.

"Plum vanished."

"Of course a thousand things could have happened to her," said Doc, and he lighted the pipe.

"Hand him up the letter, William Wallace," said Virgil. "We can't wait around till Doomsday for the net while Doc sits back thinkin'."

"I tore it up, right at the first," said William Wallace. "But I know it by heart. It said she was going to jump straight in the Pearl River and that I'd be sorry."

"Where do you come in, Virgil?" asked Doc.

"I was in the same place William Wallace sat on his neck in, all night, and done as much as he done, and come home the same time."

"You-all were out cuttin' up, so Lady Hazel has to jump in the river, is that it? Cause and effect? Anybody want to argue with me? Where do these others come in, Doyles, Malones, and what not?"

"Doc is the smartest man around," said William Wallace, turning to the solidly waiting Doyles, "but it sure takes time."

"These are the ones that's collected to drag the river for her," said Virgil.

"Of course I am not going on record to say so soon that *I* think she's drowned," Doc said, blowing out blue smoke.

"Do you think . . ." William Wallace mounted a step, and his hands both went into fists. "Do you think she was *carried off?*"

"Now that's the way to argue, see it from all sides," said Doc promptly. "But who by?"

Some Malone whistled, but not so you could tell which one.

"There's no booger around the Dover section that goes around carrying off young girls that's married," stated Doc.

"She was always scared of the Gypsies." William Wallace turned scarlet. "She'd sure turn her ring around on her finger if she passed one, and look in the other direction so they couldn't see she was pretty and carry her off. They come in the end of summer."

"Yes, there are the Gypsies, kidnappers since the world began. But was it to be you that would pay the grand ransom?" asked Doc. He pointed his finger. They all laughed then at how clever old Doc was and clapped William Wallace on the back. But that turned into a scuffle and they fell to the ground.

"Stop it, or you can't have the net," said Doc. "You're scaring my wife's chickens."

"It's time we was gone," said William Wallace.

The big barking dogs jumped to lean their front paws on the men's chests.

"My advice remains, Let well enough alone," said Doc. "Whatever this mysterious event will turn out to be, it has kept one woman from talking a while. However, Lady Hazel is the prettiest girl in Mississippi, you've never seen a prettier one and you never will. A golden-haired girl." He got to his feet with the nimbleness that was always his surprise, and said, "I'll come along with you."

The path they always followed was the Old Natchez Trace. It took them through the deep woods and led them out down below on the Pearl River, where they could begin dragging it upstream to a point near Dover. They walked in silence around William Wallace, not letting him carry anything, but the net dragged heavily and the buckets were full of clatter in a place so dim and still.

Once they went through a forest of cucumber trees and came up on a high ridge. Grady and Brucie who were running ahead all the way stopped in their tracks; a whistle had blown and far down and far away a long freight train was passing. It seemed like a little festival procession, moving with the slowness of ignorance or a dream, from distance to distance, the tiny pink and gray cars like secret boxes. Grady was counting the cars to himself, as if he could certainly see each one clearly, and Brucie watched his lips, hushed and cautious, the way he would watch a bird drinking. Tears suddenly came to Grady's eyes, but it could only be because a tiny man walked along the top of the train, walking and moving on top of the moving train.

They went down again and soon the smell of the river spread over the woods, cool and secret. Every step they took among the great walls of vines and among the passion-flowers started up a little life, a little flight.

"We're walking along in the changing-time," said Doc. "Any day now the change will come. It's going to turn from hot to cold, and we can kill the hog that's ripe and have fresh meat to eat. Come one of these nights and we can wander down here and tree a nice possum. Old Jack Frost will be pinching things up. Old Mr. Winter will be standing in the door. Hickory tree there will be yellow. Sweet-gum red, hickory yellow, dogwood red, sycamore yellow." He went along rapping the tree trunks with his knuckle. "Magnolia and live-oak never die. Remember that. Persimmons will all get fit to eat, and the nuts will be dropping like rain all through the woods here. And run, little quail, run, for we'll be after you too."

They went on and suddenly the woods opened upon light, and they had reached the river. Everyone stopped, but Doc talked on ahead as though nothing had happened. "Only today," he said, "today, in October sun, it's all gold—sky and tree and water. Everything just before it changes looks to be made of gold."

William Wallace looked down, as though he thought of Hazel with the shining eyes, sitting at home and looking straight before her, like a piece of pure gold, too precious to touch.

Below them the river was glimmering, narrow, soft, and skin-colored, and slowed nearly to stillness. The shining willow trees hung round them. The net that was being drawn out, so old and so long-used, it too looked golden, strung and tied with golden threads.

Standing still on the bank, all of a sudden William Wallace, on whose word they were waiting, spoke up in a voice of surprise. "What is the name of this river?"

They looked at him as if he were crazy not to know

the name of the river he had fished in all his life. But a
deep frown was on his forehead, as if he were com-
pelled to wonder what people had come to call this
river, or to think there was a mystery in the name of a
river they all knew so well, the same as if it were some
great far torrent of waves that dashed through the
mountains somewhere, and almost as if it were a river
in some dream, for they could not give him the name of
that.

"Everybody knows Pearl River is named the Pearl
River," said Doc.

A bird note suddenly bold was like a stone thrown
into the water to sound it.

"It's deep here," said Virgil, and jogged William Wallace. "Remember?"

William Wallace stood looking down at the river as if
it were still a mystery to him. There under his feet
which hung over the bank it was transparent and yellow
like an old bottle lying in the sun, filling with light.

Doc clattered all his paraphernalia.

Then all of a sudden all the Malones scattered jumping and tumbling down the bank. They gave their loud
shout. Little Brucie started after them, and looked back.

"Do you think she jumped?" Virgil asked William
Wallace.

II

Since the net was so wide, when it was all stretched it
reached from bank to bank of the Pearl River, and the
weights would hold it all the way to the bottom. Jug-
like sounds filled the air, splashes lifted in the sun, and
the party began to move upstream. The Malones with
great groans swam and pulled near the shore, the Doyles
swam and pushed from behind with Virgil to tell them
how to do it best; Grady and Brucie with his thread and
pin trotted along the sandbars hauling buckets and lines.
Sam and Robbie Bell, naked and bright, guided the old
oarless rowboat that always drifted at the shore, and in
it, sitting up tall with his hat on, was Doc—he went
along without ever touching water and without ever

taking his eyes off the net. William Wallace himself did everything but most of the time he was out of sight, swimming about under water or diving, and he had nothing to say any more.

The dogs chased up and down, in and out of the water, and in and out of the woods.

"Don't let her get too heavy, boys," Doc intoned regularly, every few minutes, "and she won't let nothing through."

"She won't let nothing through, she won't let nothing through," chanted Sam and Robbie Bell, one at his front and one at his back.

The sandbars were pink or violet drifts ahead. Where the light fell on the river, in a wandering from shore to shore, it was leaf-shaped spangles that trembled softly, while the dark of the river was calm. The willow trees leaned overhead under muscadine vines, and their trailing leaves hung like waterfalls in the morning air. The thing that seemed like silence must have been the endless cry of all the crickets and locusts in the world, rising and falling.

Every time William Wallace took hold of a big eel that slipped the net, the Malones all yelled, "Rassle with him, son!"

"Don't let her get too heavy, boys," said Doc.

"This is hard on catfish," William Wallace said once.

There were big and little fishes, dark and bright, that they caught, good ones and bad ones, the same old fish.

"This is more shoes than I ever saw got together in any store," said Virgil when they emptied the net to the bottom. "Get going!" he shouted in the next breath.

The little Rippens who had stayed ahead in the woods stayed ahead on the river. Brucie, leading them all, made small jumps and hops as he went, sometimes on one foot, sometimes on the other.

The winding river looked old sometimes, when it ran wrinkled and deep under high banks where the roots of trees hung down, and sometimes it seemed to be only a young creek, shining with the colors of wildflowers. Sometimes sandbars in the shapes of fishes lay nose to nose across, without the track of even a bird.

"Here comes some alligators," said Virgil. "Let's let them by."

They drew out on the shady side of the water, and three big alligators and four middle-sized ones went by, taking their own time.

"Look at their great big old teeth!" called a shrill voice. It was Grady making his only outcry, and the alligators were not showing their teeth at all.

"The better to eat folks with," said Doc from his boat, looking at him severely.

"Doc, you are bound to declare all you know," said Virgil. "Get going!"

When they started off again the first thing they caught in the net was the baby alligator.

"That's just what we wanted!" cried the Malones.

They set the little alligator down on a sandbar and he squatted perfectly still; they could hardly tell when it was he started to move. They watched with set faces his incredible mechanics, while the dogs after one bark stood off in inquisitive humility, until he winked.

"He's ours!" shouted all the Malones. "We're taking him home with us!"

"He ain't nothing but a little-old baby," said William Wallace.

The Malones only scoffed, as if he might be only a baby but he looked like the oldest and worst lizard.

"What are you going to do with him?" asked Virgil.

"Keep him."

"I'd be more careful what I took out of this net," said Doc.

"Tie him up and throw him in the bucket," the Malones were saying to each other, while Doc was saying, "Don't come running to me and ask me what to do when he gets big."

They kept catching more and more fish, as if there was no end in sight.

"Look, a string of lady's beads," said Virgil. "Here, Sam and Robbie Bell."

Sam wore them around his head, with a knot over his forehead and loops around his ears, and Robbie Bell walked behind and stared at them.

In a shadowy place something white flew up. It was a heron, and it went away over the dark treetops. William Wallace followed it with his eyes and Brucie clapped his hands, but Virgil gave a sigh, as if he knew that when you go looking for what is lost, everything is a sign.

An eel slid out of the net.

"Rassle with him, son!" yelled the Malones. They swam like fiends.

"The Malones are in it for the fish," said Virgil.

It was about noon that there was a little rustle on the bank.

"Who is that yonder?" asked Virgil, and he pointed to a little undersized man with short legs and a little straw hat with a band around it, who was following along on the other side of the river.

"Never saw him and don't know his brother," said Doc.

Nobody had ever seen him before.

"Who invited you?" cried Virgil hotly. "Hi . . . !" and he made signs for the little undersized man to look at him, but he would not.

"Looks like a crazy man, from here," said the Malones.

"Just don't pay any attention to him and maybe he'll go away," advised Doc.

But Virgil had already swum across and was up on the other bank. He and the stranger could be seen exchanging a word apiece and then Virgil put out his hand the way he would pat a child and patted the stranger to the ground. The little man got up again just as quickly, lifted his shoulders, turned around, and walked away with his hat tilted over his eyes.

When Virgil came back he said, "Little-old man claimed he was harmless as a baby. I told him to just try horning in on this river and anything in it."

"What did he look like up close?" asked Doc.

"I wasn't studying how he looked," said Virgil. "But I don't like anybody to come looking at me that I am not familiar with." And he shouted, "Get going!"

"Things are moving in too great a rush," said Doc.

Brucie darted ahead and ran looking into all the

bushes, lifting up their branches and looking underneath.

"Not one of the Doyles has spoke a word," said Virgil.

"That's because they're not talkers," said Doc.

All day William Wallace kept diving to the bottom. Once he dived down and down into the dark water, where it was so still that nothing stirred, not even a fish, and so dark that it was no longer the muddy world of the upper river but the dark clear world of deepness, and he must have believed this was the deepest place in the whole Pearl River, and if she was not here she would not be anywhere. He was gone such a long time that the others stared hard at the surface of the water, through which the bubbles came from below. So far down and all alone, had he found Hazel? Had he suspected down there, like some secret, the real, the true trouble that Hazel had fallen into, about which words in a letter could not speak . . . how (who knew?) she had been filled to the brim with that elation that they all remembered, like their own secret, the elation that comes of great hopes and changes, sometimes simply of the harvest time, that comes with a little course of its own like a tune to run in the head, and there was nothing she could do about it—they knew—and so it had turned into this? It could be nothing but the old trouble that William Wallace was finding out, reaching and turning in the gloom of such depths.

"Look down yonder," said Grady softly to Brucie.

He pointed to the surface, where their reflections lay colorless and still side by side. He touched his brother gently as though to impress him.

"That's you and me," he said.

Brucie swayed precariously over the edge, and Grady caught him by the seat of his overalls. Brucie looked, but showed no recognition. Instead, he backed away, and seemed all at once unconcerned and spiritless, and pressed the nickel William Wallace had given him into his palm, rubbing it into his skin. Grady's inflamed eyes rested on the brown water. Without warning he saw something . . . perhaps the image in the river seemed to be his father, the drowned man—with arms open, eyes open, mouth open. . . . Grady stared and blinked, again something wrinkled up his face.

And when William Wallace came up it was in an agony from submersion, which seemed an agony of the blood and of the very heart, so woeful he looked. He was staring and glaring around in astonishment, as if a long time had gone by, away from the pale world where the brown light of the sun and the river and the little party watching him trembled before his eyes.

"What did you bring up?" somebody called—was it Virgil?

One of his hands was holding fast to a little green ribbon of plant, root and all. He was surprised, and let it go.

It was afternoon. The trees spread softly, the clouds hung wet and tinted. A buzzard turned a few slow wheels in the sky, and drifted upwards. The dogs promenaded the banks.

"It's time we ate fish," said Virgil.

On a wide sandbar on which seashells lay they dragged up the haul and built a fire.

Then for a long time among clouds of odors and smoke, all half-naked except Doc, they cooked and ate catfish. They ate until the Malones groaned and all the Doyles stretched out on their faces, though for long after, Sam and Robbie Bell sat up to their own little table on a cypress stump and ate on and on. Then they all were silent and still, and one by one fell asleep.

"There ain't a thing better than fish," muttered William Wallace. He lay stretched on his back in the glimmer and shade of trampled sand. His sunburned forehead and cheeks seemed to glow with fire. His eyelids fell. The shadow of a willow branch dipped and moved over him. "There is nothing in the world as good as . . . fish. The fish of Pearl River." Then slowly he smiled. He was asleep.

But it seemed almost at once that he was leaping up, and one by one up sat the others in their ring and looked at him, for it was impossible to stop and sleep by the river.

"You're feeling as good as you felt last night," said Virgil, setting his head on one side.

"The excursion is the same when you go looking for your sorrow as when you go looking for your joy," said Doc.

But William Wallace answered none of them anything, for he was leaping all over the place and all, over them and the feast and the bones of the feast, trampling the sand, up and down, and doing a dance so crazy that he would die next. He took a big catfish and hooked it to his belt buckle and went up and down so that they all hollered, and the tears of laughter streaming down his cheeks made him put his hand up, and the two days' growth of beard began to jump out, bright red.

But all of a sudden there was an even louder cry, something almost like a cheer, from everybody at once, and all pointed fingers moved from William Wallace to the river. In the center of three light-gold rings across the water was lifted first an old hoary head ("It has whiskers!" a voice cried) and then in an undulation loop after loop and hump after hump of a long dark body, until there were a dozen rings of ripples, one behind the other, stretching all across the river, like a necklace.

"The King of the Snakes!" cried all the Malones at once, in high tenor voices and leaning together.

"The King of the Snakes," intoned old Doc in his profound bass.

"He looked you in the eye."

William Wallace stared back at the King of the Snakes with all his might.

It was Brucie that darted forward, dangling his little thread with the pin tied to it, going toward the water.

"That's the King of the Snakes!" cried Grady, who always looked after him.

Then the snake went down.

The little boy stopped with one leg in the air, spun around on the other, and sank to the ground.

"Git up," Grady whispered. "It was just the King of the Snakes. He went off whistling. Git up. It wasn't a thing but the King of the Snakes."

Brucie's green eyes opened, his tongue darted out, and he sprang up; his feet were heavy, his head light, and he rose like a bubble coming to the surface.

Then thunder like a stone loosened and rolled down the bank.

They all stood unwilling on the sandbar, holding to the net. In the eastern sky were the familiar castles and the round towers to which they were used, gray, pink, and blue, growing darker and filling with thunder. Lightning flickered in the sun along their thick walls. But in the west the sun shone with such a violence that in an illumination like a long-prolonged glare of lightning the heavens looked black and white; all color left the world, the goldenness of everything was like a memory, and only heat, a kind of glamor and oppression, lay on their heads. The thick heavy trees on the other side of the river were brushed with mile-long streaks of silver, and a wind touched each man on the forehead. At the same time there was a long roll of thunder that began behind them, came up and down mountains and valleys of air, passed over their heads, and left them listening still. With a small, near noise a mockingbird followed it, the little white bars of its body flashing over the willow trees.

"We are here for a storm now," Virgil said. "We will have to stay till it's over."

They retreated a little, and hard drops fell in the leathery leaves at their shoulders and about their heads.

"Magnolia's the loudest tree there is in a storm," said Doc.

Then the light changed the water, until all about them the woods in the rising wind seemed to grow taller and blow inward together and suddenly turn dark. The rain struck heavily. A huge tail seemed to lash through the air and the river broke in a wound of silver. In silence the party crouched and stooped beside the trunk of the great tree, which in the push of the storm rose full of a fragrance and unyielding weight. Where they all stared, past their tree, was another tree, and beyond that another and another, all the way down the bank of the river, all towering and darkened in the storm.

"The outside world is full of endurance," said Doc. "Full of endurance."

Robbie Bell and Sam squatted down low and embraced each other from the start.

"Runs in our family to get struck by lightnin'," said Robbie Bell. "Lightnin' drawed a pitchfork right on our grandpappy's cheek, stayed till he died. Pappy got struck by some bolts of lightnin' and was dead three days, dead as that-there axe."

There was a succession of glares and crashes.

"This'n's goin' to be either me or you," said Sam. "Here come a little bug. If he go to the left, be me, and to the right, be you."

But at the next flare a big tree on the hill seemed to turn into fire before their eyes, every branch, twig, and leaf, and a purple cloud hung over it.

"Did you hear that crack?" asked Robbie Bell. "That were its bones."

"Why do you little niggers talk so much!" said Doc. "Nobody's profiting by this information."

"We always talks this much," said Sam, "but now everybody so quiet, they hears us."

The great tree, split and on fire, fell roaring to earth. Just at its moment of falling, a tree like it on the opposite bank split wide open and fell in two parts.

"Hope they ain't goin' to be no balls of fire come rollin' over the water and fry all the fishes with they scales on," said Robbie Bell.

The water in the river had turned purple and was filled with sudden currents and whirlpools. The little willow trees bent almost to its surface, bowing one after another down the bank and almost breaking under the storm. A great curtain of wet leaves was borne along before a blast of wind, and every human being was covered.

"Now us got scales," wailed Sam. "Us is the fishes."

"Hush up, little-old colored children," said Virgil.

"This isn't the way to act when somebody takes you out to drag a river."

"Poor lady's-ghost, I bet it is scareder than us," said Sam.

"All I hoping is, us don't find her!" screamed Robbie Bell.

William Wallace bent down and knocked their heads together. After that they clung silently in each other's arms, the two black heads resting, with wind-filled cheeks and tight-closed eyes, one upon the other until the storm was over.

"Right over yonder is Dover," said Virgil. "We've come all the way. William Wallace, you have walked on a sharp rock and cut your foot open."

III

In Dover it had rained, and the town looked somehow like new. The wavy heat of late afternoon came down from the watertank and fell over everything like shiny mosquito-netting. At the wide place where the road was paved and patched with tar, it seemed newly embedded with Coca-Cola tops. The old circus posters on the store were nearly gone, only bits, the snowflakes of white horses, clinging to its side. Morning-glory vines started almost visibly to grow over the roofs and cling round the ties of the railroad track, where bluejays lighted on the rails, and umbrella chinaberry trees hung heavily over the whole town, dripping intermittently upon the tin roofs.

Each with his counted fish on a string the members of the river-dragging party walked through the town. They went toward the town well, and there was Hazel's mother's house, but no sign of her yet coming out. They all drank a dipper of the water, and still there was not a soul on the street. Even the bench in front of the store was empty, except for a little corn-shuck doll.

But something told them somebody had come, for after one moment people began to look out of the store and out of the postoffice. All the bird dogs woke up to see the Doyle dogs and such a large number of men and boys materialize suddenly with such a big catch of fish,

and they ran out barking. The Doyle dogs joyously
barked back. The bluejays flashed up and screeched
above the town, whipping through their tunnels in the
chinaberry trees. In the café a nickel clattered inside a
music box and a love song began to play. The whole
town of Dover began to throb in its wood and tin, like
an old tired heart, when the men walked through once
more, coming around again and going down the street
carrying the fish, so drenched, exhausted, and muddy
that no one could help but admire them.

William Wallace walked through the town as though
he did not see anybody or hear anything. Yet he carried
his great string of fish held high where it could be seen
by all. Virgil came next, imitating William Wallace exactly, then the modest Doyles crowded by the Malones,
who were holding up their alligator, tossing it in the air,
even, like a father tossing his child. Following behind
and pointing authoritatively at the ones in front strolled
Doc, with Sam and Robbie Bell still chanting in his
wake. In and out of the whole little line Grady and
Brucie jerked about. Grady, with his head ducked, and
stiff as a rod, walked with a springy limp; it made him
look forever angry and unapproachable. Under his
breath he was whispering, "Sty, sty, git out of my eye,
and git on somebody passin' by." He traveled on with
narrowed shoulders, and kept his eye unerringly upon
his little brother, wary and at the same time proud, as
though he held a flying June-bug on a string. Brucie,
making a twanging noise with his lips, had shot forth
again, and he was darting rapidly everywhere at once,
delighted and tantalized, running in circles around William Wallace, pointing to his fish. A frown of pleasure
like the print of a bird's foot was stamped between his
faint brows, and he trotted in some unknown realm of
delight.

"Did you ever see so many fish?" said the people in
Dover.

"How much are your fish, mister?"

"Would you sell your fish?"

"Is that all the fish in Pearl River?"

"How much you sell them all for? Everybody's?"

"Three dollars," said William Wallace suddenly, and loud.

The Malones were upon him and shouting, but it was too late.

And just as William Wallace was taking the money in his hand, Hazel's mother walked solidly out of her front door and saw it.

"You can't head her mother off," said Virgil. "Here she comes in full bloom."

But William Wallace turned his back on her, that was all, and on everybody, for that matter, and that was the breaking-up of the party.

Just as the sun went down, Doc climbed his back steps, sat in his chair on the back porch where he sat in the evenings, and lighted his pipe. William Wallace hung out the net and came back and Virgil was waiting for him, so they could say good evening to Doc.

"All in all," said Doc, when they came up, "I've never been on a better river-dragging, or seen better behavior. If it took catching catfish to move the Rock of Gibraltar, I believe this outfit could move it."

"Well, we didn't catch Hazel," said Virgil.

"What did you say?" asked Doc.

"He don't really pay attention," said Virgil. "I said, 'We didn't catch Hazel.'"

"Who says Hazel was to be caught?" asked Doc. "She wasn't in there. Girls don't like the water—remember that. Girls don't just haul off and go jumping in the river to get back at their husbands. They got other ways."

"Didn't you ever think she was in there?" asked William Wallace. "The whole time?"

"Nary once," said Doc.

"He's just smart," said Virgil, putting his hand on William Wallace's arm. "It's only because we didn't find her that he wasn't looking for her."

"I'm beholden to you for the net, anyway," said William Wallace.

"You're welcome to borry it again," said Doc.

*

On the way home Virgil kept saying, "Calm down, calm down, William Wallace."

"If he wasn't such an old skinny man I'd have wrung his neck for him," said William Wallace. "He had no business coming."

"He's too big for his britches," said Virgil. "Don't nobody know everything. And just because it's his net. Why does it have to be his net?"

"If it wasn't for being polite to old men, I'd have skinned him alive," said William Wallace.

"I guess he don't really know nothing about wives at all, his wife's so deaf," said Virgil.

"He don't know Hazel," said William Wallace. "I'm the only man alive knows Hazel: would she jump in the river or not, and I say she would. She jumped in because I was sitting on the back of my neck in a ditch singing, and that's just what she ought to done. Doc ain't got no right to say one word about it."

"Calm down, calm down, William Wallace," said Virgil.

"If it had been you that talked like that, I'd have broke every bone in your body," said William Wallace. "Just let you talk like that. You're my age and size."

"But I ain't going to talk like that," said Virgil. "What have I done the whole time but keep this river-dragging going straight and running even, without no hitches? You couldn't have drug the river a foot without me."

"What are you talking about! Without who!" cried William Wallace. "This wasn't your river-dragging! It wasn't your wife!" He jumped on Virgil and they began to fight.

"Let me up." Virgil was breathing heavily.

"Say it was my wife. Say it was my river-dragging."

"Yours!" Virgil was on the ground with William Wallace's hand putting dirt in his mouth.

"Say it was my net."

"Your net!"

"Get up then."

They walked along getting their breath, and smelling the honeysuckle in the evening. On a hill William Wallace looked down, and at the same time there went drifting by the sweet sounds of music outdoors. They were having the Sacred Harp Sing on the grounds of an old white church glimmering there at the crossroads, far below. He stared away as if he saw it minutely, as if he could see a lady in white take a flowered cover off the organ, which was set on a little slant in the shade, dust the keys, and start to pump and play. . . . He smiled faintly, as he would at his mother, and at Hazel, and at the singing women in his life, now all one young girl standing up to sing under the trees the oldest and longest ballads there were.

Virgil told him good night and went into his own house and the door shut on him.

When he got to his own house, William Wallace saw to his surprise that it had not rained at all. But there, curved over the roof, was something he had never seen before as long as he could remember, a rainbow at night. In the light of the moon, which had risen again, it looked small and of gauzy material, like a lady's summer dress, a faint veil through which the stars showed.

He went up on the porch and in at the door, and all exhausted he had walked through the front room and through the kitchen when he heard his name called. After a moment, he smiled, as if no matter what he might have hoped for in his wildest heart, it was better than that to hear his name called out in the house. The voice came out of the bedroom.

"What do you want?" he yelled, standing stock-still.

Then she opened the bedroom door with the old complaining creak, and there she stood. She was not changed a bit.

"How do you feel?" he said.

"I feel pretty good. Not too good," Hazel said, looking mysterious.

"I cut my foot," said William Wallace, taking his shoe off so she could see the blood.

"How in the world did you do that?" she cried, with a step back.

"Dragging the river. But it don't hurt any longer."

"You ought to have been more careful," she said.

"Supper's ready and I wondered if you would ever come home, or if it would be last night all over again. Go and make yourself fit to be seen," she said, and ran away from him.

After supper they sat on the front steps a while.

"Where were you this morning when I came in?" asked William Wallace when they were ready to go in the house.

"I was hiding," she said. "I was still writing on the letter. And then you tore it up."

"Did you watch me when I was reading it?"

"Yes, and you could have put out your hand and touched me, I was so close."

But he bit his lip, and gave her a little tap and slap, and then turned her up and spanked her.

"Do you think you will do it again?" he asked.

"I'll tell my mother on you for this!"

"Will you do it again?"

"No!" she cried.

"Then pick yourself up off my knee."

It was just as if he had chased her and captured her again. She lay smiling in the crook of his arm. It was the same as any other chase in the end.

"I will do it again if I get ready," she said. "Next time will be different, too."

Then she was ready to go in, and rose up and looked out from the top step, out across their yard where the China tree was and beyond, into the dark fields where the lightning-bugs flickered away. He climbed to his feet too and stood beside her, with the frown on his face, trying to look where she looked. And after a few minutes she took him by the hand and led him into the house, smiling as if she were smiling down on him.

Old Mr. Marblehall

Old Mr. Marblehall never did anything, never got married until he was sixty. You can see him out taking a walk. Watch and you'll see how preciously old people come to think they are made—the way they walk, like conspirators, bent over a little, filled with protection. They stand long on the corners but more impatiently than anyone, as if they expect traffic to take notice of them, rear up the horses and throw on the brakes, so they can go where they want to go. That's Mr. Marblehall. He has short white bangs, and a bit of snapdragon in his lapel. He walks with a big polished stick, a present. That's what people think of him. Everybody says to his face, "So well preserved!" Behind his back they say cheerfully, "One foot in the grave." He has on his thick, beautiful, glowing coat—tweed, but he looks as gratified as an animal in its own tingling fur. You see, even in summer he wears it, because he is cold all the time. He looks quaintly secretive and prepared for anything, out walking very luxuriously on Catherine Street.

His wife, back at home in the parlor standing up to think, is a large, elongated old woman with electric-looking hair and curly lips. She has spent her life trying to escape from the parlor-like jaws of self-consciousness. Her late marriage has set in upon her nerves like a

retriever nosing and puffing through old dead leaves out
in the woods. When she walks around the room she
looks remote and nebulous, out on the fringe of habita-
tion, and rather as if she must have been cruelly trained
—otherwise she couldn't do actual, immediate things,
like answering the telephone or putting on a hat. But
she has gone further than you'd think: into club work.
Surrounded by other more suitably exclaiming women,
she belongs to the Daughters of the American Revolution and the United Daughters of the Confederacy, attending teas. Her long, disquieted figure towering in the
candlelight of other women's houses looks like something accidental. Any occasion, and she dresses her hair
like a unicorn horn. She even sings, and is requested to
sing. She even writes some of the songs she sings ("O
Trees in the Evening"). She has a voice that dizzies
other ladies like an organ note, and amuses men like a
halloo down the well. It's full of a hollow wind and
echo, winding out through the wavery hope of her
mouth. Do people know of her perpetual amazement?
Back in safety she wonders, her untidy head trembles in
the domestic dark. She remembers how everyone in
Natchez will suddenly grow quiet around her. Old Mrs.
Marblehall, Mr. Marblehall's wife: she even goes out in
the rain, which Southern women despise above everything, in big neat biscuit-colored galoshes, for which she
"ordered off." She is only looking around—servile, unde-
lighted, sleepy, expensive, tortured Mrs. Marblehall, pinning her mind with a pin to her husband's diet. She
wants to tempt him, she tells him. What would he like
best, that he can have?

There is Mr. Marblehall's ancestral home. It's not so
wonderfully large—it has only four columns—but you
always look toward it, the way you always glance into
tunnels and see nothing. The river is after it now, and
the little back garden has assuredly crumbled away, but
the box maze is there on the edge like a trap, to con-
found the Mississippi River. Deep in the red wall waits
the front door—it weighs such a lot, it is perfectly solid,
all one piece, black mahogany. . . . And you see—one
of *them* is always going in it. There is a knocker shaped

like a gasping fish on the door. You have every reason
in the world to imagine the inside is dark, with old
things about. There's many a big, deathly-looking tapes-
try, wrinkling and thin, many a sofa shaped like an S.
Brocades as tall as the wicked queens in Italian tales
stand gathered before the windows. Everything is
draped and hooded and shaded, of course, unaffec-
tionate but close. Such rosy lamps! The only sound
would be a breath against the prisms, a stirring of the
chandelier. It's like old eyelids, the house with one of
its shutters, in careful working order, slowly opening
outward. Then the little son softly comes and stares out
like a kitten, with button nose and pointed ears and
little fuzz of silky hair running along the top of his
head.

The son is the worst of all. Mr. and Mrs. Marblehall
had a child! When both of them were terribly old, they
had this little, amazing, fascinating son. You can see
how people are taken aback, how they jerk and throw
up their hands every time they so much as think about
it. At least, Mr. Marblehall sees them. He thinks
Natchez people do nothing themselves, and really, most
of them have done or could do the same thing. This son
is six years old now. Close up, he has a monkey look, a
very penetrating look. He has very sparse Japanese hair,
tiny little pearly teeth, long little wilted fingers. Every
day he is slowly and expensively dressed and taken to
the Catholic school. He looks quietly and maliciously
absurd, out walking with old Mr. Marblehall or old
Mrs. Marblehall, placing his small booted foot on a
little green worm, while they stop and wait on him.
Everybody passing by thinks that he looks quite as if he
thinks his parents had him just to show they could. You
see, it becomes complicated, full of vindictiveness.

But now, as Mr. Marblehall walks as briskly as possible toward the river where there is sun, you have to
merge him back into his proper blur, into the little
party-giving town he lives in. Why look twice at him?
There has been an old Mr. Marblehall in Natchez ever
since the first one arrived back in 1818—with a theat-

rical presentation of Otway's *Venice,* ending with *A Laughable Combat between Two Blind Fiddlers*—an actor! Mr. Marblehall isn't so important. His name is on the list, he is forgiven, but nobody gives a hoot about any old Mr. Marblehall. He could die, for all they care; some people even say, "Oh, is he still alive?" Mr. Marblehall walks and walks, and now and then he is driven in his ancient fringed carriage with the candle burners like empty eyes in front. And yes, he is supposed to travel for his health. But why consider his absence? There isn't any other place besides Natchez, and even if there were, it would hardly be likely to change Mr. Marblehall if it were brought up against him. Big fingers could pick him up off the Esplanade and take him through the air, his old legs still measuredly walking in a dangle, and set him down where he could continue that same old Natchez stroll of his in the East or the West or Kingdom Come. What difference could anything make now about old Mr. Marblehall—so late? A week or two would go by in Natchez and then there would be Mr. Marblehall, walking down Catherine Street again, still exactly in the same degree alive and old.

People naturally get bored. They say, "Well, he waited till he was sixty years old to marry, and what did he want to marry for?" as though what he did were the excuse for their boredom and their lack of concern. Even the thought of his having a stroke right in front of one of the Pilgrimage houses during Pilgrimage Week makes them only sigh, as if to say it's nobody's fault but his own if he wants to be so insultingly and precariously well-preserved. He ought to have a little black boy to follow around after him. Oh, his precious old health, which never had reason to be so inspiring! Mr. Marblehall has a formal, reproachful look as he stands on the corners arranging himself to go out into the traffic to cross the streets. It's as if he's thinking of shaking his stick and saying, "Well, look! I've done it, don't you see?" But really, nobody pays much attention to his look. He is just like other people to them. He could have easily danced with a troupe of angels in Paradise every night, and they wouldn't have guessed. Nobody is likely to find out that he is leading a double life.

The funny thing is he just recently began to lead this double life. He waited until he was sixty years old. Isn't he crazy? Before that, he'd never done anything. He didn't know what to do. Everything was for all the world like his first party. He stood about, and looked in his father's books, and long ago he went to France, but he didn't like it.

Drive out any of these streets in and under the hills and you find yourself lost. You see those scores of little galleried houses nearly alike. See the yellowing China trees at the eaves, the round flower beds in the front yards, like bites in the grass, listen to the screen doors whining, the ice wagons dragging by, the twittering noises of children. Nobody ever looks to see who is living in a house like that. These people come out themselves and sprinkle the hose over the street at this time of day to settle the dust, and after they sit on the porch, they go back into the house, and you hear the radio for the next two hours. It seems to mourn and cry for them. They go to bed early.

Well, old Mr. Marblehall can easily be seen standing beside a row of zinnias growing down the walk in front of that little house, bending over, easy, easy, so as not to strain anything, to stare at the flowers. Of course he planted them! They are covered with brown—each petal is a little heart-shaped pocket of dust. They don't have any smell, you know. It's twilight, all amplified with locusts screaming; nobody could see anything. Just what Mr. Marblehall is bending over the zinnias for is a mystery, any way you look at it. But there he is, quite visible, alive and old, leading his double life.

There's his other wife, standing on the night-stained porch by a potted fern, screaming things to a neighbor. This wife is really worse than the other one. She is more solid, fatter, shorter, and while not so ugly, funnier looking. She looks like funny furniture—an unornamented stair post in one of these little houses, with her small monotonous round stupid head—or sometimes like a woodcut of a Bavarian witch, forefinger pointing, with scratches in the air all around her. But she's so static she scarcely moves, from her thick shoulders down past her cylindered brown dress to her short, stubby house slippers. She stands still and screams to the neighbors.

This wife thinks Mr. Marblehall's name is Mr. Bird. She says, "I declare I told Mr. Bird to go to bed, and look at him! I don't understand him!" All her devotion is combustible and goes up in despair. This wife tells everything she knows. Later, after she tells the neighbors, she will tell Mr. Marblehall. Cymbal-breasted, she fills the house with wifely complaints. She calls, "After I get Mr. Bird to bed, what does he do then? He lies there stretched out with his clothes on and don't have one word to say. Know what he does?"

And she goes on, while her husband bends over the zinnias, to tell what Mr. Marblehall (or Mr. Bird) does in bed. She does tell the truth. He reads *Terror Tales* and *Astonishing Stories*. She can't see anything to them: they scare her to death. These stories are about horrible and fantastic things happening to nude women and scientists. In one of them, when the characters open bureau drawers, they find a woman's leg with a stocking and garter on. Mrs. Bird had to shut the magazine. "The glutinous shadows," these stories say, "the red-eyed, muttering old crone," "the moonlight on her thigh," "an ancient cult of sun worshipers," "an altar suspiciously stained . . ." Mr. Marblehall doesn't feel as terrified as all that, but he reads on and on. He is killing time. It is richness without taste, like some holiday food. The clock gets a fruity bursting tick, to get through midnight—then leisurely, leisurely on. When time is passing it's like a bug in his ear. And then Mr. Bird—he doesn't even want a shade on the light, this wife moans respectably. He reads under a bulb. She can tell you how he goes straight through a stack of magazines. "He might just as well not have a family," she always ends, unjustly, and rolls back into the house as if she had been on a little wheel all this time.

But the worst of them all is the other little boy. Another little boy just like the first one. He wanders around the bungalow full of tiny little schemes and jokes. He has lost his front tooth, and in this way he looks slightly different from Mr. Marblehall's other little boy—more shocking. Otherwise, you couldn't tell them apart if you wanted to. They both have that look of cunning little jugglers, violently small under some spotlight beam, preoccupied and silent, amusing themselves. Both of the children will go into sudden fits and tantrums that frighten their mothers and Mr. Marblehall to death. Then they can get anything they want. But this little boy, the one who's lost the tooth, is the smarter. For a long time he supposed that his mother was totally solid, down to her thick separated ankles. But when she stands there on the porch screaming to the neighbors, she reminds him of those flares that charm him so, that they leave burning in the street at night—the dark solid ball, then, tongue-like, the wicked, yellow, continuous, enslaving blaze on the stem. He knows what his father thinks.

Perhaps one day, while Mr. Marblehall is standing there gently bent over the zinnias, this little boy is going to write on a fence, "Papa leads a double life." He finds out things you wouldn't find out. He is a monkey.

You see, one night he is going to follow Mr. Marblehall (or Mr. Bird) out of the house. Mr. Marblehall has said as usual that he is leaving for one of his health trips. He is one of those correct old gentlemen who are still going to the wells and drinking the waters—exactly like his father, the late old Mr. Marblehall. But why does he leave on foot? This will occur to the little boy.

So he will follow his father. He will follow him all the way across town. He will see the shining river come winding around. He will see the house where Mr. Marblehall turns in at the wrought-iron gate. He will see a big speechless woman come out and lead him in by the heavy door. He will not miss those rosy lamps beyond the many-folded draperies at the windows. He will run around the fountains and around the Japonica trees, past the stone figure of the pigtailed courtier mounted on the goat, down to the back of the house. From there he can look far up at the strange upstairs rooms. In one window the other wife will be standing like a giant, in a long-sleeved gathered nightgown, combing her electric hair and breaking it off each time in the comb. From the next window the other little boy will look out secretly into the night, and see him—or not see him. That would be an interesting thing, a moment of strange telepathies. (Mr. Marblehall can imagine it.) Then in the corner room there will suddenly be turned on the bright, naked light. Aha! Father!

Mr. Marblehall's little boy will easily climb a tree there and peep through the window. There, under a stark shadeless bulb, on a great four-poster with carved griffins, will be Mr. Marblehall, reading *Terror Tales,* stretched out and motionless.

Then everything will come out.

At first, nobody will believe it.

Or maybe the policeman will say, "Stop! How dare you!"

Maybe, better than that, Mr. Marblehall himself will confess his duplicity—how he has led two totally different lives, with completely different families, two sons instead of one. What an astonishing, unbelievable, electrifying confession that would be, and how his two wives would topple over, how his sons would cringe! To say nothing of most men aged sixty-six. So thinks self-consoling Mr. Marblehall.

You will think, what if nothing ever happens? What if there is no climax, even to this amazing life? Suppose old Mr. Marblehall simply remains alive, getting older by the minute, shuttling, still secretly, back and forth?

Nobody cares. Not an inhabitant of Natchez, Mississippi, cares if he is deceived by old Mr. Marblehall. Neither does anyone care that Mr. Marblehall has finally caught on, he thinks, to what people are supposed to do. This is it: they endure something inwardly—for a time secretly; they establish a past, a memory; thus they store up life. He has done this; most remarkably, he has even multiplied his life by deception; and plunging deeper and deeper he speculates upon some glorious finish, a great explosion of revelations . . . the future.

But he still has to kill time, and get through the clocking nights. Otherwise he dreams that he is a great blazing butterfly stitching up a net; which doesn't make sense.

Old Mr. Marblehall! He may have years ahead yet in which to wake up bolt upright in the bed under the naked bulb, his heart thumping, his old eyes watering and wild, imagining that if people knew about his double life, they'd die.

Keela, the Outcast Indian Maiden

One morning in summertime, when all his sons and daughters were off picking plums and Little Lee Roy was all alone, sitting on the porch and only listening to the screech owls away down in the woods, he had a surprise.

First he heard white men talking. He heard two white men coming up the path from the highway. Little Lee Roy ducked his head and held his breath; then he patted all around back of him for his crutches. The chickens all came out from under the house and waited attentively on the steps.

The men came closer. It was the young man who was doing all of the talking. But when they got through the fence, Max, the older man, interrupted him. He tapped him on the arm and pointed his thumb toward Little Lee Roy.

He said, "Bud? Yonder he is."

But the younger man kept straight on talking, in an explanatory voice.

"Bud?" said Max again. "Look, Bud, yonder's the only little clubfooted nigger man was ever around Cane Springs. Is he the party?"

They came nearer and nearer to Little Lee Roy and then stopped and stood there in the middle of the yard.

But the young man was so excited he did not seem to realize that they had arrived anywhere. He was only about twenty years old, very sunburned. He talked constantly, making only one gesture—raising his hand stiffly and then moving it a little to one side.

"They dressed it in a red dress, and it ate chickens alive," he said. "I sold tickets and I thought it was worth a dime, honest. They gimme a piece of paper with the thing wrote off I had to say. That was easy. 'Keela, the Outcast Indian Maiden!' I call it out through a pasteboard megaphone. Then ever' time it was fixin' to eat a live chicken, I blowed the sireen out front."

"Just tell me, Bud," said Max, resting back on the heels of his perforated tan-and-white sport shoes. "Is this nigger the one? Is that him sittin' there?"

Little Lee Roy sat huddled and blinking, a smile on his face. . . . But the young man did not look his way.

"Just took the job that time. I didn't mean to—I mean, I meant to go to Port Arthur because my brother was on a boat," he said. "My name is Steve, mister. But I worked with this show selling tickets for three months, and I never would of knowed it was like that if it hadn't been for that man." He arrested his gesture.

"Yeah, what man?" said Max in a hopeless voice.

Little Lee Roy was looking from one white man to the other, excited almost beyond respectful silence. He trembled all over, and a look of amazement and sudden life came into his eyes.

"Two years ago," Steve was saying impatiently. "And we was travelin' through Texas in those ole trucks.—See, the reason nobody ever come clost to it before was they give it a iron bar this long. And tole it if anybody come near, to shake the bar good at 'em, like this. But it couldn't say nothin'. Turned out they'd tole it it couldn't say nothin' to anybody ever, so it just kind of mumbled and growled, like a animal."

"Hee! hee!" This from Little Lee Roy, softly.

"Tell me again," said Max, and just from his look you could tell that everybody knew old Max. "Somehow I can't get it straight in my mind. Is this the boy? Is this little nigger boy the same as this Keela, the Outcast Indian Maiden?"

Up on the porch, above them, Little Lee Roy gave Max a glance full of hilarity, and then bent the other way to catch Steve's next words.

"Why, if anybody was to even come near it or even bresh their shoulder against the rope it'd growl and take on and shake its iron rod. When it would eat the live chickens it'd growl somethin' awful—you ought to heard it."

"Hee! hee!" It was a soft, almost incredulous laugh that began to escape from Little Lee Roy's tight lips, a little mew of delight.

"They'd throw it this chicken, and it would reach out an' grab it. Would sort of rub over the chicken's neck with its thumb an' press on it good, an' then it would bite its head off."

"O.K.," said Max.

"It skint back the feathers and stuff from the neck and sucked the blood. But ever'body said it was still alive." Steve drew closer to Max and fastened his light-colored, troubled eyes on his face.

"O.K."

"Then it would pull the feathers out easy and neat-like, awful fast, an' growl the whole time, kind of moan, an' then it would commence to eat all the white meat. I'd go in an' look at it. I reckon I seen it a thousand times."

"That was you, boy?" Max demanded of Little Lee Roy unexpectedly.

But Little Lee Roy could only say, "Hee! hee!" The little man at the head of the steps where the chickens sat, one on each step, and the two men facing each other below made a pyramid.

Steve stuck his hand out for silence. "They said—I mean, I said it, out front through the megaphone, I said it myself, that it wouldn't eat nothin' but only live meat. It was supposed to be a Indian woman, see, in this red dress an' stockin's. It didn't have on no shoes, so when it drug its foot ever'body could see. . . . When it come to the chicken's heart, it would eat that too, real fast, and the heart would still be jumpin'."

"Wait a second, Bud," said Max briefly. "Say, boy, is this white man here crazy?"

Little Lee Roy burst into hysterical, deprecatory giggles. He said, "Naw suh, don't think so." He tried to catch Steve's eye, seeking appreciation, crying, "Naw suh, don't think he crazy, mista."

Steve gripped Max's arm. "Wait! Wait!" he cried anxiously. "You ain't listenin'. I want to tell you about it. You didn't catch my name—Steve. You never did hear about that little nigger—all that happened to him? Lived in Cane Springs, Miss'ippi?"

"Bud," said Max, disengaging himself, "I don't hear anything. I got a juke box, see, so I don't have to listen."

"Look—I was really the one," said Steve more patiently, but nervously, as if he had been slowly breaking bad news. He walked up and down the bare-swept ground in front of Little Lee Roy's porch, along the row of princess feathers and snow-on-the-mountain. Little Lee Roy's turning head followed him. "I was the one— that's what I'm tellin' you."

"Suppose I was to listen to what every dope comes in Max's Place got to say, *I'd* be nuts," said Max.

"It's all me, see," said Steve. "I know that. I was the one was the cause for it goin' on an' on an' not bein' found out—such an awful thing. It was me, what I said out front through the megaphone."

He stopped still and stared at Max in despair.

"Look," said Max. He sat on the steps, and the chickens hopped off. "I know I ain't nobody but Max. I got Max's Place. I only run a place, understand, fifty yards down the highway. Liquor buried twenty feet from the premises, and no trouble yet. I ain't ever been up here before. I don't claim to been anywhere. People come to my place. Now. You're the hitchhiker. You're tellin' me, see. You claim a lot of information. If I don't get it I don't get it and I ain't complainin' about it, see. But I think you're nuts, and did from the first. I only come up here with you because I figured you's crazy."

"Maybe you don't believe I remember every word of it even now," Steve was saying gently. "I think about it at night—that an' drums on the midway. You ever hear drums on the midway?" He paused and stared politely at Max and Little Lee Roy.

"Yeh," said Max.

"Don't it make you feel sad. I remember how the drums was goin' and I was yellin', 'Ladies and gents! Do not try to touch Keela, the Outcast Indian Maiden—she will only beat your brains out with her iron rod, and eat them alive!' " Steve waved his arm gently in the air, and Little Lee Roy drew back and squealed. " 'Do not go near her, ladies and gents! I'm warnin' you!' So nobody ever did. Nobody ever come near her. Until that man."

"Sure," said Max. "That fella." He shut his eyes.

"Afterwards when he come up so bold, I remembered seein' him walk up an' buy the ticket an' go in the tent. I'll never forget that man as long as I live. To me he's a sort of—well—"

"Hero," said Max.

"I wish I could remember what he looked like. Seem like he was a tallish man with a sort of white face. Seem like he had bad teeth, but I may be wrong. I remember he frowned a lot. Kept frownin'. Whenever he'd buy a ticket, why, he'd frown."

"Ever seen him since?" asked Max cautiously, still with his eyes closed. "Ever hunt him up?"

"No, never did," said Steve. Then he went on. "He'd frown an' buy a ticket ever' day we was in these two little smelly towns in Texas, sometimes three-four times a day, whether it was fixin' to eat a chicken or not."

"O.K., so he gets in the tent," said Max.

"Well, what the man finally done was, he walked right up to the little stand where it was tied up and laid his hand out open on the planks in the platform. He just laid his hand out open there and said, 'Come here,' real low and quick, that-a-way."

Steve laid his open hand on Little Lee Roy's porch and held it there, frowning in concentration.

"I get it," said Max. "He'd caught on it was a fake."

Steve straightened up. "So ever'body yelled to git away, git away," he continued, his voice rising, "because it was growlin' an' carryin' on an' shakin' its iron bar like they tole it. When I heard all that commotion—boy! I was scared."

"You didn't know it was a fake."

Steve was silent for a moment, and Little Lee Roy held his breath, for fear everything was all over.

"Look," said Steve finally, his voice trembling. "I guess I was supposed to feel bad like this, and you wasn't. I wasn't supposed to ship out on that boat from Port Arthur and all like that. This other had to happen to me—not you all. Feelin' responsible. You'll be O.K., mister, but I won't. I feel awful about it. That poor little old thing."

"Look, you got him right here," said Max quickly. "See him? Use your eyes. He's O.K., ain't he? Looks O.K. to me. It's just you. You're nuts, is all."

"You know—when that man laid out his open hand on the boards, why, it just let go the iron bar," continued Steve, "let it fall down like that—bang—and act like it didn't know what to do. Then it drug itself over to where the fella was standin' an' leaned down an' grabbed holt onto that white man's hand as tight as it could an' cried like a baby. It didn't want to hit him!"

"Hee! hee! hee!"

"No sir, it didn't want to hit him. You know what it wanted?"

Max shook his head.

"It wanted him to help it. So the man said, 'Do you wanta get out of this place, whoever you are?' An' it never answered—none of us knowed it could talk—but it just wouldn't let that man's hand a-loose. It hung on, cryin' like a baby. So the man says, 'Well, wait here till I come back.' "

"Uh-huh?" said Max.

"Went off an' come back with the sheriff. Took us all to jail. But just the man owned the show and his son got took to the pen. They said I could go free. I kep' tellin' 'em I didn't know it wouldn't hit me with the iron bar

54

an' kep' tellin' 'em I didn't know it could tell what you was sayin' to it."

"Yeh, guess you told 'em," said Max.

"By that time I felt bad. Been feelin' bad ever since. Can't hold onto a job or stay in one place for nothin' in the world. They made it stay in jail to see if it could talk or not, and the first night it wouldn't say nothin'. Some time it cried. And they undressed it an' found out it wasn't no outcast Indian woman a-tall. It was a little clubfooted nigger man."

"Hee! hee!"

"You mean it was this boy here—yeh. It was him."

"Washed its face, and it was paint all over it made it look red. It all come off. And it could talk—as good as me or you. But they'd tole it not to, so it never did. They'd tole it if anybody was to come near it they was comin' to git it—and for it to hit 'em quick with that iron bar an' growl. So nobody ever come near it—until that man. I was yellin' outside, tellin' 'em to keep away, keep away. You could see where they'd whup it. They had to whup it some to make it eat all the chickens. It was awful dirty. They let it go back home free, to where they got it in the first place. They made them pay its ticket from Little Oil, Texas, to Cane Springs, Miss'ippi."

"You got a good memory," said Max.

"The way it *started* was," said Steve, in a wondering voice, "the show was just travelin' along in ole trucks through the country, and just seen this little deformed nigger man, sittin' on a fence, and just took it. It couldn't help it."

Little Lee Roy tossed his head back in a frenzy of amusement.

"I found it all out later. I was up on the Ferris wheel with one of the boys—got to talkin' up yonder in the peace an' quiet—an' said they just kind of happened up on it. Like a cyclone happens: it wasn't nothin' it could do. It was just took up." Steve suddenly paled through his sunburn. "An' they found out that back in Miss'ippi it had it a little bitty pair of crutches an' could just go runnin' on 'em!"

"And there they are," said Max.

Little Lee Roy held up a crutch and turned it about, and then snatched it back like a monkey.

"But if it hadn't been for that man, I wouldn't of knowed it till yet. If it wasn't for him bein' so bold. If he hadn't knowed what he was doin'."

"You remember that man this fella's talkin' about, boy?" asked Max, eying Little Lee Roy.

Little Lee Roy, in reluctance and shyness, shook his head gently.

"Naw suh, I can't say as I remembas that ve'y man, suh," he said softly, looking down where just then a sparrow alighted on his child's shoe. He added happily, as if on inspiration, "Now I remembas *this* man."

Steve did not look up, but when Max shook with silent laughter, alarm seemed to seize him like a spasm in his side. He walked painfully over and stood in the shade for a few minutes, leaning his head on a sycamore tree.

"Seemed like that man just studied it out an' knowed it was somethin' wrong," he said presently, his voice coming more remotely than ever. "But I didn't know. I can't look at nothin' an' be sure what it is. Then afterwards I know. Then I see how it was."

"Yeh, but you're nuts," said Max affably.

"You wouldn't of knowed it either!" cried Steve in sudden boyish, defensive anger. Then he came out from under the tree and stood again almost pleadingly in the sun, facing Max where he was sitting below Little Lee Roy on the steps. "You'd of let it go on an' on when they made it do those things—just like I did."

"Bet I could tell a man from a woman and an Indian from a nigger though," said Max.

Steve scuffed the dust into little puffs with his worn shoe. The chickens scattered, alarmed at last.

Little Lee Roy looked from one man to the other radiantly, his hands pressed over his grinning gums.

Then Steve sighed, and as if he did not know what else he could do, he reached out and without any warning hit Max in the jaw with his fist. Max fell off the steps.

Little Lee Roy suddenly sat as still and dark as a statue, looking on.

"Say! Say!" cried Steve. He pulled shyly at Max where he lay on the ground, with his lips pursed up like a whistler, and then stepped back. He looked horrified. "How you feel?"

"Lousy," said Max thoughtfully. "Let me alone." He raised up on one elbow and lay there looking all around, at the cabin, at Little Lee Roy sitting cross-legged on the porch, and at Steve with his hand out. Finally he got up.

"I can't figure out how I could of ever knocked down an athaletic guy like you. I had to do it," said Steve. "But I guess you don't understand. I had to hit you. First you didn't believe me, and then it didn't bother you."

"That's all O.K., only hush," said Max, and added, "Some dope is always giving me the low-down on something, but this is the first time one of 'em ever got away with a thing like this. I got to watch out."

"I hope it don't stay black long," said Steve.

"I got to be going," said Max. But he waited. "What you want to transact with Keela? You come a long way to see him." He stared at Steve with his eyes wide open now, and interested.

"Well, I was goin' to give him some money or somethin', I guess, if I ever found him, only now I ain't got any," said Steve defiantly.

"O.K.," said Max. "Here's some change for you, boy. Just take it. Go on back in the house. Go on."

Little Lee Roy took the money speechlessly, and then fell upon his yellow crutches and hopped with miraculous rapidity away through the door. Max stared after him for a moment.

"As for you"—he brushed himself off, turned to Steve and then said, "When did you eat last?"

"Well, I'll tell you," said Steve.

"Not here," said Max. "I didn't go to ask you a question. Just follow me. We serve eats at Max's Place, and I want to play the juke box. You eat, and I'll listen to the juke box."

"Well . . ." said Steve. "But when it cools off I got to catch a ride some place."

"Today while all you all was gone, and not a soul in de house," said Little Lee Roy at the supper table that night, "two white mens come heah to de house. Wouldn't come in. But talks to me about de ole times when I use to be wid de circus—"

"Hush up, Pappy," said the children.

A Worn Path

It was December—a bright frozen day in the early morning. Far out in the country there was an old Negro woman with her head tied in a red rag, coming along a path through the pinewoods. Her name was Phoenix Jackson. She was very old and small and she walked slowly in the dark pine shadows, moving a little from side to side in her steps, with the balanced heaviness and lightness of a pendulum in a grandfather clock. She carried a thin, small cane made from an umbrella, and with this she kept tapping the frozen earth in front of her. This made a grave and persistent noise in the still air, that seemed meditative like the chirping of a solitary little bird.

She wore a dark striped dress reaching down to her shoe tops, and an equally long apron of bleached sugar sacks, with a full pocket: all neat and tidy, but every time she took a step she might have fallen over her shoelaces, which dragged from her unlaced shoes. She looked straight ahead. Her eyes were blue with age. Her skin had a pattern all its own of numberless branching wrinkles and as though a whole little tree stood in the middle of her forehead, but a golden color ran underneath, and the two knobs of her cheeks were illumined by a yellow burning under the dark. Under the red rag her hair came down on her neck in the frailest of ringlets, still black, and with an odor like copper.

Now and then there was a quivering in the thicket. Old Phoenix said, "Out of my way, all you foxes, owls, beetles, jack rabbits, coons and wild animals! . . . Keep out from under these feet, little bob-whites. . . . Keep the big wild hogs out of my path. Don't let none of those come running my direction. I got a long way." Under her small black-freckled hand her cane, limber as a buggy whip, would switch at the brush as if to rouse up any hiding things.

On she went. The woods were deep and still. The sun made the pine needles almost too bright to look at, up where the wind rocked. The cones dropped as light as feathers. Down in the hollow was the mourning dove— it was not too late for him.

The path ran up a hill. "Seem like there is chains about my feet, time I get this far," she said, in the voice of argument old people keep to use with themselves. "Something always take a hold of me on this hill— pleads I should stay."

After she got to the top she turned and gave a full, severe look behind her where she had come. "Up through pines," she said at length. "Now down through oaks."

Her eyes opened their widest, and she started down gently. But before she got to the bottom of the hill a bush caught her dress.

Her fingers were busy and intent, but her skirts were full and long, so that before she could pull them free in one place they were caught in another. It was not possible to allow the dress to tear. "I in the thorny bush," she said. "Thorns, you doing your appointed work. Never want to let folks pass, no sir. Old eyes thought you was a pretty little *green* bush."

Finally, trembling all over, she stood free, and after a moment dared to stoop for her cane.

"Sun so high!" she cried, leaning back and looking, while the thick tears went over her eyes. "The time getting all gone here."

At the foot of this hill was a place where a log was laid across the creek.

"Now comes the trial," said Phoenix.

Putting her right foot out, she mounted the log and shut her eyes. Lifting her skirt, leveling her cane fiercely before her, like a festival figure in some parade, she began to march across. Then she opened her eyes and she was safe on the other side.

"I wasn't as old as I thought," she said.

But she sat down to rest. She spread her skirts on the bank around her and folded her hands over her knees. Up above her was a tree in a pearly cloud of mistletoe. She did not dare to close her eyes, and when a little boy brought her a plate with a slice of marble-cake on it she spoke to him. "That would be acceptable," she said. But when she went to take it there was just her own hand in the air.

So she left that tree, and had to go through a barbed-wire fence. There she had to creep and crawl, spreading her knees and stretching her fingers like a baby trying to climb the steps. But she talked loudly to herself: she could not let her dress be torn now, so late in the day, and she could not pay for having her arm or her leg sawed off if she got caught fast where she was.

At last she was safe through the fence and risen up out in the clearing. Big dead trees, like black men with one arm, were standing in the purple stalks of the withered cotton field. There sat a buzzard.

"Who you watching?"

In the furrow she made her way along.

"Glad this not the season for bulls," she said, looking sideways, "and the good Lord made his snakes to curl up and sleep in the winter. A pleasure I don't see no two-headed snake coming around that tree, where it come once. It took a while to get by him, back in the summer."

She passed through the old cotton and went into a field of dead corn. It whispered and shook and was taller than her head. "Through the maze now," she said, for there was no path.

Then there was something tall, black, and skinny there, moving before her.

At first she took it for a man. It could have been a man dancing in the field. But she stood still and listened, and it did not make a sound. It was as silent as a ghost.

"Ghost," she said sharply, "who be you the ghost of? For I have heard of nary death close by."

But there was no answer—only the ragged dancing in the wind.

She shut her eyes, reached out her hand, and touched a sleeve. She found a coat and inside that an emptiness, cold as ice.

"You scarecrow," she said. Her face lighted. "I ought to be shut up for good," she said with laughter. "My senses is gone. I too old. I the oldest people I ever know. Dance, old scarecrow," she said, "while I dancing with you."

She kicked her foot over the furrow, and with mouth drawn down, shook her head once or twice in a little strutting way. Some husks blew down and whirled in streamers about her skirts.

Then she went on, parting her way from side to side with the cane, through the whispering field. At last she came to the end, to a wagon track where the silver grass blew between the red ruts. The quail were walking around like pullets, seeming all dainty and unseen.

"Walk pretty," she said. "This the easy place. This the easy going."

She followed the track, swaying through the quiet bare fields, through the little strings of trees silver in their dead leaves, past cabins silver from weather, with the doors and windows boarded shut, all like old women under a spell sitting there. "I walking in their sleep," she said, nodding her head vigorously.

In a ravine she went where a spring was silently flowing through a hollow log. Old Phoenix bent and drank. "Sweet-gum makes the water sweet," she said, and drank more. "Nobody know who made this well, for it was here when I was born."

The track crossed a swampy part where the moss hung as white as lace from every limb. "Sleep on, alligators, and blow your bubbles." Then the track went into the road.

Deep, deep the road went down between the high green-colored banks. Overhead the live-oaks met, and it was as dark as a cave.

A black dog with a lolling tongue came up out of the weeds by the ditch. She was meditating, and not ready, and when he came at her she only hit him a little with her cane. Over she went in the ditch, like a little puff of milkweed.

Down there, her senses drifted away. A dream visited her, and she reached her hand up, but nothing reached down and gave her a pull. So she lay there and presently went to talking. "Old woman," she said to herself, "that black dog come up out of the weeds to stall you off, and now there he sitting on his fine tail, smiling at you."

A white man finally came along and found her—a hunter, a young man, with his dog on a chain.

"Well, Granny!" he laughed. "What are you doing there?"

"Lying on my back like a June-bug waiting to be turned over, mister," she said, reaching up her hand.

He lifted her up, gave her a swing in the air, and set her down. "Anything broken, Granny?"

"No sir, them old dead weeds is springy enough," said Phoenix, when she had got her breath. "I thank you for your trouble."

"Where do you live, Granny?" he asked, while the two dogs were growling at each other.

"Away back yonder, sir, behind the ridge. You can't even see it from here."

"On your way home?"

"No sir, I going to town."

"Why, that's too far! That's as far as I walk when I come out myself, and I get something for my trouble." He patted the stuffed bag he carried, and there hung down a little closed claw. It was one of the bob-whites, with its beak hooked bitterly to show it was dead. "Now you go on home, Granny!"

"I bound to go to town, mister," said Phoenix. "The time come around."

He gave another laugh, filling the whole landscape. "I know you old colored people! Wouldn't miss going to town to see Santa Claus!"

But something held old Phoenix very still. The deep lines in her face went into a fierce and different radiation. Without warning, she had seen with her own eyes a flashing nickel fall out of the man's pocket onto the ground.

"How old are you, Granny?" he was saying.

"There is no telling, mister," she said, "no telling."

Then she gave a little cry and clapped her hands and said, "Git on away from here, dog! Look! Look at that dog!" She laughed as if in admiration. "He ain't scared of nobody. He a big black dog." She whispered, "Sic him!"

"Watch me get rid of that cur," said the man. "Sic him, Pete! Sic him!"

Phoenix heard the dogs fighting, and heard the man running and throwing sticks. She even heard a gunshot. But she was slowly bending forward by that time, further and further forward, the lids stretched down over her eyes, as if she were doing this in her sleep. Her chin was lowered almost to her knees. The yellow palm of her hand came out from the fold of her apron. Her fingers slid down and along the ground under the piece of money with the grace and care they would have in lifting an egg from under a setting hen. Then she slowly straightened up, she stood erect, and the nickel was in her apron pocket. A bird flew by. Her lips moved. "God watching me the whole time. I come to stealing."

The man came back, and his own dog panted about them. "Well, I scared him off that time," he said, and then he laughed and lifted his gun and pointed it at Phoenix.

She stood straight and faced him.

"Doesn't the gun scare you?" he said, still pointing it.

"No, sir, I seen plenty go off closer by, in my day,

and for less than what I done," she said, holding utterly still.

He smiled, and shouldered the gun. "Well, Granny," he said, "you must be a hundred years old, and scared of nothing. I'd give you a dime if I had any money with me. But you take my advice and stay home, and nothing will happen to you."

"I bound to go on my way, mister," said Phoenix. She inclined her head in the red rag. Then they went in different directions, but she could hear the gun shooting again and again over the hill.

She walked on. The shadows hung from the oak trees to the road like curtains. Then she smelled wood-smoke, and smelled the river, and she saw a steeple and the cabins on their steep steps. Dozens of little black children whirled around her. There ahead was Natchez shining. Bells were ringing. She walked on.

In the paved city it was Christmas time. There were red and green electric lights strung and crisscrossed everywhere, and all turned on in the daytime. Old Phoenix would have been lost if she had not distrusted her eyesight and depended on her feet to know where to take her.

She paused quietly on the sidewalk where people were passing by. A lady came along in the crowd, carrying an armful of red-, green- and silver-wrapped presents; she gave off perfume like the red roses in hot summer, and Phoenix stopped her.

"Please, missy, will you lace up my shoe?" She held up her foot.

"What do you want, Grandma?"

"See my shoe," said Phoenix. "Do all right for out in the country, but wouldn't look right to go in a big building."

"Stand still then, Grandma," said the lady. She put her packages down on the sidewalk beside her and laced and tied both shoes tightly.

"Can't lace 'em with a cane," said Phoenix. "Thank you, missy. I doesn't mind asking a nice lady to tie up my shoe, when I gets out on the street."

Moving slowly and from side to side, she went into

the big building, and into a tower of steps, where she walked up and around and around until her feet knew to stop.

She entered a door, and there she saw nailed up on the wall the document that had been stamped with the gold seal and framed in the gold frame, which matched the dream that was hung up in her head.

"Here I be," she said. There was a fixed and ceremonial stiffness over her body.

"A charity case, I suppose," said an attendant who sat at the desk before her.

But Phoenix only looked above her head. There was sweat on her face, the wrinkles in her skin shone like a bright net.

"Speak up, Grandma," the woman said. "What's your name? We must have your history, you know. Have you been here before? What seems to be the trouble with you?"

Old Phoenix only gave a twitch to her face as if a fly were bothering her.

"Are you deaf?" cried the attendant.

But then the nurse came in.

"Oh, that's just old Aunt Phoenix," she said. "She doesn't come for herself—she has a little grandson. She makes these trips just as regular as clockwork. She lives away back off the Old Natchez Trace." She bent down. "Well, Aunt Phoenix, why don't you just take a seat? We won't keep you standing after your long trip." She pointed.

The old woman sat down, bolt upright in the chair.

"Now, how is the boy?" asked the nurse.

Old Phoenix did not speak.

"I said, how is the boy?"

But Phoenix only waited and stared straight ahead, her face very solemn and withdrawn into rigidity.

"Is his throat any better?" asked the nurse. "Aunt Phoenix, don't you hear me? Is your grandson's throat any better since the last time you came for the medicine?"

With her hands on her knees, the old woman waited,

silent, erect and motionless, just as if she were in armor.

"You mustn't take up our time this way, Aunt Phoenix," the nurse said. "Tell us quickly about your grandson, and get it over. He isn't dead, is he?"

At last there came a flicker and then a flame of comprehension across her face, and she spoke.

"My grandson. It was my memory had left me. There I sat and forgot why I made my long trip."

"Forgot?" The nurse frowned. "After you came so far?"

Then Phoenix was like an old woman begging a dignified forgiveness for waking up frightened in the night. "I never did go to school, I was too old at the Surrender," she said in a soft voice. "I'm an old woman without an education. It was my memory fail me. My little grandson, he is just the same, and I forgot it in the coming."

"Throat never heals, does it?" said the nurse, speaking in a loud, sure voice to old Phoenix. By now she had a card with something written on it, a little list. "Yes. Swallowed lye. When was it?—January—two-three years ago—"

Phoenix spoke unasked now. "No, missy, he not dead, he just the same. Every little while his throat begin to close up again, and he not able to swallow. He not get his breath. He not able to help himself. So the time come around, and I go on another trip for the soothing medicine."

"All right. The doctor said as long as you came to get it, you could have it," said the nurse. "But it's an obstinate case."

"My little grandson, he sit up there in the house all wrapped up, waiting by himself," Phoenix went on. "We is the only two left in the world. He suffer and it don't seem to put him back at all. He got a sweet look. He going to last. He wear a little patch quilt and peep out holding his mouth open like a little bird. I remembers so plain now. I not going to forget him again, no, the whole enduring time. I could tell him from all the others in creation."

"All right." The nurse was trying to hush her now. She brought her a bottle of medicine. "Charity.," she said, making a check mark in a book.

Old Phoenix held the bottle close to her eyes, and then carefully put it into her pocket.

"I thank you," she said.

"It's Christmas time, Grandma," said the attendant. "Could I give you a few pennies out of my purse?"

"Five pennies is a nickel," said Phoenix stiffly.

"Here's a nickel," said the attendant.

Phoenix rose carefully and held out her hand. She received the nickel and then fished the other nickel out of her pocket and laid it beside the new one. She stared at her palm closely, with her head on one side.

Then she gave a tap with her cane on the floor.

"This is what come to me to do," she said. "I going to the store and buy my child a little windmill they sells, made out of paper. He going to find it hard to believe there such a thing in the world. I'll march myself back where he waiting, holding it straight up in this hand."

She lifted her free hand, gave a little nod, turned around, and walked out of the doctor's office. Then her slow step began on the stairs, going down.

Petrified Man

"Reach in my purse and git me a cigarette without no powder in it if you kin, Mrs. Fletcher, honey," said Leota to her ten o'clock shampoo-and-set customer. "I don't like no perfumed cigarettes."

Mrs. Fletcher gladly reached over to the lavender shelf under the lavender-framed mirror, shook a hair net loose from the clasp of the patent-leather bag, and slapped her hand down quickly on a powder puff which burst out when the purse was opened.

"Why, look at the peanuts, Leota!" said Mrs. Fletcher in her marvelling voice.

"Honey, them goobers has been in my purse a week if they's been in it a day. Mrs. Pike bought them peanuts."

"Who's Mrs. Pike?" asked Mrs. Fletcher, settling back. Hidden in this den of curling fluid and henna packs, separated by a lavender swing-door from the other customers, who were being gratified in other booths, she could give her curiosity its freedom. She looked expectantly at the black part in Leota's yellow curls as she bent to light the cigarette.

"Mrs. Pike is this lady from New Orleans," said Leota, puffing, and pressing into Mrs. Fletcher's scalp with strong red-nailed fingers. "A friend, not a customer. You see, like maybe I told you last time, me and Fred and Sal and Joe all had us a fuss, so Sal and Joe up and moved out, so we didn't do a thing but rent out their room. So we rented it to Mrs. Pike. And Mr. Pike." She flicked an ash into the basket of dirty towels. "Mrs. Pike is a very decided blonde. *She* bought me the peanuts."

"She must be cute," said Mrs. Fletcher.

"Honey, 'cute' ain't the word for what she is. I'm tellin' you, Mrs. Pike is attractive. She has her a good time. She's got a sharp eye out, Mrs. Pike has."

She dashed the comb through the air, and paused dramatically as a cloud of Mrs. Fletcher's hennaed hair floated out of the lavender teeth like a small storm-cloud.

"Hair fallin'."

"Aw, Leota."

"Uh-huh, commencin' to fall out," said Leota, combing again, and letting fall another cloud.

"Is it any dandruff in it?" Mrs. Fletcher was frowning, her hair-line eyebrows diving down toward her nose, and her wrinkled, beady-lashed eyelids batting with concentration.

"Nope." She combed again. "Just fallin' out."

"Bet it was that last perm'nent you gave me that did it," Mrs. Fletcher said cruelly. "Remember you cooked me fourteen minutes."

"You had fourteen minutes comin' to you," said Leota with finality.

"Bound to be somethin'," persisted Mrs. Fletcher. "Dandruff, dandruff. I couldn't of caught a thing like that from Mr. Fletcher, could I?"

"Well," Leota answered at last, "you know what I heard in here yestiddy, one of Thelma's ladies was settin' over yonder in Thelma's booth gittin' a machineless, and I don't mean to insist or insinuate or anything, Mrs. Fletcher, but Thelma's lady just happ'med to throw out—I forgotten what she was talkin' about at the time—that you was p-r-e-g., and lots of times that'll make your hair do awful funny, fall out and God knows what all. It just ain't our fault, is the way I look at it."

There was a pause. The women stared at each other in the mirror.

"Who was it?" demanded Mrs. Fletcher.

"Honey, I really couldn't say," said Leota. "Not that you look it."

"Where's Thelma? I'll get it out of her," said Mrs. Fletcher.

"Now, honey, I wouldn't go and git mad over a little thing like that," Leota said, combing hastily, as though to hold Mrs. Fletcher down by the hair. "I'm sure it was somebody didn't mean no harm in the world. How far gone are you?"

"Just wait," said Mrs. Fletcher, and shrieked for Thelma, who came in and took a drag from Leota's cigarette.

"Thelma, honey, throw your mind back to yestiddy if you kin," said Leota, drenching Mrs. Fletcher's hair with a thick fluid and catching the overflow in a cold wet towel at her neck.

"Well, I got my lady half wound for a spiral," said Thelma doubtfully.

"This won't take but a minute," said Leota. "Who is it you got in there, old Horse Face? Just cast your mind back and try to remember who your lady was yestiddy who happ'm to mention that my customer was pregnant, that's all. She's dead to know."

Thelma drooped her blood-red lips and looked over Mrs. Fletcher's head into the mirror. "Why, honey, I ain't got the faintest," she breathed. "I really don't recollect the faintest. But I'm sure she meant no harm. I declare, I forgot my hair finally got combed and thought it was a stranger behind me."

"Was it that Mrs. Hutchinson?" Mrs. Fletcher was tensely polite.

"Mrs. Hutchinson? Oh, Mrs. Hutchinson." Thelma batted her eyes. "Naw, precious, she come on Thursday and didn't ev'm mention your name. I doubt if she ev'm knows you're on the way."

"Thelma!" cried Leota staunchly.

"All I know is, whoever it is 'll be sorry some day. Why, I just barely knew it myself!" cried Mrs Fletcher. "Just let her wait!"

"Why? What're you gonna do to her?"

It was a child's voice, and the women looked down. A little boy was making tents with aluminum wave pinchers on the floor under the sink.

"Billy Boy, hon, mustn't bother nice ladies." Leota smiled. She slapped him brightly and behind her back waved Thelma out of the booth. "Ain't Billy Boy a sight? Only three years old and already just nuts about the beauty-parlor business."

"I never saw him here before," said Mrs. Fletcher, still unmollified.

"He ain't been here before, that's how come," said Leota. "He belongs to Mrs. Pike. She got her a job but it was Fay's Millinery. He oughtn't to try on those ladies' hats, they come down over his eyes like I don't know what. They just git to look ridiculous, that's what, an' of course he's gonna put 'em on: hats. They tole Mrs. Pike they didn't appreciate him hangin' around there. Here, he couldn't hurt a thing."

"Well! I don't like children that much," said Mrs. Fletcher.

"Well!" said Leota moodily.

"Well! I'm almost tempted not to have this one," said Mrs. Fletcher. "That Mrs. Hutchinson! Just looks straight through you when she sees you on the street and then spits at you behind your back."

"Mr. Fletcher would beat you on the head if you didn't have it now," said Leota reasonably. "After going this far."

Mrs. Fletcher sat up straight. "Mr. Fletcher can't do a thing with me."

"He can't!" Leota winked at herself in the mirror.

"No, siree, he can't. If he so much as raises his voice against me, he knows good and well I'll have one of my sick headaches, and then I'm just not fit to live with. And if I really look that pregnant already—"

"Well, now, honey, I just want you to know—I

habm't told any of my ladies and I ain't goin' to tell 'em —even that you're losin' your hair. You just get you one of those Stork-a-Lure dresses and stop worryin'. What people don't know don't hurt nobody, as Mrs. Pike says."

"Did you tell Mrs. Pike?" asked Mrs. Fletcher sulkily.

"Well, Mrs. Fletcher, look, you ain't ever goin' to lay eyes on Mrs. Pike or her lay eyes on you, so what diffunce does it make in the long run?"

"I knew it!" Mrs. Fletcher deliberately nodded her head so as to destroy a ringlet Leota was working on behind her ear. "Mrs. Pike!"

Leota sighed. "I reckon I might as well tell you. It wasn't any more Thelma's lady tole me you was pregnant than a bat."

"Not Mrs. Hutchinson?"

"Naw, Lord! It was Mrs. Pike."

"Mrs. Pike!" Mrs. Fletcher could only sputter and let curling fluid roll into her ear. "How could Mrs. Pike possibly know I was pregnant or otherwise, when she doesn't even know me? The nerve of some people!"

"Well, here's how it was. Remember Sunday?"

"Yes," said Mrs. Fletcher.

"Sunday, Mrs. Pike an' me was all by ourself. Mr. Pike and Fred had gone over to Eagle Lake, sayin' they was goin' to catch 'em some fish, but they didn't a course. So we was settin' in Mrs. Pike's car, it's a 1939 Dodge—"

"1939, eh," said Mrs. Fletcher.

"—An' we was gettin' us a Jax beer apiece—that's the beer that Mrs. Pike says is made right in N.O., so she won't drink no other kind. So I seen you drive up to the drugstore an' run in for just a secont, leavin' I reckon Mr. Fletcher in the car, an' come runnin' out with looked like a perscription. So I says to Mrs. Pike, just to be makin' talk, 'Right yonder's Mrs. Fletcher, and I reckon that's Mr. Fletcher—she's one of my regular customers,' I says."

"I had on a figured print," said Mrs. Fletcher tentatively.

"You sure did," agreed Leota. "So Mrs. Pike, she give you a good look—she's very observant, a good judge of character, cute as a minute, you know—and she says, 'I bet you another Jax that lady's three months on the way.' "

"What gall!" said Mrs. Fletcher. "Mrs. Pike!"

"Mrs. Pike ain't goin' to bite you," said Leota. "Mrs. Pike is a lovely girl, you'd be crazy about her, Mrs. Fletcher. But she can't sit still a minute. We went to the travellin' freak show yestiddy after work. I got through early—nine o'clock. In the vacant store next door. What, you ain't been?"

"No, I despise freaks," declared Mrs. Fletcher.

"Aw. Well, honey, talkin' about bein' pregnant an' all, you ought to see those twins in a bottle, you really owe it to yourself."

"What twins?" asked Mrs. Fletcher out of the side of her mouth.

"Well, honey, they got these two twins in a bottle, see? Born joined plumb together—dead a course." Leota dropped her voice into a soft lyrical hum. "They was about this long—pardon—must of been full time, all right, wouldn't you say?—an' they had these two heads an' two faces an' four arms an' four legs, all kind of joined *here*. See, this face looked this-a-way, and the other face looked that-a-way, over their shoulder, see. Kinda pathetic."

"Glah!" said Mrs. Fletcher disapprovingly.

"Well, ugly? Honey, I mean to tell you—their parents was first cousins and all like that. Billy Boy, git me a fresh towel from off Teeny's stack—this 'n's wringin' wet—an' quit ticklin' my ankles with that curler. I declare! He don't miss nothin'."

"Me and Mr. Fletcher aren't one speck of kin, or he could never of had me," said Mrs. Fletcher placidly.

"Of course not!" protested Leota. "Neither is me an' Fred, not that we know of. Well, honey, what Mrs. Pike liked was the pygmies. They've got these pygmies down there, too, an' Mrs. Pike was just wild about 'em. You know, the teeniest men in the universe? Well, honey, they can just rest back on their little bohunkus an' roll around an' you can't hardly tell if they're sittin' or standin'. That'll give you some idea. They're about forty-two years old. Just suppose it was your husband!"

"Well, Mr. Fletcher is five foot nine and one half," said Mrs. Fletcher quickly.

"Fred's five foot ten," said Leota, "but I tell him he's still a shrimp, account of I'm so tall." She made a deep wave over Mrs. Fletcher's other temple with the comb. "Well, these pygmies are a kind of a dark brown, Mrs. Fletcher. Not bad-lookin' for what they are, you know."

"I wouldn't care for them," said Mrs. Fletcher. "What does that Mrs. Pike see in them?"

"Aw, I don't know," said Leota. "She's just cute, that's all. But they got this man, this petrified man, that ever'thing ever since he was nine years old, when it goes through his digestion, see, somehow Mrs. Pike says it goes to his joints and has been turning to stone."

"How awful!" said Mrs. Fletcher.

"He's forty-two too. That looks like a bad age."

"Who said so, that Mrs. Pike? I bet she's forty-two," said Mrs. Fletcher.

"Naw," said Leota, "Mrs. Pike's thirty-three, born in January, an Aquarian. He could move his head—like this. A course his head and mind ain't a joint, so to speak, and I guess his stomach ain't, either—not yet, anyways. But see—his food, he eats it, and it goes down, see, and then he digests it"—Leota rose on her toes for an instant—"and it goes out to his joints and before you can say 'Jack Robinson,' it's stone—pure stone. He's turning to stone. How'd you like to be married to a guy like that? All he can do, he can move his head just a quarter of an inch. A course he *looks* just *terrible*."

"I should think he would," said Mrs. Fletcher frostily. "Mr. Fletcher takes bending exercises every night of the world. I make him."

"All Fred does is lay around the house like a rug. I wouldn't be surprised if he woke up some day and couldn't move. The petrified man just sat there moving his quarter of an inch though," said Leota reminiscently.

"Did Mrs. Pike like the petrified man?" asked Mrs. Fletcher.

"Not as much as she did the others," said Leota deprecatingly. "And then she likes a man to be a good dresser, and all that."

"Is Mr. Pike a good dresser?" asked Mrs. Fletcher sceptically.

"Oh, well, yeah," said Leota, "but he's twelve or fourteen years older'n her. She ast Lady Evangeline about him."

"Who's Lady Evangeline?" asked Mrs. Fletcher.

"Well, it's this mind reader they got in the freak show," said Leota. "Was real good. Lady Evangeline is her name, and if I had another dollar I wouldn't do a thing but have my other palm read. She had what Mrs. Pike said was the 'sixth mind' but she had the worst manicure I ever saw on a living person."

"What did she tell Mrs. Pike?" asked Mrs. Fletcher.

"She told her Mr. Pike was as true to her as he could be and besides, would come into some money."

"Humph!" said Mrs. Fletcher. "What does he do?"

"I can't tell," said Leota, "because he don't work. Lady Evangeline didn't tell me enough about my nature or anything. And I would like to go back and find out some more about this boy. Used to go with this boy until he got married to this girl. Oh, shoot, that was about three and a half years ago, when you was still goin' to the Robert E. Lee Beauty Shop in Jackson. He married her for her money. Another fortune-teller tole me that at the time. So I'm not in love with him any more, anyway, besides being married to Fred, but Mrs. Pike thought, just for the hell of it, see, to ask Lady Evangeline was he happy."

"Does Mrs. Pike know everything about you already?" asked Mrs. Fletcher unbelievingly. "Mercy!"

"Oh, yeah, I tole her ever'thing about ever'thing, from now on back to I don't know when—to when I first started goin' out," said Leota. "So I ast Lady

Evangeline for one of my questions, was he happily married, and she says, just like she was glad I ask her, 'Honey,' she says, 'naw, he idn't. You write down this day, March 8, 1941,' she says, 'and mock it down: three years from today him and her won't be occupyin' the same bed.' There it is, up on the wall with them other dates—see, Mrs. Fletcher? And she says, 'Child, you ought to be glad you didn't git him, because he's so mercenary.' So I'm glad I married Fred. He sure ain't mercenary, money don't mean a thing to him. But I sure would like to go back and have my other palm read."

"Did Mrs. Pike believe in what the fortune-teller said?" asked Mrs. Fletcher in a superior tone of voice.

"Lord, yes, she's from New Orleans. Ever'body in New Orleans believes ever'thing spooky. One of 'em in New Orleans before it was raided says to Mrs. Pike one summer she was goin' to go from State to State and meet some grey-headed men, and, sure enough, she says she went on a beautician convention up to Chicago. . . ."

"Oh!" said Mrs. Fletcher. "Oh, is Mrs. Pike a beautician too?"

"Sure she is," protested Leota. "She's a beautician. I'm goin' to git her in here if I can. Before she married. But it don't leave you. She says sure enough, there was three men who was a very large part of making her trip what it was, and they all three had grey in their hair and they went in six States. Got Christmas cards from 'em. Billy Boy, go see if Thelma's got any dry cotton. Look how Mrs. Fletcher's a-drippin'."

"Where did Mrs. Pike meet Mr. Pike?" asked Mrs. Fletcher primly.

"On another train," said Leota.

"I met Mr. Fletcher, or rather he met me, in a rental library," said Mrs. Fletcher with dignity, as she watched the net come down over her head.

"Honey, me an' Fred, we met in a rumble seat eight months ago and we was practically on what you might call the way to the altar inside of half an hour," said Leota in a guttural voice, and bit a bobby pin open.

"Course it don't last. Mrs. Pike says nothin' like that ever lasts."

"Mr. Fletcher and myself are as much in love as the day we married," said Mrs. Fletcher belligerently as Leota stuffed cotton into her ears.

"Mrs. Pike says it don't last," repeated Leota in a louder voice. "Now go git under the dryer. You can turn yourself on, can't you? I'll be back to comb you out. Durin' lunch I promised to give Mrs. Pike a facial. You know—free. Her bein' in the business, so to speak."

"I bet she needs one," said Mrs. Fletcher, letting the swing-door fly back against Leota. "Oh, pardon me."

A week later, on time for her appointment, Mrs. Fletcher sank heavily into Leota's chair after first removing a drug-store rental book, called *Life Is Like That*, from the seat. She stared in a discouraged way into the mirror.

"You can tell it when I'm sitting down, all right," she said.

Leota seemed preoccupied and stood shaking out a lavender cloth. She began to pin it around Mrs. Fletcher's neck in silence.

"I said you sure can tell it when I'm sitting straight on and coming at you this way," Mrs. Fletcher said.

"Why, honey, naw you can't," said Leota gloomily. "Why, I'd never know. If somebody was to come up to me on the street and say, 'Mrs. Fletcher is pregnant!' I'd say, 'Heck, she don't look it to me.' "

"If a certain party hadn't found it out and spread it around, it wouldn't be too late even now," said Mrs. Fletcher frostily, but Leota was almost choking her with the cloth, pinning it so tight, and she couldn't speak clearly. She paddled her hands in the air until Leota wearily loosened her.

"Listen, honey, you're just a virgin compared to Mrs. Montjoy," Leota was going on, still absent-minded. She bent Mrs. Fletcher back in the chair and, sighing, tossed liquid from a teacup on to her head and dug both hands

78

into her scalp. "You know Mrs. Montjoy—her husband's that premature-grey-headed fella?"

"She's in the Trojan Garden Club, is all I know," said Mrs. Fletcher.

"Well, honey," said Leota, but in a weary voice, "she come in here not the week before and not the day before she had her baby—she come in here the very selfsame day, I mean to tell you. Child, we was all plumb scared to death. There she was! Come for her shampoo an' set. Why, Mrs. Fletcher, in an hour an' twenty minutes she was layin' up there in the Babtist Hospital with a seb'm-pound son. It was that close a shave. I declare, if I hadn't been so tired I would of drank up a bottle of gin that night."

"What gall," said Mrs. Fletcher. "I never knew her at all well."

"See, her husband was waitin' outside in the car, and her bags was all packed an' in the back seat, an' she was all ready, 'cept she wanted her shampoo an' set. An' havin' one pain right after another. Her husband kep' comin' in here, scared-like, but couldn't do nothin' with her a course. She yelled bloody murder, too, but she always yelled her head off when I give her a perm'nent."

"She must of been crazy," said Mrs. Fletcher. "How did she look?"

"Shoot!" said Leota.

"Well, I can guess," said Mrs. Fletcher. "Awful."

"Just wanted to look pretty while she was havin' her baby, is all," said Leota airily. "Course, we was glad to give the lady what she was after—that's our motto—but I bet a hour later she wasn't payin' no mind to them little end curls. I bet she wasn't thinkin' about she ought to have on a net. It wouldn't of done her no good if she had."

"No, I don't suppose it would," said Mrs. Fletcher.

"Yeah man! She was a-yellin'. Just like when I give her perm'nent."

"Her husband ought to make her behave. Don't it seem that way to you?" asked Mrs. Fletcher. "He ought to put his foot down."

"Ha," said Leota. "A lot he could do. Maybe some women is soft."

"Oh, you mistake me, I don't mean for her to get soft —far from it! Women have to stand up for themselves, or there's just no telling. But now you take me—I ask Mr. Fletcher's advice now and then, and he appreciates it, especially on something important, like is it time for a permanent—not that I've told him about the baby. He says, 'Why, dear, go ahead!' Just ask their *advice*."

"Huh! If I ever ast Fred's advice we'd be floatin' down the Yazoo River on a houseboat or somethin' by this time," said Leota. "I'm sick of Fred. I told him to go over to Vicksburg."

"Is he going?" demanded Mrs. Fletcher.

"Sure. See, the fortune-teller—I went back and had my other palm read, since we've got to rent the room agin—said my lover was goin' to work in Vicksburg, so I don't know who she could mean, unless she meant Fred. And Fred ain't workin' here—that much is so."

"Is he going to work in Vicksburg?" asked Mrs. Fletcher. "And—"

"Sure. Lady Evangeline said so. Said the future is going to be brighter than the present. He don't want to go, but I ain't gonna put up with nothin' like that. Lays around the house an' bulls—did bull—with that good-for-nothin' Mr. Pike. He says if he goes who'll cook, but I says I never get to eat anyway—not meals. Billy Boy, take Mrs. Grover that *Screen Secrets* and leg it."

Mrs. Fletcher heard stamping feet go out the door.

"Is that that Mrs. Pike's little boy here again?" she asked, sitting up gingerly.

"Yeah, that's still him." Leota stuck out her tongue.

Mrs. Fletcher could hardly believe her eyes. "Well! How's Mrs. Pike, your attractive new friend with the sharp eyes who spreads it around town that perfect strangers are pregnant?" she asked in a sweetened tone.

"Oh, Mizziz Pike." Leota combed Mrs. Fletcher's hair with heavy strokes.

"You act like you're tired," said Mrs. Fletcher.

"Tired? Feel like it's four o'clock in the afternoon already," said Leota. "I ain't told you the awful luck we had, me and Fred? It's the worst thing you ever heard of. Maybe *you* think Mrs. Pike's got sharp eyes. Shoot, there's a limit! Well, you know, we rented out our room to this Mr. and Mrs. Pike from New Orleans when Sal an' Joe Fentress got mad at us 'cause they drank up some home-brew we had in the closet—Sal an' Joe did. So, a week ago Sat'day Mr. and Mrs. Pike moved in. Well, I kinda fixed up the room, you know—put a sofa pillow on the couch and picked some ragged robbins and put in a vase, but they never did say they appreciated it. Anyway, then I put some old magazines on the table."

"I think that was lovely," said Mrs. Fletcher.

"Wait. So, come night 'fore last, Fred and this Mr. Pike, who Fred just took up with, was back from they said they was fishin', bein' as neither one of 'em has got a job to his name, and we was all settin' around in their room. So Mrs. Pike was settin' there, readin' a old *Startling G-Man Tales* that was mine, mind you, I'd bought it myself, and all of a sudden she jumps!—into the air—you'd 'a' thought she'd set on a spider—an' says, 'Canfield'—ain't that silly, that's Mr. Pike—'Canfield, my God A'mighty,' she says, 'honey,' she says, 'we're rich, and you won't have to work.' Not that he turned one hand anyway. Well, me and Fred rushes over to her, and Mr. Pike, too, and there she sets, pointin' her finger at a photo in my copy of *Startling G-Man*. 'See that man?' yells Mrs. Pike. 'Remember him, Canfield?' 'Never forget a face,' says Mr. Pike. 'It's Mr. Petrie, that we stayed with him in the apartment next to ours in Toulouse Street in N.O. for six weeks. Mr. Petrie.' 'Well,' says Mrs. Pike, like she can't hold out one secont longer, 'Mr. Petrie is wanted for five hundred dollars cash, for rapin' four women in California, and I know where he is.' "

"Mercy!" said Mrs. Fletcher. "Where was he?"

At some time Leota had washed her hair and now she yanked her up by the back locks and sat her up.

"Know where he was?"

"I certainly don't," Mrs. Fletcher said. Her scalp hurt all over.

Leota flung a towel around the top of her customer's head. "Nowhere else but in that freak show! I saw him just as plain as Mrs. Pike. *He* was the petrified man!"

"Who would ever have thought that!" cried Mrs. Fletcher sympathetically.

"So Mr. Pike says, 'Well whatta you know about that,' an' he looks real hard at the photo and whistles. And she starts dancin' and singin' about their good luck. She meant our bad luck! I made a point of tellin' that fortune-teller the next time I saw her. I said, 'Listen, that magazine was layin' around the house for a month, and there was the freak show runnin' night an' day, not two steps away from my own beauty parlor, with Mr. Petrie just settin' there waitin'. An' it had to be Mr. and Mrs. Pike, almost perfect strangers.' "

"What gall," said Mrs. Fletcher. She was only sitting there, wrapped in a turban, but she did not mind.

"Fortune-tellers don't care. And Mrs. Pike, she goes around actin' like she thinks she was Mrs. God," said Leota. "So they're goin' to leave tomorrow, Mr. and Mrs. Pike. And in the meantime I got to keep that mean, bad little ole kid here, gettin' under my feet ever' minute of the day an' talkin' back too."

"Have they gotten the five hundred dollars' reward already?" asked Mrs. Fletcher.

"Well," said Leota, "at first Mr. Pike didn't want to do anything about it. Can you feature that? Said he kinda liked that ole bird and said he was real nice to 'em, lent 'em money or somethin'. But Mrs. Pike simply tole him he could just go to hell, and I can see her point. She says, 'You ain't worked a lick in six months, and here I make five hundred dollars in two seconts, and what thanks do I get for it? You go to hell, Canfield,' she says. So," Leota went on in a despondent voice, "they called up the cops and they caught the ole bird, all right, right there in the freak show where I saw him with my own eyes, thinkin' he was petrified. He's the one. Did it under his real name—Mr. Petrie. Four women in California, all in the month of August. So Mrs. Pike gits five hundred dollars. And my magazine, and right next door to my beauty parlor. I cried all night, but Fred said it wasn't a bit of use and to go to sleep, because the whole thing was just a sort of coincidence—you know: can't do nothin' about it. He says it put him clean out of the notion of goin' to Vicksburg for a few days till we rent out the room agin—no tellin' who we'll git this time."

"But can you imagine anybody knowing this old man, that's raped four women?" persisted Mrs. Fletcher, and she shuddered audibly. "Did Mrs. Pike *speak* to him when she met him in the freak show?"

Leota had begun to comb Mrs. Fletcher's hair. "I says to her, I says. 'I didn't notice you fallin' on his neck when he was the petrified man—don't tell me you didn't recognize your fine friend?' And she says, 'I didn't recognize him with that white powder all over his face. He just looked familiar,' Mrs. Pike says, 'and lots of people look familiar.' But she says that ole petrified man did put her in mind of somebody. She wondered who it was! Kep' her awake, which man she'd ever knew it reminded her of. So when she seen the photo, it all come to her. Like a flash. Mr. Petrie. The way he'd turn his head and look at her when she took him in his breakfast."

"Took him in his breakfast!" shrieked Mrs. Fletcher. "Listen—don't tell me. I'd 'a' felt something."

"Four women. I guess those women didn't have the faintest notion at the time they'd be worth a hunderd an' twenty-five bucks apiece some day to Mrs. Pike. We ast her how old the fella was then, an' she says he musta had one foot in the grave, at least. Can you beat it?"

"Not really petrified at all, of course," said Mrs. Fletcher meditatively. She drew herself up. "I'd 'a' felt something," she said proudly.

"Shoot! I did feel somethin'," said Leota. "I tole Fred when I got home I felt so funny. I said, 'Fred, that ole petrified man sure did leave me with a funny feelin'.' He says, 'Funny-haha or funny-peculiar?' and I says, 'Funny-peculiar.'" She pointed her comb into the air emphatically.

"I'll bet you did," said Mrs. Fletcher.

They both heard a crackling noise.

Leota screamed, "Billy Boy! What you doin' in my purse?"

"Aw, I'm just eatin' these ole stale peanuts up," said Billy Boy.

"You come here to me!" screamed Leota, recklessly flinging down the comb, which scattered a whole ash-tray full of bobby pins and knocked down a row of Coca-Cola bottles. "This is the last straw!"

"I caught him! I caught him!" giggled Mrs. Fletcher. "I'll hold him on my lap. You bad, bad boy, you! I guess I better learn how to spank little old bad boys," she said.

Leota's eleven o'clock customer pushed open the swing-door upon Leota paddling him heartily with the brush, while he gave angry but belittling screams which penetrated beyond the booth and filled the whole curious beauty parlor. From everywhere ladies began to gather round to watch the paddling. Billy Boy kicked both Leota and Mrs. Fletcher as hard as he could, Mrs. Fletcher with her new fixed smile.

Billy Boy stomped through the group of wild-haired ladies and went out the door, but flung back the words, "If you're so smart, why ain't you rich?"

A Still Moment

Lorenzo Dow rode the Old Natchez Trace at top speed upon a race horse, and the cry of the itinerant Man of God, "I must have souls! And souls I must have!" rang in his own windy ears. He rode as if never to stop, toward his night's appointment.

It was the hour of sunset. All the souls that he had saved and all those he had not took dusky shapes in the mist that hung between the high banks, and seemed by their great number and density to block his way, and showed no signs of melting or changing back into mist, so that he feared his passage was to be difficult forever. The poor souls that were not saved were darker and more pitiful than those that were, and still there was not any of the radiance he would have hoped to see in such a congregation.

"Light up, in God's name!" he called, in the pain of his disappointment.

Then a whole swarm of fireflies instantly flickered all around him, up and down, back and forth, first one golden light and then another, flashing without any of the weariness that had held back the souls. These were the signs sent from God that he had not seen the accumulated radiance of saved souls because he was not

able, and that his eyes were more able to see the fireflies of the Lord than His blessed souls.

"Lord, give me the strength to see the angels when I
am in Paradise," he said. "Do not let my eyes remain in
this failing proportion to my loving heart always."

He gasped and held on. It was that day's complexity
of horse-trading that had left him in the end with a
Spanish race horse for which he was bound to send
money in November from Georgia. Riding faster on the
beast and still faster until he felt as if he were flying he
sent thoughts of love with matching speed to his wife
Peggy in Massachusetts. He found it effortless to love at
a distance. He could look at the flowering trees and love
Peggy in fullness, just as he could see his visions and
love God. And Peggy, to whom he had not spoken until
he could speak fateful words ("Would she accept of
such an object as him?"), Peggy, the bride, with whom
he had spent a few hours of time, showing of herself a
small round handwriting, declared all in one letter, her
first, that she felt the same as he, and that the fear was
never of separation, but only of death.

Lorenzo well knew that it was Death that opened
underfoot, that rippled by at night, that was the silence
the birds did their singing in. He was close to death,
closer than any animal or bird. On the back of one
horse after another, winding them all, he was always
riding toward it or away from it, and the Lord sent him
directions with protection in His mind.

Just then he rode into a thicket of Indians taking aim
with their new guns. One stepped out and took the
horse by the bridle, it stopped at a touch, and the rest
made a closing circle. The guns pointed.

"Incline!" The inner voice spoke sternly and with its
customary lightning-quickness.

Lorenzo inclined all the way forward and put his
head to the horse's silky mane, his body to its body,
until a bullet meant for him would endanger the horse
and make his death of no value. Prone he rode out
through the circle of Indians, his obedience to the voice
leaving him almost fearless, almost careless with joy.

But as he straightened and pressed ahead, care caught up with him again. Turning half-beast and half-divine, dividing himself like a heathen Centaur, he had escaped his death once more. But was it to be always by some metamorphosis of himself that he escaped, some humiliation of his faith, some admission to strength and argumentation and not frailty? Each time when he acted so it was at the command of an instinct that he took at once as the word of an angel, until too late, when he knew it was the word of the devil. He had roared like a tiger at Indians, he had submerged himself in water blowing the savage bubbles of the alligator, and they skirted him by. He had prostrated himself to appear dead, and deceived bears. But all the time God would have protected him in His own way, less hurried, more divine.

Even now he saw a serpent crossing the Trace, giving out knowing glances.

He cried, "I know you now!", and the serpent gave him one look out of which all the fire had been taken, and went away in two darts into the tangle.

He rode on, all expectation, and the voices in the throats of the wild beasts went, almost without his noticing when, into words. "Praise God," they said. "Deliver us from one another." Birds especially sang of divine love which was the one ceaseless protection. "Peace, in peace," were their words so many times when they spoke from the briars, in a courteous sort of inflection, and he turned his countenance toward all perched creatures with a benevolence striving to match their own.

He rode on past the little intersecting trails, letting himself be guided by voices and by lights. It was battle-sounds he heard most, sending him on, but sometimes ocean sounds, that long beat of waves that would make his heart pound and retreat as heavily as they, and he despaired again in his failure in Ireland when he took a voyage and persuaded with the Catholics with his back against the door, and then ran away to their cries of "Mind the white hat!" But when he heard singing it was not the militant and sharp sound of Wesley's hymns, but a soft, tireless and tender air that had no beginning and no end, and the softness of distance, and he had pleaded with the Lord to find out if all this meant that it was wicked, but no answer had come.

Soon night would descend, and a camp-meeting ground ahead would fill with its sinners like the sky with its stars. How he hungered for them! He looked in prescience with a longing of love over the throng that waited while the flames of the torches threw change, change, change over their faces. How could he bring them enough, if it were not divine love and sufficient warning of all that could threaten them? He rode on faster. He was a filler of appointments, and he filled more and more, until his journeys up and down creation were nothing but a shuttle, driving back and forth upon the rich expanse of his vision. He was homeless by his own choice, he must be everywhere at some time, and somewhere soon. There hastening in the wilderness on his flying horse he gave the night's torch-lit crowd a premature benediction, he could not wait. He spread his arms out, one at a time for safety, and he wished, when they would all be gathered in by his tin horn blasts and the inspired words would go out over their heads, to brood above the entire and passionate life of the wide world, to become its rightful part.

He peered ahead. "Inhabitants of Time! The wilderness is your souls on earth!" he shouted ahead into the treetops. "Look about you, if you would view the conditions of your spirit, put here by the good Lord to show you and afright you. These wild places and these trails of awesome loneliness lie nowhere, nowhere, but in your heart."

A dark man, who was James Murrell the outlaw, rode his horse out of a cane brake and began going along beside Lorenzo without looking at him. He had the alternately proud and aggrieved look of a man believing himself to be an instrument in the hands of a power, and when he was young he said at once to strangers that he was being used by Evil, or sometimes he stopped a traveler by shouting, "Stop! I'm the Devil!"

He rode along now talking and drawing out his talk, by some deep control of the voice gradually slowing the speed of Lorenzo's horse down until both the horses were softly trotting. He would have wondered that nothing he said was heard, not knowing that Lorenzo listened only to voices of whose heavenly origin he was more certain.

Murrell riding along with his victim-to-be, Murrell riding, was Murrell talking. He told away at his long tales, with always a distance and a long length of time flowing through them, and all centered about a silent man. In each the silent man would have done a piece of evil, a robbery or a murder, in a place of long ago, and it was all made for the revelation in the end that the silent man was Murrell himself, and the long story had happened yesterday, and the place *here*—the Natchez Trace. It would only take one dawning look for the victim to see that all of this was another story and he himself had listened his way into it, and that he too was about to recede in time (to where the dread was forgotten) for some listener and to live for a listener in the long ago. Destroy the present!—that must have been the first thing that was whispered in Murrell's heart—the living moment and the man that lives in it must die before you can go on. It was his habit to bring the journey—which might even take days—to a close with a kind of ceremony. Turning his face at last into the face of the victim, for he had never seen him before now, he would tower up with the sudden height of a man no longer the tale teller but the speechless protagonist, silent at last, one degree nearer the hero. Then he would murder the man.

But it would always start over. This man going forward was going backward with talk. He saw nothing, observed no world at all. The two ends of his journey pulled at him always and held him in a nowhere, half asleep, smiling and witty, dangling his predicament. He was a murderer whose final stroke was over-long postponed, who had to bring himself through the greatest tedium to act, as if the whole wilderness, where he was born, were his impediment. But behind him and before him he kept in sight a victim, he saw a man fixed and stayed at the point of death—no matter how the man's eyes denied it, a victim, hands spreading to reach as if for the first time for life. Contempt! That is what Murrell gave that man.

Lorenzo might have understood, if he had not been in haste, that Murrell in laying hold of a man meant to solve his mystery of being. It was as if other men, all but himself, would lighten their hold on the secret, upon assault, and let it fly free at death. In his violence he was only treating of enigma. The violence shook his own body first, like a force gathering, and now he turned in the saddle.

Lorenzo's despair had to be kindled as well as his ecstasy, and could not come without that kindling. Before the awe-filled moment when the faces were turned up under the flares, as though an angel hand tipped their chins, he had no way of telling whether he would enter the sermon by sorrow or by joy. But at this moment the face of Murrell was turned toward him, turning at last, all solitary, in its full, and Lorenzo would have seized the man at once by his black coat and shaken him like prey for a lost soul, so instantly was he certain that the false fire was in his heart instead of the true fire. But Murrell, quick when he was quick, had put his own hand out, a restraining hand, and laid it on the wavelike flesh of the Spanish race horse, which quivered and shuddered at the touch.

They had come to a great live-oak tree at the edge of a low marsh-land. The burning sun hung low, like a head lowered on folded arms, and over the long reaches of violet trees the evening seemed still with thought. Lorenzo knew the place from having seen it among many in dreams, and he stopped readily and willingly. He drew rein, and Murrell drew rein, he dismounted and Murrell dismounted, he took a step, and Murrell was there too; and Lorenzo was not surprised at the closeness, how Murrell in his long dark coat and over it his dark face darkening still, stood beside him like a brother seeking light.

But in that moment instead of two men coming to stop by the great forked tree, there were three.

From far away, a student, Audubon, had been approaching lightly on the wilderness floor, disturbing nothing in his lightness. The long day of beauty had led him this certain distance. A flock of purple finches that he tried for the first moment to count went over his head. He made a spelling of the soft *pet* of the ivory-billed woodpecker. He told himself always: remember.

Coming upon the Trace, he looked at the high cedars, azure and still as distant smoke overhead, with their silver roots trailing down on either side like the veins of deepness in this place, and he noted some fact to his memory—this earth that wears but will not crumble or slide or turn to dust, they say it exists in one other spot in the world, Egypt—and then forgot it. He walked quietly. All life used this Trace, and he liked to see the animals move along it in direct, oblivious journeys, for they had begun it and made it, the buffalo and deer and the small running creatures before man ever knew where he wanted to go, and birds flew a great mirrored course above. Walking beneath them Audubon remembered how in the cities he had seen these very birds in his imagination, calling them up whenever he wished, even in the hard and glittering outer parlors where if an artist were humble enough to wait, some idle hand held up promised money. He walked lightly and he went as carefully as he had started at two that morning, crayon and paper, a gun, and a small bottle of spirits disposed about his body. (*Note: "The mocking birds so gentle that they would scarcely move out of the way."*) He looked with care; great abundance had ceased to startle him, and he could see things one by one. In Natchez they had told him of many strange and marvelous birds that were to be found here. Their descriptions had been exact, complete, and wildly varying, and he took them for inventions and believed that like all the worldly things that came out of Natchez, they would be disposed of and shamed by any man's excursion into the reality of Nature.

In the valley he appeared under the tree, a sure man, very sure and tender, as if the touch of all the earth rubbed upon him and the stains of the flowery swamp had made him so.

Lorenzo welcomed him and turned fond eyes upon him. To transmute a man into an angel was the hope that drove him all over the world and never let him flinch from a meeting or withhold good-byes for long. This hope insistently divided his life into only two parts, journey and rest. There could be no night and day and love and despair and longing and satisfaction to make partitions in the single ecstasy of this alternation. All things were speech.

"God created the world," said Lorenzo, "and it exists to give testimony. Life is the tongue: speak."

But instead of speech there happened a moment of deepest silence.

Audubon said nothing because he had gone without speaking a word for days. He did not regard his thoughts for the birds and animals as susceptible, in their first change, to words. His long playing on the flute was not in its origin a talking to himself. Rather than speak to order or describe, he would always draw a deer with a stroke across it to communicate his need of venison to an Indian. He had only found words when he discovered that there is much otherwise lost that can be noted down each item in its own day, and he wrote often now in a journal, not wanting anything to be lost the way it had been, all the past, and he would write about a day, "Only sorry that the Sun Sets."

Murrell, his cheated hand hiding the gun, could only continue to smile at Lorenzo, but he remembered in malice that he had disguised himself once as an Evangelist, and his final words to this victim would have been, "One of my disguises was what you are."

Then in Murrell Audubon saw what he thought of as "acquired sorrow"—that cumbrousness and darkness from which the naked Indian, coming just as he was made from God's hand, was so lightly free. He noted the eyes—the dark kind that loved to look through chinks, and saw neither closeness nor distance, light nor shade, wonder nor familiarity. They were narrowed to contract the heart, narrowed to make an averting plan. Audubon knew the finest-drawn tendons of the body and the working of their power, for he had touched them, and he supposed then that in man the enlargement of the eye to see started a motion in the hands to make or do, and that the narrowing of the eye stopped the hand and contracted the heart. Now Murrell's eyes followed an ant on a blade of grass, up the blade and down, many times in the single moment. Audubon had examined the Cave-In Rock where one robber had lived his hiding life, and the air in the cave was the cavelike air that enclosed this man, the same odor, flinty and dark. O secret life, he thought—is it true that the secret is withdrawn from the true disclosure, that man is a cave man, and that the openness I see, the ways through forests, the rivers brimming light, the wide arches where the birds fly, are dreams of freedom? If my origin is withheld from me, is my end to be unknown too? Is the radiance I see closed into an interval between two darks, or can it not illuminate them both and discover at last, though it cannot be spoken, what was thought hidden and lost?

In that quiet moment a solitary snowy heron flew down not far away and began to feed beside the marsh water.

At the single streak of flight, the ears of the race horse lifted, and the eyes of both horses filled with the soft lights of sunset, which in the next instant were reflected in the eyes of the men too as they all looked into the west toward the heron, and all eyes seemed infused with a sort of wildness.

Lorenzo gave the bird a triumphant look, such as a man may bestow upon his own vision, and thought, Nearness is near, lighted in a marsh-land, feeding at sunset. Praise God, His love has come visible.

Murrell, in suspicion pursuing all glances, blinking into a haze, saw only whiteness ensconced in darkness, as if it were a little luminous shell that drew in and held the eyesight. When he shaded his eyes, the brand "H.T." on his thumb thrust itself into his own vision, and he

looked at the bird with the whole plan of the Mystic
Rebellion darting from him as if in rays of the bright
reflected light, and he stood looking proudly, leader as
he was bound to become of the slaves, the brigands and
outcasts of the entire Natchez country, with plans,
dates, maps burning like a brand into his brain, and he
saw himself proudly in a moment of prophecy going
down rank after rank of successively bowing slaves to
unroll and flaunt an awesome great picture of the Devil
colored on a banner.

Audubon's eyes embraced the object in the distance
and he could see it as carefully as if he held it in his
hand. It was a snowy heron alone out of its flock. He
watched it steadily, in his care noting the exact inevita-
ble things. When it feeds it muddies the water with its
foot. . . . It was as if each detail about the heron happened slowly in time, and only once. He felt again the
old stab of wonder—what structure of life bridged the
reptile's scale and the heron's feather? That knowledge
too had been lost. He watched without moving. The
bird was defenseless in the world except for the intensity of its life, and he wondered, how can heat of blood
and speed of heart defend it? Then he thought, as always as if it were new and unbelievable, it has nothing
in space or time to prevent its flight. And he waited,
knowing that some birds will wait for a sense of their
presence to travel to men before they will fly away from
them.

Fixed in its pure white profile it stood in the precipi-
tous moment, a plumicorn on its head, its breeding
dress extended in rays, eating steadily the little water
creatures. There was a little space between each man
and the others, where they stood overwhelmed. No one
could say the three had ever met, or that this moment
of intersection had ever come in their lives, or its promise fulfilled. But before them the white heron rested in
the grasses with the evening all around it, lighter and
more serene than the evening, flight closed in its body,
the circuit of its beauty closed, a bird seen and a bird
still, its motion calm as if it were offered: Take my
flight. . . .

What each of them had wanted was simply *all*. To save all souls, to destroy all men, to see and to record all life that filled this world—all, all—but now a single frail yearning seemed to go out of the three of them for a moment and to stretch toward this one snowy, shy bird in the marshes. It was as if three whirlwinds had drawn together at some center, to find there feeding in peace a snowy heron. Its own slow spiral of flight could take it away in its own time, but for a little it held them still, it laid quiet over them, and they stood for a moment unburdened. . . .

Murrell wore no mask, for his face was that, a face that was aware while he was somnolent, a face that watched for him, and listened for him, alert and nearly brutal, the guard of a planner. He was quick without that he might be slow within, he staved off time, he wandered and plotted, and yet his whole desire mounted in him toward the end (was this the end—the sight of a bird feeding at dusk?), toward the instant of confession. His incessant deeds were thick in his heart now, and flinging himself to the ground he thought wearily, when all these trees are cut down, and the Trace lost, then my Conspiracy that is yet to spread itself will be disclosed, and all the stone-loaded bodies of murdered men will be pulled up, and all everywhere will know poor Murrell. His look pressed upon Lorenzo, who stared upward, and Audubon, who was taking out his gun, and his eyes squinted up to them in pleading, as if to say, "How soon may I speak, and how soon will you pity me?" Then he looked back to the bird, and he thought if it would look at him a dread penetration would fill and gratify his heart.

Audubon in each act of life was aware of the mysterious origin he half-concealed and half-sought for. People along the way asked him in their kindness or their rudeness if it were true, that he was born a prince, and was the Lost Dauphin, and some said it was his secret, and some said that that was what he wished to find out before he died. But if it was his identity that he wished to discover, or if it was what a man had to seize beyond that, the way for him was by endless examination, by the care for every bird that flew in his path and every serpent that shone underfoot. Not one was enough; he looked deeper and deeper, on and on, as if for a particular beast or some legendary bird. Some men's eyes persisted in looking outward when they opened to look inward, and to their delight, there outflung was the astonishing world under the sky. When a man at last brought himself to face some mirror-surface he still saw the world looking back at him, and if he continued to look, to look closer and closer, what then? The gaze that looks outward must be trained without rest, to be indomitable. It must see as slowly as Murrell's ant in the grass, as exhaustively as Lorenzo's angel of God, and then, Audubon dreamed, with his mind going to his pointed brush, it must see like this, and he tightened his hand on the trigger of the gun and pulled it, and his eyes went closed. In memory the heron was all its solitude, its total beauty. All its whiteness could be seen from all sides at once, its pure feathers were as if counted and known and their array one upon the other would never be lost. But it was not from that memory that he could paint.

His opening eyes met Lorenzo's, close and flashing, and it was on seeing horror deep in them, like fires in abysses, that he recognized it for the first time. He had never seen horror in its purity and clarity until now, in bright blue eyes. He went and picked up the bird. He had thought it to be a female, just as one sees the moon as female; and so it was. He put it in his bag, and started away. But Lorenzo had already gone on, leaning a-tilt on the horse which went slowly.

Murrell was left behind, but he was proud of the dispersal, as if he had done it, as if he had always known that three men in simply being together and doing a thing can, by their obstinacy, take the pride out of one another. Each must go away alone, each send the others away alone. He himself had purposely kept to the wildest country in the world, and would have sought it out, the loneliest road. He looked about with satisfaction, and hid. Travelers were forever innocent, he believed: that was his faith. He lay in wait; his faith was

in innocence and his knowledge was of ruin; and had
these things been shaken? Now, what could possibly be
outside his grasp? Churning all about him like a cloud
about the sun was the great folding descent of his
thought. Plans of deeds made his thoughts, and they
rolled and mingled about his ears as if he heard a dark
voice that rose up to overcome the wilderness voice, or
was one with it. The night would soon come; and he
had gone through the day.

Audubon, splattered and wet, turned back into the
wilderness with the heron warm under his hand, his
head still light in a kind of trance. It was undeniable, on
some Sunday mornings, when he turned over and over
his drawings they seemed beautiful to him, through
what was dramatic in the conflict of life, or what was
exact. What he would draw, and what he had seen,
became for a moment one to him then. Yet soon
enough, and it seemed to come in that same moment,
like Lorenzo's horror and the gun's firing, he knew that
even the sight of the heron which surely he alone had
appreciated, had not been all his belonging, and that
never could any vision, even any simple sight, belong to
him or to any man. He knew that the best he could
make would be, after it was apart from his hand, a dead
thing and not a live thing, never the essence, only a sum
of parts; and that it would always meet with a stranger's
sight, and never be one with the beauty in any other
man's head in the world. As he had seen the bird most
purely at its moment of death, in some fatal way, in his
care for looking outward, he saw his long labor most
revealingly at the point where it met its limit. Still carefully, for he was trained to see well in the dark, he
walked on into the deeper woods, noting all sights, all
sounds, and was gentler than they as he went.

In the woods that echoed yet in his ears, Lorenzo
riding slowly looked back. The hair rose on his head
and his hands began to shake with cold, and suddenly it
seemed to him that God Himself, just now, thought of
the Idea of Separateness. For surely He had never
thought of it before, when the little white heron was
flying down to feed. He could understand God's giving

Separateness first and then giving Love to follow and heal in its wonder; but God had reversed this, and given Love first and then Separateness, as though it did not matter to Him which came first. Perhaps it was that God never counted the moments of Time; Lorenzo did that, among his tasks of love. Time did not occur to God. Therefore—did He even know of it? How to explain Time and Separateness back to God, Who had never thought of them, Who could let the whole world come to grief in a scattering moment?

Lorenzo brought his cold hands together in a clasp and stared through the distance at the place where the bird had been as if he saw it still; as if nothing could really take away what had happened to him, the beautiful little vision of the feeding bird. Its beauty had been greater than he could account for. The sweat of rapture poured down from his forehead, and then he shouted into the marshes.

"Tempter!"

He whirled forward in the saddle and began to hurry the horse to its high speed. His camp ground was far away still, though even now they must be lighting the torches and gathering in the multitudes, so that at the appointed time he would duly appear in their midst, to deliver his address on the subject of "In that day when all hearts shall be disclosed."

Then the sun dropped below the trees, and the new moon, slender and white, hung shyly in the west.

Lily Daw and the Three Ladies

Mrs. Watts and Mrs. Carson were both in the post office in Victory when the letter came from the Ellisville Institute for the Feeble-Minded of Mississippi. Aimee Slocum, with her hand still full of mail, ran out in front and handed it straight to Mrs. Watts, and they all three read it together. Mrs. Watts held it taut between her pink hands, and Mrs. Carson underscored each line slowly with her thimbled finger. Everybody else in the post office wondered what was up now.

"What will Lily say," beamed Mrs. Carson at last, "when we tell her we're sending her to Ellisville!"

"She'll be tickled to death," said Mrs. Watts, and added in a guttural voice to a deaf lady, "Lily Daw's getting in at Ellisville!"

"Don't you all dare go off and tell Lily without me!" called Aimee Slocum, trotting back to finish putting up the mail.

"Do you suppose they'll look after her down there?" Mrs. Carson began to carry on a conversation with a group of Baptist ladies waiting in the post office. She was the Baptist preacher's wife.

"I've always heard it was lovely down there, but crowded," said one.

"Lily lets people walk over her so," said another.

"Last night at the tent show—" said another, and then popped her hand over her mouth.

"Don't mind me, I know there are such things in the world," said Mrs. Carson, looking down and fingering the tape measure which hung over her bosom.

"Oh, Mrs. Carson. Well, anyway, last night at the tent show, why, the man was just before making Lily buy a ticket to get in."

"A ticket!"

"Till my husband went up and explained she wasn't bright, and so did everybody else."

The ladies all clucked their tongues.

"Oh, it was a very nice show," said the lady who had gone. "And Lily acted so nice. She was a perfect lady— just set in her seat and stared."

"Oh, she can be a lady—she can be," said Mrs. Carson, shaking her head and turning her eyes up. "That's just what breaks your heart."

"Yes'm, she kept her eyes on—what's that thing makes all the commotion?—the xylophone," said the lady. "Didn't turn her head to the right or to the left the whole time. Set in front of me."

"The point is, what did she do after the show?" asked Mrs. Watts practically. "Lily has gotten so she is very mature for her age."

"Oh, Etta!" protested Mrs. Carson, looking at her wildly for a moment.

"And that's how come we are sending her to Ellisville," finished Mrs. Watts.

"I'm ready, you all," said Aimee Slocum, running out with white powder all over her face. "Mail's up. I don't know how good it's up."

"Well, of course, I do hope it's for the best," said several of the other ladies. They did not go at once to take their mail out of their boxes; they felt a little left out.

The three women stood at the foot of the water tank.

"To find Lily is a different thing," said Aimee Slocum.

"Where in the wide world do you suppose she'd be?" It was Mrs. Watts who was carrying the letter.

"I don't see a sign of her either on this side of the street or on the other side," Mrs. Carson declared as they walked along.

Ed Newton was stringing Redbird school tablets on the wire across the store.

"If you're after Lily, she come in here while ago and tole me she was fixin' to git married," he said.

"Ed Newton!" cried the ladies all together, clutching one another. Mrs. Watts began to fan herself at once with the letter from Ellisville. She wore widow's black, and the least thing made her hot.

"Why she is not. She's going to Ellisville, Ed," said Mrs. Carson gently. "Mrs. Watts and I and Aimee Slocum are paying her way out of our own pockets. Besides, the boys of Victory are on their honor. Lily's not going to get married, that's just an idea she's got in her head."

"More power to you, ladies," said Ed Newton, spanking himself with a tablet.

When they came to the bridge over the railroad tracks, there was Estelle Mabers, sitting on a rail. She was slowly drinking an orange Ne-Hi.

"Have you seen Lily?" they asked her.

"I'm supposed to be out here watching for her now," said the Mabers girl, as though she weren't there yet. "But for Jewel—Jewel says Lily come in the store while ago and picked out a two-ninety-eight hat and wore it off. Jewel wants to swap her something else for it."

"Oh, Estelle, Lily says she's going to get married!" cried Aimee Slocum.

"Well, I declare," said Estelle; she never understood anything.

Loralee Adkins came riding by in her Willys-Knight, tooting the horn to find out what they were talking about.

Aimee threw up her hands and ran out into the street. "Loralee, Loralee, you got to ride us up to Lily Daws'. She's up yonder fixing to get married!"

"Hop in, my land!"

"Well, that just goes to show you right now," said Mrs. Watts, groaning as she was helped into the back seat. "What we've got to do is persuade Lily it will be nicer to go to Ellisville."

"Just to think!"

While they rode around the corner Mrs. Carson was going on in her sad voice, sad as the soft noises in the hen house at twilight. "We buried Lily's poor defenseless mother. We gave Lily all her food and kindling and every stitch she had on. Sent her to Sunday school to learn the Lord's teachings, had her baptized a Baptist. And when her old father commenced beating her and tried to cut her head off with the butcher knife, why, we went and took her away from him and gave her a place to stay."

The paintless frame house with all the weather vanes was three stories high in places and had yellow and violet stained-glass windows in front and gingerbread around the porch. It leaned steeply to one side, toward the railroad, and the front steps were gone. The car full of ladies drew up under the cedar tree.

"Now Lily's almost grown up," Mrs. Carson continued. "In fact, she's grown," she concluded, getting out.

"Talking about getting married," said Mrs. Watts disgustedly. "Thanks, Loralee, you run on home."

They climbed over the dusty zinnias onto the porch and walked through the open door without knocking.

"There certainly is always a funny smell in this house. I say it every time I come," said Aimee Slocum.

Lily was there, in the dark of the hall, kneeling on the floor by a small open trunk.

When she saw them she put a zinnia in her mouth, and held still.

"Hello, Lily," said Mrs. Carson reproachfully.

"Hello," said Lily. In a minute she gave a suck on the zinnia stem that sounded exactly like a jay bird. There she sat, wearing a petticoat for a dress, one of the things Mrs. Carson kept after her about. Her milky-yellow hair streamed freely down from under a new hat. You could see the wavy scar on her throat if you knew it was there.

Mrs. Carson and Mrs. Watts, the two fattest, sat in the double rocker. Aimee Slocum sat on the wire chair donated from the drugstore that burned.

"Well, what are you doing, Lily?" asked Mrs. Watts, who led the rocking.

Lily smiled.

The trunk was old and lined with yellow and brown paper, with an asterisk pattern showing in darker circles and rings. Mutely the ladies indicated to each other that they did not know where in the world it had come from. It was empty except for two bars of soap and a green washcloth, which Lily was now trying to arrange in the bottom.

"Go on and tell us what you're doing, Lily," said Aimee Slocum.

"Packing, silly," said Lily.

"Where are you going?"

"Going to get married, and I bet you wish you was me now," said Lily. But shyness overcame her suddenly, and she popped the zinnia back into her mouth.

"Talk to me, dear," said Mrs. Carson. "Tell old Mrs. Carson why you want to get married."

"No," said Lily, after a moment's hesitation.

"Well, we've thought of something that will be so much nicer," said Mrs. Carson. "Why don't you go to Ellisville!"

"Won't that be lovely?" said Mrs. Watts. "Goodness, yes."

"It's a lovely place," said Aimee Slocum uncertainly.

"You've got bumps on your face," said Lily.

"Aimee, dear, you stay out of this, if you don't mind," said Mrs. Carson anxiously. "I don't know what it is comes over Lily when you come around her."

Lily stared at Aimee Slocum meditatively.

"There! Wouldn't you like to go to Ellisville now?" asked Mrs. Carson.

"No'm," said Lily.

"Why not?" All the ladies leaned down toward her in impressive astonishment.

" 'Cause I'm goin' to get married," said Lily.

"Well, and who are you going to marry, dear?" asked Mrs. Watts. She knew how to pin people down and make them deny what they'd already said.

Lily bit her lip and began to smile. She reached into the trunk and held up both cakes of soap and wagged them.

"Tell us," challenged Mrs. Watts. "Who you're going to marry, now."

"A man last night."

There was a gasp from each lady. The possible reality of a lover descended suddenly like a summer hail over their heads. Mrs. Watts stood up and balanced herself.

"One of those show fellows! A musician!" she cried.

Lily looked up in admiration.

"Did he—did he do anything to you?" In the long run, it was still only Mrs. Watts who could take charge.

"Oh, yes'm," said Lily. She patted the cakes of soap fastidiously with the tips of her small fingers and tucked them in with the washcloth.

"What?" demanded Aimee Slocum, rising up and tottering before her scream. "What?" she called out in the hall.

"Don't ask her what," said Mrs. Carson, coming up behind. "Tell me, Lily—just yes or no—are you the same as you were?"

"He had a red coat," said Lily graciously. "He took little sticks and went *ping-pong! ding-dong!*"

"Oh, I think I'm going to faint," said Aimee Slocum, but they said, "No, you're not."

"The xylophone!" cried Mrs. Watts. "The xylophone player! Why, the coward, he ought to be run out of town on a rail!"

"Out of town? He is out of town, by now," cried Aimee. "Can't you read?—the sign in the café—Victory on the ninth, Como on the tenth? He's in Como. Como!"

"All right! We'll bring him back!" cried Mrs. Watts. "He can't get away from me!"

"Hush," said Mrs. Carson. "I don't think it's any use following that line of reasoning at all. It's better in the long run for him to be gone out of our lives for good and all. That kind of a man. He was after Lily's body alone and he wouldn't ever in this world make the poor little thing happy, even if we went out and forced him to marry her like he ought—at the point of a gun."

"Still—" began Aimee, her eyes widening.

"Shut up," said Mrs. Watts. "Mrs. Carson, you're right, I expect."

"This is my hope chest—see?" said Lily politely in the pause that followed. "You haven't even looked at it. I've already got soap and a washrag. And I have my hat —on. What are you all going to give me?"

"Lily," said Mrs. Watts, starting over, "we'll give you lots of gorgeous things if you'll only go to Ellisville instead of getting married."

"What will you give me?" asked Lily.

"I'll give you a pair of hemstitched pillowcases," said Mrs. Carson.

"I'll give you a big caramel cake," said Mrs. Watts.

"I'll give you a souvenir from Jackson—a little toy bank," said Aimee Slocum. "Now will you go?"

"No," said Lily.

"I'll give you a pretty little Bible with your name on it in real gold," said Mrs. Carson.

"What if I was to give you a pink crêpe de Chine brassière with adjustable shoulder straps?" asked Mrs. Watts grimly.

"Oh, Etta."

"Well, she needs it," said Mrs. Watts. "What would they think if she ran all over Ellisville in a petticoat looking like a Fiji?"

"I wish *I* could go to Ellisville," said Aimee Slocum luringly.

"What will they have for me down there?" asked Lily softly.

"Oh! lots of things. You'll have baskets to weave, I expect. . . ." Mrs. Carson looked vaguely at the others.

"Oh, yes indeed, they will let you make all sorts of baskets," said Mrs. Watts; then her voice too trailed off.

"No'm, I'd rather get married," said Lily.

"Lily Daw! Now that's just plain stubbornness!" cried Mrs. Watts. "You almost said you'd go and then you took it back!"

"We've all asked God, Lily," said Mrs. Carson finally, "and God seemed to tell us—Mr. Carson, too—that the place where you ought to be, so as to be happy, was Ellisville."

Lily looked reverent, but still stubborn.

"We've really just got to get her there—now!" screamed Aimee Slocum all at once. "Suppose—! She can't stay here!"

"Oh, no, no, no," said Mrs. Carson hurriedly. "We mustn't think that."

They sat sunken in despair.

"Could I take my hope chest—to go to Ellisville?" asked Lily shyly, looking at them sidewise.

"Why, yes," said Mrs. Carson blankly.

Silently they rose once more to their feet.

"Oh, if I could just take my hope chest!"

"All the time it was just her hope chest," Aimee whispered.

Mrs. Watts struck her palms together. "It's settled!"

"Praise the fathers," murmured Mrs. Carson.

Lily looked up at them, and her eyes gleamed. She cocked her head and spoke out in a proud imitation of someone—someone utterly unknown.

"O.K.—Toots!"

The ladies had been nodding and smiling and backing away toward the door.

"I think I'd better stay," said Mrs. Carson, stopping in her tracks. "Where—where could she have learned that terrible expression?"

"Pack up," said Mrs. Watts. "Lily Daw is leaving for Ellisville on Number One."

In the station the train was puffing. Nearly everyone in Victory was hanging around waiting for it to leave. The Victory Civic Band had assembled without any orders and was scattered through the crowd. Ed Newton gave false signals to start on his bass horn. A crate full of baby chickens got loose on the platform. Everybody wanted to see Lily all dressed up, but Mrs. Carson and Mrs. Watts had sneaked her into the train from the other side of the tracks.

The two ladies were going to travel as far as Jackson to help Lily change trains and be sure she went in the right direction.

Lily sat between them on the plush seat with her hair combed and pinned up into a knot under a small blue hat which was Jewel's exchange for the pretty one. She wore a traveling dress made out of part of Mrs. Watts's last summer's mourning. Pink straps glowed through. She had a purse and a Bible and a warm cake in a box, all in her lap.

Aimee Slocum had been getting the outgoing mail stamped and bundled. She stood in the aisle of the coach now, tears shaking from her eyes.

"Good-bye, Lily," she said. She was the one who felt things.

"Good-bye, silly," said Lily.

"Oh, dear, I hope they get our telegram to meet her in Ellisville!" Aimee cried sorrowfully, as she thought how far away it was. "And it was so hard to get it all in ten words, too."

"Get off, Aimee, before the train starts and you break your neck," said Mrs. Watts, all settled and waving her dressy fan gaily. "I declare, it's so hot, as soon as we get a few miles out of town I'm going to slip my corset down."

"Oh, Lily, don't cry down there. Just be good, and do what they tell you—it's all because they love you." Aimee drew her mouth down. She was backing away, down the aisle.

Lily laughed. She pointed across Mrs. Carson's bosom out the window toward a man. He had stepped off the train and just stood there, by himself. He was a stranger and wore a cap.

"Look," she said, laughing softly through her fingers.

"Don't—look," said Mrs. Carson very distinctly, as if, out of all she had ever spoken, she would impress these two solemn words upon Lily's soft little brain. She added, "Don't look at anything till you get to Ellisville."

Outside, Aimee Slocum was crying so hard she almost ran into the stranger. He wore a cap and was short and seemed to have on perfume, if such a thing could be.

"Could you tell me, madam," he said, "where a little lady lives in this burg name of Miss Lily Daw?" He lifted his cap—and he had red hair.

"What do you want to know for?" Aimee asked before she knew it.

"Talk louder," said the stranger. He almost whispered, himself.

"She's gone away—she's gone to Ellisville!"

"Gone?"

"Gone to Ellisville!"

"Well, I like that!" The man stuck out his bottom lip and puffed till his hair jumped.

"What business did you have with Lily?" cried Aimee suddenly.

"We was only going to get married, that's all," said the man.

Aimee Slocum started to scream in front of all those people. She almost pointed to the long black box she saw lying on the ground at the man's feet. Then she jumped back in fright.

"The xylophone! The xylophone!" she cried, looking back and forth from the man to the hissing train. Which was more terrible? The bell began to ring hollowly, and the man was talking.

"Did you say Ellisville? That in the state of Mississippi?" Like lightning he had pulled out a red notebook entitled, "Permanent Facts & Data." He wrote down something. "I don't hear well."

Aimee nodded her head up and down, and circled around him.

Under "Ellis-Ville Miss" he was drawing a line; now he was flicking it with two little marks. "Maybe she didn't say she would. Maybe she said she wouldn't." He suddenly laughed very loudly, after the way he had whispered. Aimee jumped back. "Women!— Well, if we play anywheres near Ellisville, Miss., in the future I may look her up and I may not," he said.

The bass horn sounded the true signal for the band to begin. White steam rushed out of the engine. Usually the train stopped for only a minute in Victory, but the engineer knew Lily from waving at her, and he knew this was her big day.

"Wait!" Aimee Slocum did scream. "Wait, mister! I can get her for you. Wait, Mister Engineer! Don't go!"

Then there she was back on the train, screaming in Mrs. Carson's and Mrs. Watts's faces.

"The xylophone player! The xylophone player to marry her! Yonder he is!"

"Nonsense," murmured Mrs. Watts, peering over the others to look where Aimee pointed. "If he's there I don't see him. Where is he? You're looking at One-Eye Beasley."

"The little man with the cap—no, with the red hair! Hurry!"

"Is that really him?" Mrs. Carson asked Mrs. Watts in wonder. "Mercy! He's small, isn't he?"

"Never saw him before in my life!" cried Mrs. Watts. But suddenly she shut up her fan.

"Come on! This is a train we're on!" cried Aimee Slocum. Her nerves were all unstrung.

"All right, don't have a conniption fit, girl," said Mrs. Watts. "Come on," she said thickly to Mrs. Carson.

"Where are we going now?" asked Lily as they struggled down the aisle.

"We're taking you to get married," said Mrs. Watts. "Mrs. Carson, you'd better phone up your husband right there in the station."

"But I don't want to git married," said Lily, beginning to whimper. "I'm going to Ellisville."

"Hush, and we'll all have some ice-cream cones later," whispered Mrs. Carson.

Just as they climbed down the steps at the back end of the train, the band went into "Independence March."

The xylophone player was still there, patting his foot. He came up and said, "Hello, Toots. What's up—

tricks?" and kissed Lily with a smack, after which she hung her head.

"So you're the young man we've heard so much about," said Mrs. Watts. Her smile was brilliant. "Here's your little Lily."

"What say?" asked the xylophone player.

"My husband happens to be the Baptist preacher of Victory," said Mrs. Carson in a loud, clear voice. "Isn't that lucky? I can get him here in five minutes: I know exactly where he is."

They were in a circle around the xylophone player, all going into the white waiting room.

"Oh, I feel just like crying, at a time like this," said Aimee Slocum. She looked back and saw the train moving slowly away, going under the bridge at Main Street. Then it disappeared around the curve.

"Oh, the hope chest!" Aimee cried in a stricken voice.

"And whom have we the pleasure of addressing?" Mrs. Watts was shouting, while Mrs. Carson was ringing up the telephone.

The band went on playing. Some of the people thought Lily was on the train, and some swore she wasn't. Everybody cheered, though, and a straw hat was thrown into the telephone wires.

The Hitch-Hikers

Tom Harris, a thirty-year-old salesman traveling in office supplies, got out of Victory a little after noon and saw people in Midnight and Louise, but went on toward Memphis. It was a base, and he was thinking he would like to do something that night.

Toward evening, somewhere in the middle of the Delta, he slowed down to pick up two hitch-hikers. One of them stood still by the side of the pavement, with his foot stuck out like an old root, but the other was playing a yellow guitar which caught the late sun as it came in a long straight bar across the fields.

Harris would get sleepy driving. On the road he did some things rather out of a dream. And the recurring sight of hitch-hikers waiting against the sky gave him the flash of a sensation he had known as a child: standing still, with nothing to touch him, feeling tall and having the world come all at once into its round shape underfoot and rush and turn through space and make his stand very precarious and lonely. He opened the car door.

"How you do?"

"How you do?"

Harris spoke to hitch-hikers almost formally. Now resuming his speed, he moved over a little in the seat.

There was no room in the back for anybody. The man with the guitar was riding with it between his legs. Harris reached over and flicked on the radio.

"Well, music!" said the man with the guitar. Presently he began to smile. "Well, we been there a whole day in that one spot," he said softly. "Seen the sun go clear over. Course, part of the time we laid down under that one tree and taken our ease."

They rode without talking while the sun went down in red clouds and the radio program changed a few times. Harris switched on his lights. Once the man with the guitar started to sing "The One Rose That's Left in My Heart," which came over the air, played by the Aloha Boys. Then in shyness he stopped, but made a streak on the radio dial with his blackly calloused finger tip.

"I 'preciate them big 'lectric gittars some have," he said.

"Where are you going?"

"Looks like north."

"It's north," said Harris. "Smoke?"

The other man held out his hand.

"Well . . . rarely," said the man with the guitar.

At the use of the unexpected word, Harris's cheek twitched, and he handed over his pack of cigarettes. All three lighted up. The silent man held his cigarette in front of him like a piece of money, between his thumb and forefinger. Harris realized that he wasn't smoking it, but was watching it burn.

"My! gittin' night agin," said the man with the guitar in a voice that could assume any social surprise.

"Anything to eat?" asked Harris.

The man gave a pluck to a low string and glanced at him.

"Dewberries," said the other man. It was his only remark, and it was delivered in a slow and pondering voice.

"Some nice little rabbit come skinnin' by," said the man with the guitar, nudging Harris with a slight punch in his side, "but it run off the way it come."

The other man was so bogged in inarticulate anger

that Harris could imagine him running down a cotton row after the rabbit. He smiled but did not look around.

"Now to look out for a place to sleep—is that it?" he remarked doggedly.

A pluck of the strings again, and the man yawned.

There was a little town coming up; the lights showed for twenty miles in the flat land.

"Is that Dulcie?" Harris yawned too.

"I bet you ain't got no idea where all I've slep'," the man said, turning around in his seat and speaking directly to Harris, with laughter in his face that in the light of a road sign appeared strangely teasing.

"I could eat a hamburger," said Harris, swinging out of the road under the sign in some automatic gesture of evasion. He looked out of the window, and a girl in red pants leaped onto the running board.

"Three and three beers?" she asked, smiling, with her head poked in. "Hi," she said to Harris.

"How are you?" said Harris. "That's right."

"My," said the man with the guitar. "Red sailor-boy britches." Harris listened for the guitar note, but it did not come. "But not purty," he said.

The screen door of the joint whined, and a man's voice called, "Come on in, boys, we got girls."

Harris cut off the radio, and they listened to the nickelodeon which was playing inside the joint and turning the window blue, red and green in turn.

"Hi," said the car-hop again as she came out with the tray. "Looks like rain."

They ate the hamburgers rapidly, without talking. A girl came and looked out of the window of the joint, leaning on her hand. The same couple kept dancing by behind her. There was something brassy playing, a swing record of "Love, Oh Love, Oh Careless Love."

"Same songs ever'where," said the man with the guitar softly. "I come down from the hills. . . . We had us owls for chickens and fox for yard dogs but we sung true."

Nearly every time the man spoke Harris's cheek twitched. He was easily amused. Also, he recognized at once any sort of attempt to confide, and then its certain and hasty retreat. And the more anyone said, the further he was drawn into a willingness to listen. I'll hear him play his guitar yet, he thought. It had got to be a pattern in his days and nights, it was almost automatic, his listening, like the way his hand went to his pocket for money.

"That'n's most the same as a ballat," said the man, licking mustard off his finger. "My ma, she was the one for ballats. Little in the waist as a dirt-dauber, but her voice carried. Had her a whole lot of tunes. Long ago dead an' gone. Pa'd come home from the courthouse drunk as a wheelbarrow, and she'd just pick up an' go sit on the front step facin' the hill an' sing. Ever'thing she knowed, she'd sing. Dead an' gone, an' the house burned down." He gulped at his beer. His foot was patting.

"This," said Harris, touching one of the keys on the guitar. "Couldn't you stop somewhere along here and make money playing this?"

Of course it was by the guitar that he had known at once that they were not mere hitch-hikers. They were tramps. They were full blown, abandoned to this. Both of them were. But when he touched it he knew obscurely that it was the yellow guitar, that bold and gay burden in the tramp's arms, that had caused him to stop and pick them up.

The man hit it flat with the palm of his hand.

"This box? Just play it for myself."

Harris laughed delightedly, but somehow he had a desire to tease him, to make him swear to his freedom.

"You wouldn't stop and play somewhere like this? For them to dance? When you know all the songs?"

Now the fellow laughed out loud. He turned and spoke completely as if the other man could not hear him. "Well, but right now I got *him*."

"Him?" Harris stared ahead.

"He'd gripe. He don't like foolin' around. He wants to git on. You always git a partner got notions."

The other tramp belched. Harris laid his hand on the horn.

"Hurry back," said the car-hop, opening a heart-shaped pocket over her heart and dropping the tip courteously within.

"Aw river!" sang out the man with the guitar.

As they pulled out into the road again, the other man began to lift a beer bottle, and stared beseechingly, with his mouth full, at the man with the guitar.

"Drive back, mister. Sobby forgot to give her back her bottle. Drive back."

"Too late," said Harris rather firmly, speeding on into Dulcie, thinking, I was about to take directions from him.

Harris stopped the car in front of the Dulcie Hotel on the square.

" 'Preciated it," said the man, taking up his guitar.

"Wait here."

They stood on the walk, one lighted by the street light, the other in the shadow of the statue of the Confederate soldier, both caved in and giving out an odor of dust, both sighing with obedience.

Harris went across the yard and up the one step into the hotel.

Mr. Gene, the proprietor, a white-haired man with little dark freckles all over his face and hands, looked up and shoved out his arm at the same time.

"If he ain't back." He grinned. "Been about a month to the day—I was just remarking."

"Mr. Gene, I ought to go on, but I got two fellows out front. O.K., but they've just got nowhere to sleep tonight, and you know that little back porch."

"Why, it's a beautiful night out!" bellowed Mr. Gene, and he laughed silently.

"They'd get fleas in your bed," said Harris, showing the back of his hand. "But you know that old porch. It's not so bad. I slept out there once, I forget how."

The proprietor let his laugh out like a flood. Then he sobered abruptly.

"Sure. O.K.," he said. "Wait a minute—Mike's sick. Come here, Mike, it's just old Harris passin' through."

Mike was an ancient collie dog. He rose from a quilt near the door and moved over the square brown rug, stiffly, like a table walking, and shoved himself between the men, swinging his long head from Mr. Gene's hand to Harris's and bearing down motionless with his jaw in Harris's palm.

"You sick, Mike?" asked Harris.

"Dyin' of old age, that's what he's doin'!" blurted the proprietor as if in anger.

Harris began to stroke the dog, but the familiarity in his hands changed to slowness and hesitancy. Mike looked up out of his eyes.

"His spirit's gone. You see?" said Mr. Gene pleadingly.

"Say, look," said a voice at the front door.

"Come in, Cato, and see poor old Mike," said Mr. Gene.

"I knew that was your car, Mr. Harris," said the boy. He was nervously trying to tuck a Bing Crosby cretonne shirt into his pants like a real shirt. Then he looked up and said, "They was tryin' to take your car, and down the street one of 'em like to bust the other one's head wide op'm with a bottle. Looks like you would 'a' heard the commotion. Everybody's out there. I said, 'That's Mr. Tom Harris's car, look at the out-of-town license and look at all the stuff he all time carries around with him, all bloody.' "

"He's not dead though," said Harris, kneeling on the seat of his car.

It was the man with the guitar. The ceiling light had been turned on. With blood streaming from his broken head, he was slumped down upon the guitar, his legs bowed around it, his arms at either side, his whole body limp in the posture of a bareback rider. Harris was aware of the other face not a yard away: the man the guitar player had called Sobby was standing on the curb, with two men unnecessarily holding him. He looked more like a bystander than any of the rest, except that he still held the beer bottle in his right hand.

"Looks like if he was fixin' to hit him, *he* would of

hit *him* with that gittar," said a voice. "That 'd be a real good thing to hit somebody with. Whang!"

"The way I figure this thing out is," said a penetrating voice, as if a woman were explaining it all to her husband, "the men was left to 'emselves. So—that 'n' yonder wanted to make off with the car—he's the bad one. So the good one says, 'Naw, that ain't right.' "

Or was it the other way around? thought Harris dreamily.

"So the other one says bam! bam! He whacked him over the head. And so dumb—right where the movie was letting out."

"Who's got my car keys!" Harris kept shouting. He had, without realizing it, kicked away the prop, the guitar; and he had stopped the blood with something.

Nobody had to tell him where the ramshackle little hospital was—he had been there once before, on a Delta trip. With the constable scuttling along after and then riding on the running board, glasses held tenderly in one fist, the handcuffed Sobby dragged alongside by the other, with a long line of little boys in flowered shirts accompanying him on bicycles, riding in and out of the headlight beam, with the rain falling in front of him and with Mr. Gene shouting in a sort of plea from the hotel behind and Mike beginning to echo the barking of the rest of the dogs, Harris drove in all carefulness down the long tree-dark street, with his wet hand pressed on the horn.

The old doctor came down the walk and, joining them in the car, slowly took the guitar player by the shoulders.

"I 'spec' he gonna die though," said a colored child's voice mournfully. "Wonder who goin' to git his box?"

In a room on the second floor of the two-story hotel Harris put on clean clothes, while Mr. Gene lay on the bed with Mike across his stomach.

"Ruined that Christmas tie you came in." The proprietor was talking in short breaths. "It took it out of Mike, I'm tellin' you." He sighed. "First time he's barked since Bud Milton shot up that Chinese." He lifted his head and took a long swallow of the hotel whisky, and tears appeared in his warm brown eyes. "Suppose they'd done it on the porch."

The phone rang.

"See, everybody knows you're here," said Mr. Gene.

"Ruth?" he said, lifting the receiver, his voice almost contrite.

But it was for the proprietor.

When he had hung up he said, "That little peanut—he ain't ever goin' to learn which end is up. The constable. Got a nigger already in the jail, so he's runnin' round to find a place to put this fella of yours with the bottle, and damned if all he can think of ain't the hotel!"

"Hell, is he going to spend the night with me?"

"Well, the same thing. Across the hall. The other fella may die. Only place in town with a key but the bank, he says."

"What time is it?" asked Harris all at once.

"Oh, it ain't *late*," said Mr. Gene.

He opened the door for Mike, and the two men followed the dog slowly down the stairs. The light was out on the landing. Harris looked out of the old half-open stained-glass window.

"Is that rain?"

"It's been rainin' since dark, but you don't ever know a thing like that—it's proverbial." At the desk he held up a brown package. "Here. I sent Cato after some Memphis whisky for you. He had to do something."

"Thanks."

"I'll see you. I don't guess you're goin' to get away very shortly in the mornin'. I'm real sorry they did it in your car if they were goin' to do it."

"That's all right," said Harris. "You'd better have a little of this."

"That? It'd kill me," said Mr. Gene.

In a drugstore Harris phoned Ruth, a woman he knew in town, and found her at home having a party.

"Tom Harris! Sent by heaven!" she cried. "I was wondering what I'd do about Carol—this *baby!*"

"What's the matter with her?"

"No date."

Some other people wanted to say hello from the party. He listened awhile and said he'd be out.

This had postponed the call to the hospital. He put in another nickel. . . . There was nothing new about the guitar player.

"Like I told you," the doctor said, "we don't have the facilities for giving transfusions, and he's been moved plenty without you taking him to Memphis."

Walking over to the party, so as not to use his car, making the only sounds in the dark wet street, and only partly aware of the indeterminate shapes of houses with their soft-shining fanlights marking them off, there with the rain falling mist-like through the trees, he almost forgot what town he was in and which house he was bound for.

Ruth, in a long dark dress, leaned against an open door, laughing. From inside came the sounds of at least two people playing a duet on the piano.

"He would come like this and get all wet!" she cried over her shoulder into the room. She was leaning back on her hands. "What's the matter with your little blue car? I hope you brought us a present."

He went in with her and began shaking hands, and set the bottle wrapped in the paper sack on a table

"He never forgets!" cried Ruth.

"Drinkin' whisky!" Everybody was noisy again.

"So this is the famous 'he' that everybody talks about all the time," pouted a girl in a white dress. "Is he one of your cousins, Ruth?"

"No kin of mine, he's nothing but a vagabond," said Ruth, and led Harris off to the kitchen by the hand.

I wish they'd call me "you" when I've got here, he thought tiredly.

"More has gone on than a little bit," she said, and told him the news while he poured fresh drinks into the glasses. When she accused him of nothing, of no carelessness or disregard of her feelings, he was fairly sure she had not heard about the assault in his car.

She was looking at him closely. "Where did you get that sunburn?"

"Well, I had to go to the Coast last week," he said.

"What did you do?"

"Same old thing." He laughed; he had started to tell her about something funny in Bay St. Louis, where an eloping couple had flagged him down in the residential section and threatened to break up if he would not carry them to the next town. Then he remembered how Ruth looked when he mentioned other places where he stopped on trips.

Somewhere in the house the phone rang and rang, and he caught himself jumping. Nobody was answering it.

"I thought you'd quit drinking," she said, picking up the bottle.

"I start and quit," he said, taking it from her and pouring his drink. "Where's my date?"

"Oh, she's in Leland," said Ruth.

They all drove over in two cars to get her.

She was a slight little thing, with her nightgown in some sort of little bag. She came out when they blew the horn, before he could go in after her. . . .

"Let's go holler off the bridge," said somebody in the car ahead.

They drove over a little gravel road, miles through the misty fields, and came to the bridge out in the middle of nowhere.

"Let's dance," said one of the boys. He grabbed Carol around the waist, and they began to tango over the boards.

"Did you miss me?" asked Ruth. She stayed by him, standing in the road.

"Woo-hoo!" they cried.

"I wish I knew what makes it holler back," said one girl."There's nothing anywhere. Some of my kinfolks can't even hear it."

"Yes, it's funny," said Harris, with a cigarette in his mouth.

"Some people say it's an old steamboat got lost once."

"Might be."

They drove around and waited to see if it would stop raining.

Back in the lighted rooms at Ruth's he saw Carol, his date, give him a strange little glance. At the moment he was serving her with a drink from the tray.

"Are you the one everybody's 'miratin' and gyratin' over?" she said, before she would put her hand out.

"Yes," he said, "I come from afar." He placed the strongest drink from the tray in her hand, with a little flourish.

"Hurry back!" called Ruth.

In the pantry Ruth came over and stood by him while he set more glasses on the tray and then followed him out to the kitchen. Was she at all curious about him? he wondered. For a moment, when they were simply close together, her lips parted, and she stared off at nothing; her jealousy seemed to let her go free. The rainy wind from the back porch stirred her hair.

As if under some illusion, he set the tray down and told her about the two hitch-hikers.

Her eyes flashed.

"What a—stupid thing!" Furiously she seized the tray when he reached for it.

The phone was ringing again. Ruth glared at him.

It was as though he had made a previous engagement with the hitch-hikers.

Everybody was meeting them at the kitchen door.

"Aha!" cried one of the men, Jackson. "He tries to put one over on you, girls. Somebody just called up, Ruth, about the murder in Tom's car."

"Did he die?" asked Harris, without moving.

"I knew all about it!" cried Ruth, her cheeks flaming. "He told me all about it. It practically ruined his car. Didn't it!"

"Wouldn't he get into something crazy like that?"

"It's because he's an angel," said the girl named Carol, his date, speaking in a hollow voice from her highball glass.

"Who phoned?" asked Harris.

"Old Mrs. Daggett, that old lady about a million years old that's always calling up. She was right there."

Harris phoned the doctor's home and woke the doctor's wife. The guitar player was still the same.

"This is so exciting, tell us all," said a fat boy. Harris knew he lived fifty miles up the river and had driven down under the impression that there would be a bridge game.

"It was just a fight."

"Oh, he wouldn't tell you, he never talks. I'll tell you," said Ruth. "Get your drinks, for goodness' sake."

So the incident became a story. Harris grew very tired of it.

"It's marvelous the way he always gets in with somebody and then something happens," said Ruth, her eyes completely black.

"Oh, he's my hero," said Carol, and she went out and stood on the back porch.

"Maybe you'll still be here tomorrow," Ruth said to Harris, taking his arm. "Will you be detained, maybe?"

"If he dies," said Harris.

He told them all good-bye.

"Let's all go to Greenville and get a Coke," said Ruth.

"No," he said. "Good night."

" 'Aw river,' " said the girl in the white dress. "Isn't that what the little man said?"

"Yes," said Harris, the rain falling on him, and he refused to spend the night or to be taken in a car back to the hotel.

In the antlered lobby, Mr. Gene bent over asleep under a lamp by the desk phone. His freckles seemed to come out darker when he was asleep.

Harris woke him. "Go to bed," he said. "What was the idea? Anything happened?"

"I just wanted to tell you that little buzzard's up in 202. Locked and double-locked, handcuffed to the bed, but I wanted to tell you."

"Oh. Much obliged."

"All a gentleman could do," said Mr. Gene. He was drunk. "Warn you what's sleepin' under your roof."

"Thanks," said Harris. "It's almost morning. Look."

"Poor Mike can't sleep," said Mr. Gene. "He scrapes somethin' when he breathes. Did the other fella poop out?"

"Still unconscious. No change," said Harris. He took the bunch of keys which the proprietor was handing him.

"You keep 'em," said Mr. Gene.

In the next moment Harris saw his hand tremble and he took hold of it.

"A murderer!" whispered Mr. Gene. All his freckles stood out. "Here he came . . . with not a word to say . . ."

"Not a murderer yet," said Harris, starting to grin.

When he passed 202 and heard no sound, he remembered what old Sobby had said, standing handcuffed in front of the hospital, with nobody listening to him. "I was jist tired of him always uppin' an' makin' a noise about ever'thing."

In his room, Harris lay down on the bed without undressing or turning out the light. He was too tired to sleep. Half blinded by the unshaded bulb he stared at the bare plaster walls and the equally white surface of the mirror above the empty dresser. Presently he got up and turned on the ceiling fan, to create some motion and sound in the room. It was a defective fan which clicked with each revolution, on and on. He lay perfectly still beneath it, with his clothes on, unconsciously breathing in a rhythm related to the beat of the fan.

He shut his eyes suddenly. When they were closed, in the red darkness he felt all patience leave him. It was like the beginning of desire. He remembered the girl dropping money into her heart-shaped pocket, and remembered a disturbing possessiveness, which meant nothing, Ruth leaning on her hands. He knew he would not be held by any of it. It was for relief, almost, that his thoughts turned to pity, to wonder about the two tramps, their conflict, the sudden brutality when his back was turned. How would it turn out? It was in this suspense that it was more acceptable to him to feel the helplessness of his life.

He could forgive nothing in this evening. But it was too like other evenings, this town was too like other towns, for him to move out of this lying still clothed on the bed, even into comfort or despair. Even the rain— there was often rain, there was often a party, and there had been other violence not of his doing—other fights, not quite so pointless, but fights in his car; fights, unheralded confessions, sudden love-making—none of any of this his, not his to keep, but belonging to the people of these towns he passed through, coming out of their rooted pasts and their mock rambles, coming out of their time. He himself had no time. He was free; helpless. He wished he knew how the guitar player was, if he was still unconscious, if he felt pain.

He sat up on the bed and then got up and walked to the window.

"Tom!" said a voice outside in the dark.

Automatically he answered and listened. It was a girl. He could not see her, but she must have been standing on the little plot of grass that ran around the side of the hotel. Wet feet, pneumonia, he thought. And he was so tired he thought of a girl from the wrong town.

He went down and unlocked the door. She ran in as far as the middle of the lobby as though from impetus. It was Carol, from the party.

"You're wet," he said. He touched her.

"Always raining." She looked up at him, stepping back. "How are you?"

"O.K., fine," he said.

"I was wondering," she said nervously. "I knew the light would be you. I hope I didn't wake up anybody." Was old Sobby asleep? he wondered.

"Would you like a drink? Or do you want to go to the All-Nite and get a Coca-Cola?" he said.

"It's open," she said, making a gesture with her hand. "The All-Nite's open—I just passed it."

They went out into the mist, and she put his coat on

with silent protest, in the dark street not drunken but womanly.

"You didn't remember me at the party," she said, and did not look up when he made his exclamation. "They say you never forget anybody, so I found out they were wrong about that anyway."

"They're often wrong," he said, and then hurriedly, "Who are you?"

"We used to stay at the Manning Hotel on the Coast every summer—I wasn't grown. Carol Thames. Just dances and all, but you had just started to travel then, it was on your trips, and you—you talked at intermission."

He laughed shortly, but she added:

"You talked about yourself."

They walked past the tall wet church, and their steps echoed.

"Oh, it wasn't so long ago—five years," she said. Under a magnolia tree she put her hand out and stopped him, looking up at him with her child's face. "But when I saw you again tonight I wanted to know how you were getting along."

He said nothing, and she went on.

"You used to play the piano."

They passed under a street light, and she glanced up as if to look for the little tic in his cheek.

"Out on the big porch where they danced," she said, walking on. "Paper lanterns . . ."

"I'd forgotten that, is one thing sure," he said. "Maybe you've got the wrong man. I've got cousins galore who all play the piano."

"You'd put your hands down on the keyboard like you'd say, 'Now this is how it really is!' " she cried, and turned her head away. "I guess I was crazy about you, though."

"Crazy about me then?" He struck a match and held a cigarette between his teeth.

"No—yes, and now too!" she cried sharply, as if driven to deny him.

They came to the little depot where a restless switch engine was hissing, and crossed the black street. The past and present joined like this, he thought, it never happened often to me, and it probably won't happen again. He took her arm and led her through the dirty screen door of the All-Nite.

He waited at the counter while she sat down by the wall table and wiped her face all over with her handkerchief. He carried the black coffees over to the table himself, smiling at her from a little distance. They sat under a calendar with some picture of giant trees being cut down.

They said little. A fly bothered her. When the coffee was all gone he put her into the old Cadillac taxi that always stood in front of the depot.

Before he shut the taxi door he said, frowning, "I appreciate it. . . . You're sweet."

Now she had torn her handkerchief. She held it up and began to cry. "What's sweet about me?" It was the look of bewilderment in her face that he would remember.

"To come out, like this—in the rain—to be here. . . ." He shut the door, partly from weariness.

She was holding her breath. "I hope your friend doesn't die," she said. "All I hope is your friend gets well."

But when he woke up the next morning and phoned the hospital, the guitar player was dead. He had been dying while Harris was sitting in the All-Nite.

"It *was* a murderer," said Mr. Gene, pulling Mike's ears. "That was just plain murder. No way anybody could call that an affair of honor."

The man called Sobby did not oppose an invitation to confess. He stood erect and turning his head about a little, and almost smiled at all the men who had come to see him. After one look at him Mr. Gene, who had come with Harris, went out and slammed the door behind him.

All the same, Sobby had found little in the night, asleep or awake, to say about it. "I done it, sure," he said. "Didn't ever'body see me, or was they blind?"

They asked him about the man he had killed.

"Name Sanford," he said, standing still, with his foot out, as if he were trying to recall something particular and minute. "But he didn't have nothing and he didn't have no folks. No more'n me. Him and me, we took up together two weeks back." He looked up at their faces as if for support. "He was uppity, though. He bragged. He carried a gittar around." He whimpered. "It was his notion to run off with the car."

Harris, fresh from the barbershop, was standing in the filling station where his car was being polished.

A ring of little boys in bright shirt-tails surrounded him and the car, with some colored boys waiting behind them.

"Could they git all the blood off the seat and the steerin' wheel, Mr. Harris?"

He nodded. They ran away.

"Mr. Harris," said a little colored boy who stayed. "Does you want the box?"

"The what?"

He pointed, to where it lay in the back seat with the sample cases. "The po' kilt man's gittar. Even the police-mans didn't want it."

"No," said Harris, and handed it over.

Powerhouse

Powerhouse is playing!

He's here on tour from the city—"Powerhouse and His Keyboard"—"Powerhouse and His Tasmanians"—think of the things he calls himself! There's no one in the world like him. You can't tell what he is. "Nigger man"?—he looks more Asiatic, monkey, Jewish, Babylonian, Peruvian, fanatic, devil. He has pale gray eyes, heavy lids, maybe horny like a lizard's, but big glowing eyes when they're open. He has African feet of the greatest size, stomping, both together, on each side of the pedals. He's not coal black—beverage colored—looks like a preacher when his mouth is shut, but then it opens—vast and obscene. And his mouth is going every minute: like a monkey's when it looks for something. Improvising, coming on a light and childish melody—*smooch*—he loves it with his mouth.

Is it possible that he could be this! When you have him there performing for you, that's what you feel. You know people on a stage—and people of a darker race—so likely to be marvelous, frightening.

This is a white dance. Powerhouse is not a show-off like the Harlem boys, not drunk, not crazy—he's in a trance; he's a person of joy, a fanatic. He listens as much as he performs, a look of hideous, powerful rapture on his face. Big arched eyebrows that never stop traveling, like a Jew's—wandering-Jew eyebrows. When he plays he beats down piano and seat and wears them away. He is in motion every moment—what could be more obscene? There he is with his great head, fat stomach, and little round piston legs, and long yellow-sectioned strong big fingers, at rest about the size of bananas. Of course you know how he sounds—you've heard him on records—but still you need to see him. He's going all the time, like skating around the skating rink or rowing a boat. It makes everybody crowd around, here in this shadowless steel-trussed hall with the rose-like posters of Nelson Eddy and the testimonial for the mind-reading horse in handwriting magnified five hundred times. Then all quietly he lays his finger on a key with the promise and serenity of a sibyl touching the book.

Powerhouse is so monstrous he sends everybody into oblivion. When any group, any performers, come to town, don't people always come out and hover near, leaning inward about them, to learn what it is? What is it? Listen. Remember how it was with the acrobats. Watch them carefully, hear the least word, especially what they say to one another, in another language—don't let them escape you; it's the only time for hallucination, the last time. They can't stay. They'll be somewhere else this time tomorrow.

Powerhouse has as much as possible done by signals. Everybody, laughing as if to hide a weakness, will sooner or later hand him up a written request. Powerhouse reads each one, studying with a secret face: that is the face which looks like a mask—anybody's; there is a moment when he makes a decision. Then a light slides under his eyelids, and he says, "92!" or some combination of figures—never a name. Before a number the band is all frantic, misbehaving, pushing, like children in a schoolroom, and he is the teacher getting silence. His hands over the keys, he says sternly, "You-all ready? You-all ready to do some serious walking?"—waits—then, STAMP. Quiet. STAMP, for the second time. This is absolute. Then a set of rhythmic kicks against the floor to communicate the tempo. Then, O Lord! say the distended eyes from beyond the boundary of the trumpets, Hello and good-bye, and they are all down the first note like a waterfall.

This note marks the end of any known discipline. Powerhouse seems to abandon them all—he himself seems lost—down in the song, yelling up like somebody in a whirlpool—not guiding them—hailing them only. But he knows, really. He cries out, but he must know exactly. "Mercy! . . . What I say! Yeah!" And then drifting, listening—"Where that skin beater?"—wanting drums, and starting up and pouring it out in the greatest delight and brutality. On the sweet pieces such a leer for everybody! He looks down so benevolently upon all our faces and whispers the lyrics to us. And if you could hear him at this moment on "Marie, the Dawn is Breaking"! He's going up the keyboard with a few fingers in some very derogatory triplet-routine, he gets higher and higher, and then he looks over the end of the piano, as if over a cliff. But not in a show-off way —the song makes him do it.

He loves the way they all play, too—all those next to him. The far section of the band is all studious, wearing glasses, every one—they don't count. Only those playing around Powerhouse are the real ones. He has a bass fiddler from Vicksburg, black as pitch, named Valentine, who plays with his eyes shut and talking to himself, very young: Powerhouse has to keep encouraging him. "Go on, go on, give it up, bring it on out there!" When you heard him like that on records, did you know he was really pleading?

He calls Valentine out to take a solo.

"What you going to play?" Powerhouse looks out kindly from behind the piano; he opens his mouth and shows his tongue, listening.

Valentine looks down, drawing against his instrument, and says without a lip movement, " 'Honeysuckle Rose.' "

He has a clarinet player named Little Brother, and loves to listen to anything he does. He'll smile and say,

"Beautiful!" Little Brother takes a step forward when he plays and stands at the very front, with the whites of his eyes like fishes swimming. Once when he played a low note, Powerhouse muttered in dirty praise, "He went clear downstairs to get that one!"

After a long time, he holds up the number of fingers to tell the band how many choruses still to go—usually five. He keeps his directions down to signals.

It's a bad night outside. It's a white dance, and nobody dances, except a few straggling jitterbugs and two elderly couples. Everybody just stands around the band and watches Powerhouse. Sometimes they steal glances at one another, as if to say, Of course, you know how it is with *them*—Negroes—band leaders—they would play the same way, giving all they've got, for an audience of one. . . . When somebody, no matter who, gives everything, it makes people feel ashamed for him.

Late at night they play the one waltz they will ever consent to play—by request, "Pagan Love Song." Powerhouse's head rolls and sinks like a weight between his waving shoulders. He groans, and his fingers drag into the keys heavily, holding on to the notes, retrieving. It is a sad song.

"You know what happened to me?" says Powerhouse.

Valentine hums a response, dreaming at the bass.

"I got a telegram my wife is dead," says Powerhouse, with wandering fingers.

"Uh-huh?"

His mouth gathers and forms a barbarous O while his fingers walk up straight, unwillingly, three octaves.

"Gypsy? Why how come her to die, didn't you just phone her up in the night last night long distance?"

"Telegram say—here the words: Your wife is dead." He puts 4/4 over the 3/4.

"Not but four words?" This is the drummer, an unpopular boy named Scoot, a disbelieving maniac.

Powerhouse is shaking his vast cheeks. "What the hell was she trying to do? What was she up to?"

"What name has it got signed, if you got a telegram?" Scoot is spitting away with those wire brushes.

Little Brother, the clarinet player, who cannot now speak, glares and tilts back.

"Uranus Knockwood is the name signed." Powerhouse lifts his eyes open. "Ever heard of him?" A bubble shoots out on his lip like a plate on a counter.

Valentine is beating slowly on with his palm and scratching the strings with his long blue nails. He is fond of a waltz. Powerhouse interrupts him.

"I don't know him. Don't know who he is." Valentine shakes his head with the closed eyes.

"Say it agin."

"Uranus Knockwood."

"That ain't Lenox Avenue."

"It ain't Broadway."

"Ain't ever seen it wrote out in any print, even for horse racing."

"Hell, that's on a star, boy, ain't it?" Crash of the cymbals.

"What the hell was she up to?" Powerhouse shudders. "Tell me, tell me, tell me." He makes triplets, and begins a new chorus. He holds three fingers up.

"You say you got a telegram." This is Valentine, patient and sleepy, beginning again.

Powerhouse is elaborate. "Yas, the time I go out, go way downstairs along a long cor-ri-dor to where they puts us: coming back along the cor-ri-dor: steps out and hands me a telegram: Your wife is dead."

"Gypsy?" The drummer like a spider over his drums.

"Aaaaaaaaa!" shouts Powerhouse, flinging out both powerful arms for three whole beats to flex his muscles, then kneading a dough of bass notes. His eyes glitter. He plays the piano like a drum sometimes—why not?

"Gypsy? Such a dancer?"

"Why you don't hear it straight from your agent? Why it ain't come from headquarters? What you been doing, getting telegrams in the *corridor*, signed nobody?"

They all laugh. End of that chorus.

"What time is it?" Powerhouse calls. "What the hell place is this? Where is my watch and chain?"

"I hang it on you," whimpers Valentine. "It still there."

There it rides on Powerhouse's great stomach, down where he can never see it.

"Sure did hear some clock striking twelve while ago. Must be *midnight*."

"It going to be intermission," Powerhouse declares, lifting up his finger with the signet ring.

He draws the chorus to an end. He pulls a big Northern hotel towel out of the deep pocket in his vast, special-cut tux pants and pushes his forehead into it.

"If she went and killed herself!" he says with a hidden face. "If she up and jumped out that window!" He gets to his feet, turning vaguely, wearing the towel on his head.

"Ha, ha!"

"Sheik, sheik!"

"She wouldn't do that." Little Brother sets down his clarinet like a precious vase, and speaks. He still looks like an East Indian queen, implacable, divine, and full of snakes. "You ain't going to expect people doing what they says over long distance."

"Come on!" roars Powerhouse. He is already at the back door, he has pulled it wide open, and with a wild, gathered-up face is smelling the terrible night.

Powerhouse, Valentine, Scoot and Little Brother step outside into the drenching rain.

"Well, they emptying buckets," says Powerhouse in a mollified voice. On the street he holds his hands out and turns up the blanched palms like sieves.

A hundred dark, ragged, silent, delighted Negroes have come around from under the eaves of the hall, and follow wherever they go.

"Watch out Little Brother don't shrink," says Powerhouse. "You just the right size now, clarinet don't suck you in. You got a dry throat, Little Brother, you in the desert?" He reaches into the pocket and pulls out a paper of mints. "Now hold 'em in your mouth—don't chew 'em. I don't carry around nothing without limit."

"Go in that joint and have a beer," says Scoot, who walks ahead.

"Beer? Beer? You know what beer is? What do they say is beer? What's beer? Where I been?"

"Down yonder where it say World Café—that do?" They are in Negrotown now.

Valentine patters over and holds open a screen door warped like a sea shell, bitter in the wet, and they walk in, stained darker with the rain and leaving footprints. Inside, sheltered dry smells stand like screens around a table covered with a red-checkered cloth, in the center of which flies hang onto an obelisk-shaped ketchup bottle. The midnight walls are checkered again with admonishing "Not Responsible" signs and black-figured, smoky calendars. It is a waiting, silent, limp room. There is a burned-out-looking nickelodeon and right beside it a long-necked wall instrument labeled "Business Phone, Don't Keep Talking." Circled phone numbers are written up everywhere. There is a worn-out peacock feather hanging by a thread to an old, thin, pink, exposed light bulb, where it slowly turns around and around, whoever breathes.

A waitress watches.

"Come here, living statue, and get all this big order of beer we fixing to give."

"Never seen you before anywhere." The waitress moves and comes forward and slowly shows little gold leaves and tendrils over her teeth. She shoves up her shoulders and breasts. "How I going to know who you might be? Robbers? Coming in out of the black of night right at midnight, setting down so big at my table?"

"Boogers," says Powerhouse, his eyes opening lazily as in a cave.

The girl screams delicately with pleasure. O Lord, she likes talk and scares.

"Where you going to find enough beer to put out on this here table?"

She runs to the kitchen with bent elbows and sliding steps.

"Here's a million nickels," says Powerhouse, pulling his hand out of his pocket and sprinkling coins out, all but the last one, which he makes vanish like a magician.

Valentine and Scoot take the money over to the nickelodeon, which looks as battered as a slot machine, and read all the names of the records out loud.

"Whose 'Tuxedo Junction'?" asks Powerhouse.

"You know whose."

"Nickelodeon, I request you please to play 'Empty Bed Blues' and let Bessie Smith sing."

Silence: they hold it like a measure.

"Bring me all those nickels on back here," says Powerhouse. "Look at that! What you tell me the name of this place?"

"White dance, week night, raining, Alligator, Mississippi, long ways from home."

"Uh-huh."

"Sent for You Yesterday and Here You Come Today" plays.

The waitress, setting the tray of beer down on a back table, comes up taut and apprehensive as a hen. "Says in the kitchen, back there putting their eyes to little hole peeping out, that you is Mr. Powerhouse. . . . They knows from a picture they seen."

"They seeing right tonight, that is him," says Little Brother.

"You him?"

"That is him in the flesh," says Scoot.

"Does you wish to touch him?" asks Valentine. "Because he don't bite."

"You passing through?"

"Now you got everything right."

She waits like a drop, hands languishing together in front.

"Little-Bit, ain't you going to bring the beer?"

She brings it, and goes behind the cash register and smiles, turning different ways. The little fillet of gold in her mouth is gleaming.

"The Mississippi River's here," she says once.

Now all the watching Negroes press in gently and bright-eyed through the door, as many as can get in. One is a little boy in a straw sombrero which has been coated with aluminum paint all over.

Powerhouse, Valentine, Scoot and Little Brother drink beer, and their eyelids come together like curtains.

The wall and the rain and the humble beautiful waitress waiting on them and the other Negroes watching enclose them.

"Listen!" whispers Powerhouse, looking into the ketchup bottle and slowly spreading his performer's hands over the damp, wrinkling cloth with the red squares. "Listen how it is. My wife gets missing me. Gypsy. She goes to the window. She looks out and sees you know what. Street. Sign saying Hotel. People walking. Somebody looks up. Old man. She looks down, out the window. Well? . . . *Ssssst! Plooey!* What she do? Jump out and bust her brains all over the world."

He opens his eyes.

"That's it," agrees Valentine. "You gets a telegram."

"Sure she misses you," Little Brother adds.

"No, it's night time." How softly he tells them! "Sure. It's the night time. She say, What do I hear? Footsteps walking up the hall? That him? Footsteps go on off. It's not me. I'm in Alligator, Mississippi, she's crazy. Shaking all over. Listens till her ears and all grow out like old music-box horns but still she can't hear a thing. She says, All right! I'll jump out the window then. Got on her nightgown. I know that nightgown, and her thinking there. Says, Ho hum, all right, and jumps out the window. Is she mad at me! Is she crazy! She don't leave *nothing* behind her!"

"Ya! Ha!"

"Brains and insides everywhere, Lord, Lord."

All the watching Negroes stir in their delight, and to their higher delight he says affectionately, "Listen! Rats in here."

"That must be the way, boss."

"Only, naw, Powerhouse, that ain't true. That sound too *bad*."

"Does? I even know who finds her," cries Powerhouse. "That no-good pussyfooted crooning creeper, that creeper that follow around after me, coming up like weeds behind me, following around after me everything I do and messing around on the trail I leave. Bets my numbers, sings my songs, gets close to my agent like a Betsy-bug; when I going out he just coming in. I got him now! I got my eye on him."

"Know who he is?"

"Why, it's that old Uranus Knockwood!"

"Ya! Ha!"

"Yeah, and he coming now, he going to find Gypsy. There he is, coming around that corner, and Gypsy kadoodling down, oh-oh, watch out! Ssssst! Plooey! See, there she is in her little old nightgown, and her insides and brains all scattered round."

A sigh fills the room.

"Hush about her brains. Hush about her insides."

"Ya! Ha! You talking about her brains and insides— old Uranus Knockwood," says Powerhouse, "look down and say Jesus! He say, Look here what I'm walking round in!"

They all burst into halloos of laughter. Powerhouse's face looks like a big hot iron stove.

"Why, he picks her up and carries her off!" he says.

"Ya! Ha!"

"Carries her *back* around the corner. . . ."

"Oh, Powerhouse!"

"You know him."

"Uranus Knockwood!"

"Yeahhh!"

"He take our wives when we gone!"

"He come in when we goes out!"

"Uh-huh!"

"He go out when we comes in!"

"Yeahhh!"

"He standing behind the door!"

"Old Uranus Knockwood."

"You know him."

"Middle-size man."

"Wears a hat."

"That's him."

Everybody in the room moans with pleasure. The little boy in the fine silver hat opens a paper and divides out a jelly roll among his followers.

And out of the breathless ring somebody moves forward like a slave, leading a great logy Negro with bursting eyes, and says, "This here is Sugar-Stick Thompson, that dove down to the bottom of July Creek and pulled up all those drownded white people fall out of a boat. Last summer, pulled up fourteen."

"Hello," says Powerhouse, turning and looking around at them all with his great daring face until they nearly suffocate.

Sugar-Stick, their instrument, cannot speak; he can only look back at the others.

"Can't even swim. Done it by holding his breath," says the fellow with the hero.

Powerhouse looks at him seekingly.

"I his half brother," the fellow puts in.

They step back.

"Gypsy say," Powerhouse rumbles gently again, looking at *them*, " 'What is the use? I'm gonna jump out so far—so far. . . .' *Sssst—!*"

"Don't, boss, don't do it agin," says Little Brother.

"It's awful," says the waitress. "I hates that Mr. Knockwoods. All that the truth?"

"Want to see the telegram I got from him?" Powerhouse's hand goes to the vast pocket.

"Now wait, now wait, boss." They all watch him.

"It must be the real truth," says the waitress, sucking in her lower lip, her luminous eyes turning sadly, seeking the windows.

"No, babe, it ain't the truth." His eyebrows fly up, and he begins to whisper to her out of his vast oven mouth. His hand stays in his pocket. "Truth is something worse, I ain't said what, yet. It's something hasn't come to me, but I ain't saying it won't. And when it does, then want me to tell you?" He sniffs all at once, his eyes come open and turn up, almost too far. He is dreamily smiling.

"Don't, boss, don't, Powerhouse!"

"Oh!" the waitress screams.

"Go on git out of here!" bellows Powerhouse, taking his hand out of his pocket and clapping after her red dress.

The ring of watchers breaks and falls away.

"*Look* at that! Intermission is up," says Powerhouse.

He folds money under a glass, and after they go out, Valentine leans back in and drops a nickel in the nickelodeon behind them, and it lights up and begins to play "The Goona Goo." The feather dangles still.

"Take a telegram!" Powerhouse shouts suddenly up into the rain over the street. "Take a answer. Now what was that name?"

They get a little tired.

"Uranus Knockwood."

"You ought to know."

"Yas? Spell it to me."

They spell it all the ways it could be spelled. It puts them in a wonderful humor.

"Here's the answer. I got it right here. 'What in the hell you talking about? Don't make any difference: I gotcha.' Name signed: Powerhouse."

"That going to reach him, Powerhouse?" Valentine speaks in a maternal voice.

"Yas, yas."

All hushing, following him up the dark street at a distance, like old rained-on black ghosts, the Negroes are afraid they will die laughing.

Powerhouse throws back his vast head into the steaming rain, and a look of hopeful desire seems to blow somehow like a vapor from his own dilated nostrils over his face and bring a mist to his eyes.

"Reach him and come out the other side."

"That's it, Powerhouse, that's it. You got him now."

Powerhouse lets out a long sigh.

"But ain't you going back there to call up Gypsy long distance, the way you did last night in that other place? I seen a telephone. . . . Just to see if she there at home?"

There is a measure of silence. That is one crazy drummer that's going to get his neck broken some day.

"No," growls Powerhouse. "No! How many thousand times tonight I got to say No?"

He holds up his arm in the rain.

"You sure-enough unroll your voice some night, it

about reach up yonder to her," says Little Brother, dismayed.

They go on up the street, shaking the rain off and on them like birds.

Back in the dance hall, they play "San" (99). The jitterbugs start up like windmills stationed over the floor, and in their orbits—one circle, another, a long stretch and a zigzag—dance the elderly couples with old smoothness, undisturbed and stately.

When Powerhouse first came back from intermission, no doubt full of beer, they said, he got the band tuned up again in his own way. He didn't strike the piano keys for pitch—he simply opened his mouth and gave falsetto howls—in A, D and so on—they tuned by him. Then he took hold of the piano, as if he saw it for the first time in his life, and tested it for strength, hit it down in the bass, played an octave with his elbow, lifted the top, looked inside, and leaned against it with all his might. He sat down and played it for a few minutes with outrageous force and got it under his power—a bass deep and coarse as a sea net—then produced something glimmering and fragile, and smiled. And who could ever remember any of the things he says? They are just inspired remarks that roll out of his mouth like smoke.

They've requested "Somebody Loves Me," and he's already done twelve or fourteen choruses, piling them up nobody knows how, and it will be a wonder if he ever gets through. Now and then he calls and shouts, "'Somebody loves me! Somebody loves me, I wonder who!'" His mouth gets to be nothing but a volcano. "I wonder who!"

"Maybe . . ." He uses all his right hand on a trill.

"Maybe . . ." He pulls back his spread fingers, and looks out upon the place where he is. A vast, impersonal and yet furious grimace transfigures his wet face.

". . . Maybe it's you!"

Why I Live at the P.O.

I was getting along fine with Mama, Papa-Daddy and
Uncle Rondo until my sister Stella-Rondo just separated from her husband and came back home again. Mr.
Whitaker! Of course I went with Mr. Whitaker first,
when he first appeared here in China Grove, taking
"Pose Yourself" photos, and Stella-Rondo broke us up.
Told him I was one-sided. Bigger on one side than the
other, which is a deliberate, calculated falsehood: I'm
the same. Stella-Rondo is exactly twelve months to the
day younger than I am and for that reason she's spoiled.

She's always had anything in the world she wanted
and then she'd throw it away. Papa-Daddy gave her this
gorgeous Add-a-Pearl necklace when she was eight
years old and she threw it away playing baseball when
she was nine, with only two pearls.

So as soon as she got married and moved away from
home the first thing she did was separate! From Mr.
Whitaker! This photographer with the popeyes she said
she trusted. Came home from one of those towns up in
Illinois and to our complete surprise brought this child
of two.

Mama said she like to made her drop dead for a
second. "Here you had this marvelous blonde child and
never so much as wrote your mother a word about it,"

says Mama. "I'm thoroughly ashamed of you." But of course she wasn't.

Stella-Rondo just calmly takes off this *hat,* I wish you could see it. She says, "Why, Mama, Shirley-T.'s adopted, I can prove it."

"How?" says Mama, but all I says was, "H'm!" There I was over the hot stove, trying to stretch two chickens over five people and a completely unexpected child into the bargain, without one moment's notice.

"What do you mean—'H'm!'?" says Stella-Rondo, and Mama says, "I heard that, Sister."

I said that oh, I didn't mean a thing, only that whoever Shirley-T. was, she was the spit-image of Papa-Daddy if he'd cut off his beard, which of course he'd never do in the world. Papa-Daddy's Mama's papa and sulks.

Stella-Rondo got furious! She said, "Sister, I don't need to tell you you got a lot of nerve and always did have and I'll thank you to make no future reference to my adopted child whatsoever."

"Very well," I said. "Very well, very well. Of course I noticed at once she looks like Mr. Whitaker's side too. That frown. She looks like a cross between Mr. Whitaker and Papa-Daddy."

"Well, all I can say is she isn't."

"She looks exactly like Shirley Temple to me," says Mama, but Shirley-T. just ran away from her. So the first thing Stella-Rondo did at the table was turn Papa-Daddy against me.

"Papa-Daddy," she says. He was trying to cut up his meat. "Papa-Daddy!" I was taken completely by surprise. Papa-Daddy is about a million years old and's got this long-long beard. "Papa-Daddy, Sister says she fails to understand why you don't cut off your beard."

So Papa-Daddy l-a-y-s down his knife and fork! He's real rich. Mama says he is, he says he isn't. So he says, "Have I heard correctly? You don't understand why I don't cut off my beard?"

"Why," I says, "Papa-Daddy, of course I understand, I did not say any such of a thing, the idea!"

He says, "Hussy!"

I says, "Papa-Daddy, you know I wouldn't any more want you to cut off your beard than the man in the moon. It was the farthest thing from my mind! Stella-Rondo sat there and made that up while she was eating breast of chicken."

But he says, "So the postmistress fails to understand why I don't cut off my beard. Which job I got you through my influence with the government. 'Bird's nest' —is that what you call it?"

Not that it isn't the next to smallest P.O. in the entire state of Mississippi.

I says, "Oh, Papa-Daddy," I says, "I didn't say any such of a thing, I never dreamed it was a bird's nest, I have always been grateful though this is the next to smallest P.O. in the state of Mississippi, and I do not enjoy being referred to as a hussy by my own grandfather."

But Stella-Rondo says, "Yes, you did say it too. Anybody in the world could of heard you, that had ears."

"Stop right there," says Mama, looking at *me*.

So I pulled my napkin straight back through the napkin ring and left the table.

As soon as I was out of the room Mama says, "Call her back, or she'll starve to death," but Papa-Daddy says, "This is the beard I started growing on the Coast when I was fifteen years old." He would of gone on till nightfall if Shirley-T. hadn't lost the Milky Way she ate in Cairo.

So Papa-Daddy says, "I am going out and lie in the hammock, and you can all sit here and remember my words: I'll never cut off my beard as long as I live, even one inch, and I don't appreciate it in you at all." Passed right by me in the hall and went straight out and got in the hammock.

It would be a holiday. It wasn't five minutes before Uncle Rondo suddenly appeared in the hall in one of Stella-Rondo's flesh-colored kimonos, all cut on the bias, like something Mr. Whitaker probably thought was gorgeous.

"Uncle Rondo!" I says. "I didn't know who that was! Where are you going?"

"Sister," he says, "get out of my way, I'm poisoned."

"If you're poisoned stay away from Papa-Daddy," I says. "Keep out of the hammock. Papa-Daddy will certainly beat you on the head if you come within forty miles of him. He thinks I deliberately said he ought to cut off his beard after he got me the P.O., and I've told him and told him and told him, and he acts like he just don't hear me. Papa-Daddy must of gone stone deaf."

"He picked a fine day to do it then," says Uncle Rondo, and before you could say "Jack Robinson" flew out in the yard.

What he'd really done, he'd drunk another bottle of that prescription. He does it every single Fourth of July as sure as shooting, and it's horribly expensive. Then he falls over in the hammock and snores. So he insisted on zigzagging right on out to the hammock, looking like a half-wit.

Papa-Daddy woke up with this horrible yell and right there without moving an inch he tried to turn Uncle Rondo against me. I heard every word he said. Oh, he told Uncle Rondo I didn't learn to read till I was eight years old and he didn't see how in the world I ever got the mail put up at the P.O., much less read it all, and he said if Uncle Rondo could only fathom the lengths he had gone to to get me that job! And he said on the other hand he thought Stella-Rondo had a brilliant mind and deserved credit for getting out of town. All the time he was just lying there swinging as pretty as you please and looping out his beard, and poor Uncle Rondo was *pleading* with him to slow down the hammock, it was making him as dizzy as a witch to watch it. But that's what Papa-Daddy likes about a hammock. So Uncle Rondo was too dizzy to get turned against me for the time being. He's Mama's only brother and is a good case of a one-track mind. Ask anybody. A certified pharmacist.

Just then I heard Stella-Rondo raising the upstairs window. While she was married she got this peculiar idea that it's cooler with the windows shut and locked. So she has to raise the window before she can make a soul hear her outdoors.

So she raises the window and says, *"Oh!"* You would have thought she was mortally wounded.

Uncle Rondo and Papa-Daddy didn't even look up, but kept right on with what they were doing. I had to laugh.

I flew up the stairs and threw the door open! I says, "What in the wide world's the matter, Stella-Rondo? You mortally wounded?"

"No," she says, "I am not mortally wounded but I wish you would do me the favor of looking out that window there and telling me what you see."

So I shade my eyes and look out the window.

"I see the front yard," I says.

"Don't you see any human beings?" she says.

"I see Uncle Rondo trying to run Papa-Daddy out of the hammock," I says. "Nothing more. Naturally, it's so suffocating-hot in the house, with all the windows shut and locked, everybody who cares to stay in their right mind will have to go out and get in the hammock before the Fourth of July is over."

"Don't you notice anything different about Uncle Rondo?" asks Stella-Rondo.

"Why, no, except he's got on some terrible-looking flesh-colored contraption I wouldn't be found dead in, is all I can see," I says.

"Never mind, you won't be found dead in it, because it happens to be part of my trousseau, and Mr. Whitaker took several dozen photographs of me in it," says Stella-Rondo. "What on earth could Uncle Rondo *mean* by wearing part of my trousseau out in the broad open daylight without saying so much as 'Kiss my foot,' *knowing* I only got home this morning after my separation and hung my negligee up on the bathroom door, just as nervous as I could be?"

"I'm sure I don't know, and what do you expect me to do about it?" I says. "Jump out the window?"

"No, I expect nothing of the kind. I simply declare that Uncle Rondo looks like a fool in it, that's all," she says. "It makes me sick to my stomach."

"Well, he looks as good as he can," I says. "As good as anybody in reason could." I stood up for Uncle

Rondo, please remember. And I said to Stella-Rondo, "I think I would do well not to criticize so freely if I were you and came home with a two-year-old child I had never said a word about, and no explanation whatever about my separation."

"I asked you the instant I entered this house not to refer one more time to my adopted child, and you gave me your word of honor you would not," was all Stella-Rondo would say, and started pulling out every one of her eyebrows with some cheap Kress tweezers.

So I merely slammed the door behind me and went down and made some green-tomato pickle. Somebody had to do it. Of course Mama had turned both the niggers loose; she always said no earthly power could hold one anyway on the Fourth of July, so she wouldn't even try. It turned out that Jaypan fell in the lake and came within a very narrow limit of drowning.

So Mama trots in. Lifts up the lid and says, "H'm! Not very good for your Uncle Rondo in his precarious condition, I must say. Or poor little adopted Shirley-T. Shame on you!"

That made me tired. I says, "Well, Stella-Rondo had better thank her lucky stars it was her instead of me came trotting in with that very peculiar-looking child. Now if it had been me that trotted in from Illinois and brought a peculiar-looking child of two, I shudder to think of the reception I'd of got, much less controlled the diet of an entire family."

"But you must remember, Sister, that you were never married to Mr. Whitaker in the first place and didn't go up to Illinois to live," says Mama, shaking a spoon in my face. "If you had I would of been just as overjoyed to see you and your little adopted girl as I was to see Stella-Rondo, when you wound up with your separation and came on back home."

"You would not," I says.

"Don't contradict me, I would," says Mama.

But I said she couldn't convince me though she talked till she was blue in the face. Then I said, "Besides, you know as well as I do that that child is not adopted."

"She most certainly is adopted," says Mama, stiff as a poker.

I says, "Why, Mama, Stella-Rondo had her just as sure as anything in this world, and just too stuck up to admit it."

"Why, Sister," said Mama. "Here I thought we were going to have a pleasant Fourth of July, and you start right out not believing a word your own baby sister tells you!"

"Just like Cousin Annie Flo. Went to her grave denying the facts of life," I remind Mama.

"I told you if you ever mentioned Annie Flo's name I'd slap your face," says Mama, and slaps my face.

"All right, you wait and see," I says.

"I," says Mama, "*I* prefer to take my children's word for anything when it's humanly possible." You ought to see Mama, she weighs two hundred pounds and has real tiny feet.

Just then something perfectly horrible occurred to me.

"Mama," I says, "can that child talk?" I simply had to whisper! "Mama, I wonder if that child can be—you know—in any way? Do you realize," I says, "that she hasn't spoken one single, solitary word to a human being up to this minute? This is the way she looks," I says, and I looked like this.

Well, Mama and I just stood there and stared at each other. It was horrible!

"I remember well that Joe Whitaker frequently drank like a fish," says Mama. "I believed to my soul he drank *chemicals*." And without another word she marches to the foot of the stairs and calls Stella-Rondo.

"Stella-Rondo? O-o-o-o-o! Stella-Rondo!"

"What?" says Stella-Rondo from upstairs. Not even the grace to get up off the bed.

"Can that child of yours talk?" asks Mama.

Stella-Rondo says, "Can she what?"

"Talk! Talk!" says Mama. "Burdyburdyburdyburdy!"

So Stella-Rondo yells back, "Who says she can't talk?"

"Sister says so," says Mama.

"You didn't have to tell me, I know whose word of honor don't mean a thing in this house," says Stella-Rondo.

And in a minute the loudest Yankee voice I ever heard in my life yells out, "OE'm Pop-OE the Sail-or-r-r-r Ma-a-an!" and then somebody jumps up and down in the upstairs hall. In another second the house would of fallen down.

"Not only talks, she can tap-dance!" calls Stella-Rondo. "Which is more than some people I won't name can do."

"Why, the little precious darling thing!" Mama says, so surprised. "Just as smart as she can be!" Starts talking baby talk right there. Then she turns on me. "Sister, you ought to be thoroughly ashamed! Run upstairs this instant and apologize to Stella-Rondo and Shirley-T."

"Apologize for what?" I says. "I merely wondered if the child was normal, that's all. Now that she's proved she is, why, I have nothing further to say."

But Mama just turned on her heel and flew out, furious. She ran right upstairs and hugged the baby. She believed it was adopted. Stella-Rondo hadn't done a thing but turn her against me from upstairs while I stood there helpless over the hot stove. So that made Mama, Papa-Daddy and the baby all on Stella-Rondo's side.

Next, Uncle Rondo.

I must say that Uncle Rondo has been marvelous to me at various times in the past and I was completely unprepared to be made to jump out of my skin, the way it turned out. Once Stella-Rondo did something perfectly horrible to him—broke a chain letter from Flanders Field—and he took the radio back he had given her and gave it to me. Stella-Rondo was furious! For six months we all had to call her Stella instead of Stella-Rondo, or she wouldn't answer. I always thought Uncle Rondo had all the brains of the entire family. Another time he sent me to Mammoth Cave, with all expenses paid.

But this would be the day he was drinking that prescription, the Fourth of July.

So at supper Stella-Rondo speaks up and says she thinks Uncle Rondo ought to try to eat a little something. So finally Uncle Rondo said he would try a little cold biscuits and ketchup, but that was all. So *she* brought it to him.

"Do you think it wise to disport with ketchup in Stella-Rondo's flesh-colored kimono?" I says. Trying to be considerate! If Stella-Rondo couldn't watch out for her trousseau, somebody had to.

"Any objections?" asks Uncle Rondo, just about to pour out all the ketchup.

"Don't mind what she says, Uncle Rondo," says Stella-Rondo. "Sister has been devoting this solid afternoon to sneering out my bedroom window at the way you look."

"What's that?" says Uncle Rondo. Uncle Rondo has got the most terrible temper in the world. Anything is liable to make him tear the house down if it comes at the wrong time.

So Stella-Rondo says, "Sister says, 'Uncle Rondo certainly does look like a fool in that pink kimono!'"

Do you remember who it was really said that?

Uncle Rondo spills out all the ketchup and jumps out of his chair and tears off the kimono and throws it down on the dirty floor and puts his foot on it. It had to be sent all the way to Jackson to the cleaners and repleated.

"So that's your opinion of your Uncle Rondo, is it?" he says. "I look like a fool, do I? Well, that's the last straw. A whole day in this house with nothing to do, and then to hear you come out with a remark like that behind my back!"

"I didn't say any such of a thing, Uncle Rondo," I says, "and I'm not saying who did, either. Why, I think you look all right. Just try to take care of yourself and not talk and eat at the same time," I says. "I think you better go lie down."

"Lie down my foot," says Uncle Rondo. I ought to of

known by that he was fixing to do something perfectly horrible.

So he didn't do anything that night in the precarious state he was in—just played Casino with Mama and Stella-Rondo and Shirley-T. and gave Shirley-T. a nickel with a head on both sides. It tickled her nearly to death, and she called him "Papa." But at 6:30 A.M. the next morning, he threw a whole five-cent package of some unsold one-inch firecrackers from the store as hard as he could into my bedroom and they every one went off. Not one bad one in the string. Anybody else, there'd be one that wouldn't go off.

Well, I'm just terribly susceptible to noise of any kind, the doctor has always told me I was the most sensitive person he had ever seen in his whole life, and I was simply prostrated. I couldn't eat! People tell me they heard it as far as the cemetery, and old Aunt Jep Patterson, that had been holding her own so good, thought it was Judgment Day and she was going to meet her whole family. It's usually so quiet here.

And I'll tell you it didn't take me any longer than a minute to make up my mind what to do. There I was with the whole entire house on Stella-Rondo's side and turned against me. If I have anything at all I have pride.

So I just decided I'd go straight down to the P.O. There's plenty of room there in the back, I says to myself.

Well! I made no bones about letting the family catch on to what I was up to. I didn't try to conceal it.

The first thing they knew, I marched in where they were all playing Old Maid and pulled the electric oscillating fan out by the plug, and everything got real hot. Next I snatched the pillow I'd done the needlepoint on right off the davenport from behind Papa-Daddy. He went "Ugh!" I beat Stella-Rondo up the stairs and finally found my charm bracelet in her bureau drawer under a picture of Nelson Eddy.

"So that's the way the land lies," says Uncle Rondo. There he was, piecing on the ham. "Well, Sister, I'll be glad to donate my army cot if you got any place to set it up, providing you'll leave right this minute and let me get some peace." Uncle Rondo was in France.

"Thank you kindly for the cot and 'peace' is hardly the word I would select if I had to resort to firecrackers at 6:30 A.M. in a young girl's bedroom," I says back to him. "And as to where I intend to go, you seem to forget my position as postmistress of China Grove, Mississippi," I says. "I've always got the P.O."

Well, that made them all sit up and take notice.

I went out front and started digging up some four-o'clocks to plant around the P.O.

"Ah-ah-ah!" says Mama, raising the window. "Those happen to be my four-o'clocks. Everything planted in that star is mine. I've never known you to make anything grow in your life."

"Very well," I says. "But I take the fern. Even you, Mama, can't stand there and deny that I'm the one watered that fern. And I happen to know where I can send in a box top and get a packet of one thousand mixed seeds, no two the same kind, free."

"Oh, where?" Mama wants to know.

But I says, "Too late. You 'tend to your house, and I'll 'tend to mine. You hear things like that all the time if you know how to listen to the radio. Perfectly marvelous offers. Get anything you want free."

So I hope to tell you I marched in and got that radio, and they could of all bit a nail in two, especially Stella-Rondo, that it used to belong to, and she well knew she couldn't get it back, I'd sue for it like a shot. And I very politely took the sewing-machine motor I helped pay the most on to give Mama for Christmas back in 1929, and a good big calendar, with the first-aid remedies on it. The thermometer and the Hawaiian ukulele certainly were rightfully mine, and I stood on the step-ladder and got all my watermelon-rind preserves and every fruit and vegetable I'd put up, every jar. Then I began to pull the tacks out of the bluebird wall vases on the archway to the dining room.

"Who told you you could have those, Miss Priss?" says Mama, fanning as hard as she could.

"I bought 'em and I'll keep track of 'em," I says. "I'll

tack 'em up one on each side the post-office window, and you can see 'em when you come to ask me for your mail, if you're so dead to see 'em."

"Not I! I'll never darken the door to that post office again if I live to be a hundred," Mama says. "Ungrateful child! After all the money we spent on you at the Normal."

"Me either," says Stella-Rondo. "You can just let my mail lie there and *rot*, for all I care. I'll never come and relieve you of a single, solitary piece."

"I should worry," I says. "And who you think's going to sit down and write you all those big fat letters and postcards, by the way? Mr. Whitaker? Just because he was the only man ever dropped down in China Grove and you got him—unfairly—is he going to sit down and write you a lengthy correspondence after you come home giving no rhyme nor reason whatsoever for your separation and no explanation for the presence of that child? I may not have your brilliant mind, but I fail to see it."

So Mama says, "Sister, I've told you a thousand times that Stella-Rondo simply got homesick, and this child is far too big to be hers," and she says, "Now, why don't you all just sit down and play Casino?"

Then Shirley-T. sticks out her tongue at me in this perfectly horrible way. She has no more manners than the man in the moon. I told her she was going to cross her eyes like that some day and they'd stick.

"It's too late to stop me now," I says. "You should have tried that yesterday. I'm going to the P.O. and the only way you can possibly see me is to visit me there."

So Papa-Daddy says, "You'll never catch me setting foot in that post office, even if I should take a notion into my head to write a letter some place." He says, "I won't have you reachin' out of that little old window with a pair of shears and cuttin' off any beard of mine. I'm too smart for you!"

"We all are," says Stella-Rondo.

But I said, "If you're so smart, where's Mr. Whitaker?"

So then Uncle Rondo says, "I'll thank you from now

on to stop reading all the orders I get on postcards and telling everybody in China Grove what you think is the matter with them," but I says, "I draw my own conclusions and will continue in the future to draw them." I says, "If people want to write their inmost secrets on penny postcards, there's nothing in the wide world you can do about it, Uncle Rondo."

"And if you think we'll ever *write* another postcard you're sadly mistaken," says Mama.

"Cutting off your nose to spite your face then," I says. "But if you're all determined to have no more to do with the U. S. mail, think of this: What will Stella-Rondo do now, if she wants to tell Mr. Whitaker to come after her?"

"Wah!" says Stella-Rondo. I knew she'd cry. She had a conniption fit right there in the kitchen.

"It will be interesting to see how long she holds out," I says. "And now—I am leaving."

"Good-bye," says Uncle Rondo.

"Oh, I declare," says Mama, "to think that a family of mine should quarrel on the Fourth of July, or the day after, over Stella-Rondo leaving old Mr. Whitaker and having the sweetest little adopted child! It looks like we'd all be glad!"

"Wah!" says Stella-Rondo, and has a fresh conniption fit.

"*He* left *her*—you mark my words," I says. "That's Mr. Whitaker. I know Mr. Whitaker. After all, I knew him first. I said from the beginning he'd up and leave her. I foretold every single thing that's happened."

"Where did he go?" asks Mama.

"Probably to the North Pole, if he knows what's good for him," I says.

But Stella-Rondo just bawled and wouldn't say another word. She flew to her room and slammed the door.

"Now look what you've gone and done, Sister," says Mama. "You go apologize."

"I haven't got time, I'm leaving," I says.

"Well, what are you waiting around for?" asks Uncle Rondo.

So I just picked up the kitchen clock and marched off, without saying "Kiss my foot" or anything, and never did tell Stella-Rondo good-bye.

There was a nigger girl going along on a little wagon right in front.

"Nigger girl," I says, "come help me haul these things down the hill, I'm going to live in the post office."

Took her nine trips in her express wagon. Uncle Rondo came out on the porch and threw her a nickel.

And that's the last I've laid eyes on any of my family or my family laid eyes on me for five solid days and nights. Stella-Rondo may be telling the most horrible tales in the world about Mr. Whitaker, but I haven't heard them. As I tell everybody, I draw my own conclusions.

But oh, I like it here. It's ideal, as I've been saying. You see, I've got everything cater-cornered, the way I like it. Hear the radio? All the war news. Radio, sewing machine, book ends, ironing board and that great big piano lamp—peace, that's what I like. Butter-bean vines planted all along the front where the strings are.

Of course, there's not much mail. My family are naturally the main people in China Grove, and if they prefer to vanish from the face of the earth, for all the mail they get or the mail they write, why, I'm not going to open my mouth. Some of the folks here in town are taking up for me and some turned against me. I know which is which. There are always people who will quit buying stamps just to get on the right side of Papa-Daddy.

But here I am, and here I'll stay. I want the world to know I'm happy.

And if Stella-Rondo should come to me this minute, on bended knees, and *attempt* to explain the incidents of her life with Mr. Whitaker, I'd simply put my fingers in both my ears and refuse to listen.

Livvie

Solomon carried Livvie twenty-one miles away from her home when he married her. He carried her away up on the Old Natchez Trace into the deep country to live in his house. She was sixteen—an only girl, then. Once people said he thought nobody would ever come along there. He told her himself that it had been a long time, and a day she did not know about, since that road was a traveled road with *people* coming and going. He was good to her, but he kept her in the house. She had not thought that she could not get back. Where she came from, people said an old man did not want anybody in the world to ever find his wife, for fear they would steal her back from him. Solomon asked her before he took her, "Would she be happy?"—very dignified, for he was a colored man that owned his land and had it written down in the courthouse; and she said, "Yes, sir," since he was an old man and she was young and just listened and answered. He asked her, if she was choosing winter, would she pine for spring, and she said, "No indeed." Whatever she said, always, was because he was an old man . . . while nine years went by. All the time, he got old, and he got so old he gave out. At last he slept the whole day in bed, and she was young still.

It was a nice house, inside and outside both. In the

first place, it had three rooms. The front room was papered in holly paper, with green palmettos from the swamp spaced at careful intervals over the walls. There was fresh newspaper cut with fancy borders on the mantel-shelf, on which were propped photographs of old or very young men printed in faint yellow—Solomon's people. Solomon had a houseful of furniture. There was a double settee, a tall scrolled rocker and an organ in the front room, all around a three-legged table with a pink marble top, on which was set a lamp with three gold feet, besides a jelly glass with pretty hen feathers in it. Behind the front room, the other room had the bright iron bed with the polished knobs like a throne, in which Solomon slept all day. There were snow-white curtains of wiry lace at the window, and a lace bed-spread belonged on the bed. But what old Solomon slept so sound under was a big feather-stitched piece-quilt in the pattern "Trip Around the World," which had twenty-one different colors, four hundred and forty pieces, and a thousand yards of thread, and that was what Solomon's mother made in her life and old age. There was a table holding the Bible, and a trunk with a key. On the wall were two calendars, and a diploma from somewhere in Solomon's family, and under that Livvie's one possession was nailed, a picture of the little white baby of the family she worked for, back in Natchez before she was married. Going through that room and on to the kitchen, there was a big wood stove and a big round table always with a wet top and with the knives and forks in one jelly glass and the spoons in another, and a cut-glass vinegar bottle between, and going out from those, many shallow dishes of pickled peaches, fig preserves, watermelon pickles and blackberry jam always sitting there. The churn sat in the sun, the doors of the safe were always both shut, and there were four baited mouse-traps in the kitchen, one in every corner.

The outside of Solomon's house looked nice. It was not painted, but across the porch was an even balance. On each side there was one easy chair with high springs, looking out, and a fern basket hanging over it from the ceiling, and a dishpan of zinnia seedlings growing at its foot on the floor. By the door was a plow-wheel, just a pretty iron circle, nailed up on one wall and a square mirror on the other, a turquoise-blue comb stuck up in the frame, with the wash stand beneath it. On the door was a wooden knob with a pearl in the end, and Solomon's black hat hung on that, if he was in the house.

Out front was a clean dirt yard with every vestige of grass patiently uprooted and the ground scarred in deep whorls from the strike of Livvie's broom. Rose bushes with tiny blood-red roses blooming every month grew in threes on either side of the steps. On one side was a peach tree, on the other a pomegranate. Then coming around up the path from the deep cut of the Natchez Trace below was a line of bare crape-myrtle trees with every branch of them ending in a colored bottle, green or blue. There was no word that fell from Solomon's lips to say what they were for, but Livvie knew that there could be a spell put in trees, and she was familiar from the time she was born with the way bottle trees kept evil spirits from coming into the house—by luring them inside the colored bottles, where they cannot get out again. Solomon had made the bottle trees with his own hands over the nine years, in labor amounting to about a tree a year, and without a sign that he had any uneasiness in his heart, for he took as much pride in his precautions against spirits coming in the house as he took in the house, and sometimes in the sun the bottle trees looked prettier than the house did.

It was a nice house. It was in a place where the days would go by and surprise anyone that they were over. The lamplight and the firelight would shine out the door after dark, over the still and breathing country, lighting the roses and the bottle trees, and all was quiet there.

But there was nobody, nobody at all, not even a white person. And if there had been anybody, Solomon would not have let Livvie look at them, just as he would not let her look at a field hand, or a field hand look at her. There was no house near, except for the cabins of the tenants that were forbidden to her, and there was no house as far as she had been, stealing away down the still, deep Trace. She felt as if she waded a river when she went, for the dead leaves on the ground reached as high as her knees, and when she was all scratched and bleeding she said it was not like a road that went anywhere. One day, climbing up the high bank, she had found a graveyard without a church, with ribbon-grass growing about the foot of an angel (she had climbed up because she thought she saw angel wings), and in the sun, trees shining like burning flames through the great caterpillar nets which enclosed them. Scarey thistles stood looking like the prophets in the Bible in Solomon's house. Indian paint brushes grew over her head, and the mourning dove made the only sound in the world. Oh for a stirring of the leaves, and a breaking of the nets! But not by a ghost, prayed Livvie, jumping down the bank. After Solomon took to his bed, she never went out, except one more time.

Livvie knew she made a nice girl to wait on anybody. She fixed things to eat on a tray like a surprise. She could keep from singing when she ironed, and to sit by a bed and fan away the flies, she could be so still she could not hear herself breathe. She could clean up the house and never drop a thing, and wash the dishes without a sound, and she would step outside to churn, for churning sounded too sad to her, like sobbing, and if it made her home-sick and not Solomon, she did not think of that.

But Solomon scarcely opened his eyes to see her, and scarcely tasted his food. He was not sick or paralyzed or in any pain that he mentioned, but he was surely wearing out in the body, and no matter what nice hot thing Livvie would bring him to taste, he would only look at it now, as if he were past seeing how he could add anything more to himself. Before she could beg him, he would go fast asleep. She could not surprise him any more, if he would not taste, and she was afraid that he was never in the world going to taste another thing she brought him—and so how could he last?

But one morning it was breakfast time and she cooked his eggs and grits, carried them in on a tray, and called his name. He was sound asleep. He lay in a dignified way with his watch beside him, on his back in the middle of the bed. One hand drew the quilt up high, though it was the first day of spring. Through the white lace curtains a little puffy wind was blowing as if it came from round cheeks. All night the frogs had sung 'out in the swamp, like a commotion in the room, and he had not stirred, though she lay wide awake and saying "Shh, frogs!" for fear he would mind them.

He looked as if he would like to sleep a little longer, and so she put back the tray and waited a little. When she tiptoed and stayed so quiet, she surrounded herself with a little reverie, and sometimes it seemed to her when she was so stealthy that the quiet she kept was for a sleeping baby, and that she had a baby and was its mother. When she stood at Solomon's bed and looked down at him, she would be thinking, "He sleeps so well," and she would hate to wake him up. And in some other way, too, she was afraid to wake him up because even in his sleep he seemed to be such a strict man.

Of course, nailed to the wall over the bed—only she would forget who it was—there was a picture of him when he was young. Then he had a fan of hair over his forehead like a king's crown. Now his hair lay down on his head, the spring had gone out of it. Solomon had a lightish face, with eyebrows scattered but rugged, the way privet grows, strong eyes, with second sight, a strict mouth, and a little gold smile. This was the way he looked in his clothes, but in bed in the daytime he looked like a different and smaller man, even when he was wide awake, and holding the Bible. He looked like somebody kin to himself. And then sometimes when he lay in sleep and she stood fanning the flies away, and the light came in, his face was like new, so smooth and clear that it was like a glass of jelly held to the window, and she could almost look through his forehead and see what he thought.

She fanned him and at length he opened his eyes and spoke her name, but he would not taste the nice eggs she had kept warm under a pan.

Back in the kitchen she ate heartily, his breakfast and hers, and looked out the open door at what went on. The whole day, and the whole night before, she had felt the stir of spring close to her. It was as present in the house as a young man would be. The moon was in the last quarter and outside they were turning the sod and planting peas and beans. Up and down the red fields, over which smoke from the brush-burning hung showing like a little skirt of sky, a white horse and a white mule pulled the plow. At intervals hoarse shouts came through the air and roused her as if she dozed neglectfully in the shade, and they were telling her, "Jump up!" She could see how over each ribbon of field were moving men and girls, on foot and mounted on mules, with hats set on their heads and bright with tall hoes and forks as if they carried streamers on them and were going to some place on a journey—and how as if at a signal now and then they would all start at once shouting, hollering, cajoling, calling and answering back, running, being leaped on and breaking away, flinging to earth with a shout and lying motionless in the trance of twelve o'clock. The old women came out of the cabins and brought them the food they had ready for them, and then all worked together, spread evenly out. The little children came too, like a bouncing stream overflowing the fields, and set upon the men, the women, the dogs, the rushing birds, and the wave-like rows of earth, their little voices almost too high to be heard. In the middle distance like some white and gold towers were the haystacks, with black cows coming around to eat their edges. High above everything, the wheel of fields, house, and cabins, and the deep road surrounding like a moat to keep them in, was the turning sky, blue with long, far-flung white mare's-tail clouds, serene and still as high flames. And sound asleep while all this went around him that was his, Solomon was like a little still spot in the middle.

Even in the house the earth was sweet to breathe. Solomon had never let Livvie go any farther than the chicken house and the well. But what if she would walk now into the heart of the fields and take a hoe and work until she fell stretched out and drenched with her efforts, like other girls, and laid her cheek against the laid-open earth, and shamed the old man with her humbleness and delight? To shame him! A cruel wish could come in uninvited and so fast while she looked out the back door. She washed the dishes and scrubbed the table. She could hear the cries of the little lambs. Her mother, that she had not seen since her wedding day, had said one time, "I rather a man be anything, than a woman be mean."

So all morning she kept tasting the chicken broth on the stove, and when it was right she poured off a nice cup-ful. She carried it in to Solomon, and there he lay having a dream. Now what did he dream about? For she saw him sigh gently as if not to disturb some whole thing he held round in his mind, like a fresh egg. So even an old man dreamed about something pretty. Did he dream of her, while his eyes were shut and sunken, and his small hand with the wedding ring curled close in sleep around the quilt? He might be dreaming of what time it was, for even through his sleep he kept track of it like a clock, and knew how much of it went by, and waked up knowing where the hands were even before he consulted the silver watch that he never let go. He would sleep with the watch in his palm, and even holding it to his cheek like a child that loves a plaything. Or he might dream of journeys and travels on a steamboat to Natchez. Yet she thought he dreamed of her; but even while she scrutinized him, the rods of the foot of the bed seemed to rise up like a rail fence between them, and she could see that people never could be sure of anything as long as one of them was asleep and the other awake. To look at him dreaming of her when he might be going to die frightened her a little, as if he might carry her with him that way, and she wanted to run out of the room. She took hold of the bed and held on, and Solomon opened his eyes and called her name, but he did not want anything. He would not taste the good broth.

Just a little after that, as she was taking up the ashes in the front room for the last time in the year, she heard a sound. It was somebody coming. She pulled the curtains together and looked through the slit.

Coming up the path under the bottle trees was a white lady. At first she looked young, but then she looked old. Marvelous to see, a little car stood steaming like a kettle out in the field-track—it had come without a road.

Livvie stood listening to the long, repeated knockings at the door, and after a while she opened it just a little. The lady came in through the crack, though she was more than middle-sized and wore a big hat.

"My name is Miss Baby Marie," she said.

Livvie gazed respectfully at the lady and at the little suitcase she was holding close to her by the handle until the proper moment. The lady's eyes were running over the room, from palmetto to palmetto, but she was saying, "I live at home . . . out from Natchez . . . and get out and show these pretty cosmetic things to the white people and the colored people both . . . all around . . . years and years. . . . Both shades of powder and rouge. . . . It's the kind of work a girl can do and not go clear 'way from home . . ." And the harder she looked, the more she talked. Suddenly she turned up her nose and said, "It is not Christian or sanitary to put feathers in a vase," and then she took a gold key out of the front of her dress and began unlocking the locks on her suitcase. Her face drew the light, the way it was covered with intense white and red, with a little patty-cake of white between the wrinkles by her upper lip. Little red tassels of hair bobbed under the rusty wires of her picture-hat, as with an air of triumph and secrecy she now drew open her little suitcase and brought out bottle after bottle and jar after jar, which she put down on the table, the mantel-piece, the settee, and the organ.

"Did you ever see so many cosmetics in your life?" cried Miss Baby Marie.

"No'm," Livvie tried to say, but the cat had her tongue.

"Have you ever applied cosmetics?" asked Miss Baby Marie next.

"No'm," Livvie tried to say.

"Then look!" she said, and pulling out the last thing of all, "Try this!" she said. And in her hand was unclenched a golden lipstick which popped open like magic. A fragrance came out of it like incense, and Livvie cried out suddenly, "Chinaberry flowers!"

Her hand took the lipstick, and in an instant she was carried away in the air through the spring, and looking down with a half-drowsy smile from a purple cloud she saw from above a chinaberry tree, dark and smooth and neatly leaved, neat as a guinea hen in the dooryard, and there was her home that she had left. On one side of the tree was her mama holding up her heavy apron, and she could see it was loaded with ripe figs, and on the other side was her papa holding a fish-pole over the pond, and she could see it transparently, the little clear fishes swimming up to the brim.

"Oh, no, not chinaberry flowers—secret ingredients," said Miss Baby Marie. "My cosmetics have secret ingredients—not chinaberry flowers."

"It's purple," Livvie breathed, and Miss Baby Marie said, "Use it freely. Rub it on."

Livvie tiptoed out to the wash stand on the front porch and before the mirror put the paint on her mouth. In the wavery surface her face danced before her like a flame. Miss Baby Marie followed her out, took a look at what she had done, and said, "That's it."

Livvie tried to say "Thank you" without moving her parted lips where the paint lay so new.

By now Miss Baby Marie stood behind Livvie and looked in the mirror over her shoulder, twisting up the tassels of her hair. "The lipstick I can let you have for only two dollars," she said, close to her neck.

"Lady, but I don't have no money, never did have," said Livvie.

"Oh, but you don't pay the first time. I make another trip, that's the way I do. I come back again—later."

"Oh," said Livvie, pretending she understood everything so as to please the lady.

"But if you don't take it now, this may be the last time I'll call at your house," said Miss Baby Marie sharply. "It's far away from anywhere, I'll tell you that. You don't live close to anywhere."

"Yes'm. My husband, he keep the *money*," said Livvie, trembling. "He is strict as he can be. He don't know *you* walk in here—Miss Baby Marie!"

"Where is he?"

"Right now, he in yonder sound asleep, an old man. I wouldn't ever ask him for anything."

Miss Baby Marie took back the lipstick and packed it up. She gathered up the jars for both black and white and got them all inside the suitcase, with the same little fuss of triumph with which she had brought them out. She started away.

"Goodbye," she said, making herself look grand from the back, but at the last minute she turned around in the door. Her old hat wobbled as she whispered, "Let me see your husband."

Livvie obediently went on tiptoe and opened the door to the other room. Miss Baby Marie came behind her and rose on her toes and looked in.

"My, what a little tiny old, old man!" she whispered, clasping her hands and shaking her head over them. "What a beautiful quilt! What a tiny old, old man!"

"He can sleep like that all day," whispered Livvie proudly.

They looked at him awhile so fast asleep, and then all at once they looked at each other. Somehow that was as if they had a secret, for he had never stirred. Livvie then politely, but all at once, closed the door.

"Well! I'd certainly like to leave you with a lipstick!" said Miss Baby Marie vivaciously. She smiled in the door.

"Lady, but I told you I don't have no money, and never did have."

"And never will?" In the air and all around, like a bright halo around the white lady's nodding head, it was a true spring day.

"Would you take eggs, lady?" asked Livvie softly.

"No, I have plenty of eggs—plenty," said Miss Baby Marie.

"I still don't have no money," said Livvie, and Miss Baby Marie took her suitcase and went on somewhere else.

Livvie stood watching her go, and all the time she felt

her heart beating in her left side. She touched the place
with her hand. It seemed as if her heart beat and her
whole face flamed from the pulsing color of her lips.
She went to sit by Solomon and when he opened his
eyes he could not see a change in her. "He's fixin' to
die," she said inside. That was the secret. That was
when she went out of the house for a little breath of air.

She went down the path and down the Natchez Trace
a way, and she did not know how far she had gone, but
it was not far, when she saw a sight. It was a man,
looking like a vision—she standing on one side of the
Old Natchez Trace and he standing on the other.

As soon as this man caught sight of her, he began to
look himself over. Starting at the bottom with his
pointed shoes, he began to look up, lifting his peg-top
pants the higher to see fully his bright socks. His coat
long and wide and leaf-green he opened like doors to
see his high-up tawny pants and his pants he smoothed
downward from the points of his collar, and he wore a
luminous baby-pink satin shirt. At the end, he reached
gently above his wide platter-shaped round hat, the
color of a plum, and one finger touched at the feather,
emerald green, blowing in the spring winds.

No matter how she looked, she could never look so
fine as he did, and she was not sorry for that, she was
pleased.

He took three jumps, one down and two up, and was
by her side.

"My name is Cash," he said.

He had a guinea pig in his pocket. They began to
walk along. She stared on and on at him, as if he were
doing some daring spectacular thing, instead of just
walking beside her. It was not simply the city way he
was dressed that made her look at him and see hope in
its insolence looking back. It was not only the way he
moved along kicking the flowers as if he could break
through everything in the way and destroy anything in
the world, that made her eyes grow bright. It might be,
if he had not appeared the way he did appear that day
she would never have looked so closely at him, but the
time people come makes a difference.

They walked through the still leaves of the Natchez Trace, the light and the shade falling through trees about them, the white irises shining like candles on the banks and the new ferns shining like green stars up in the oak branches. They came out at Solomon's house, bottle trees and all. Livvie stopped and hung her head.

Cash began whistling a little tune. She did not know what it was, but she had heard it before from a distance, and she had a revelation. Cash was a field hand. He was a transformed field hand. Cash belonged to Solomon. But he had stepped out of his overalls into this. There in front of Solomon's house he laughed. He had a round head, a round face, all of him was young, and he flung his head up, rolled it against the mare's-tail sky in his round hat, and he could laugh just to see Solomon's house sitting there. Livvie looked at it, and there was Solomon's black hat hanging on the peg on the front door, the blackest thing in the world.

"I been to Natchez," Cash said, wagging his head around against the sky. "*I* taken a trip, *I* ready for Easter!"

How was it possible to look so fine before the harvest? Cash must have stolen the money, stolen it from Solomon. He stood in the path and lifted his spread hand high and brought it down again and again in his laughter. He kicked up his heels. A little chill went through her. It was as if Cash was bringing that strong hand down to beat a drum or to rain blows upon a man, such an abandon and menace were in his laugh. Frowning, she went closer to him and his swinging arm drew her in at once and the fright was crushed from her body, as a little match-flame might be smothered out by what it lighted. She gathered the folds of his coat behind him and fastened her red lips to his mouth, and she was dazzled by herself then, the way he had been dazzled at himself to begin with.

In that instant she felt something that could not be told—that Solomon's death was at hand, that he was the same to her as if he were dead now. She cried out, and uttering little cries turned and ran for the house.

At once Cash was coming, following after, he was

running behind her. He came close, and halfway up the path he laughed and passed her. He even picked up a stone and sailed it into the bottle trees. She put her hands over her head, and sounds clattered through the bottle trees like cries of outrage. Cash stamped and plunged zigzag up the front steps and in at the door.

When she got there, he had stuck his hands in his pockets and was turning slowly about in the front room. The little guinea pig peeped out. Around Cash, the pinned-up palmettos looked as if a lazy green monkey had walked up and down and around the walls leaving green prints of his hands and feet.

She got through the room and his hands were still in his pockets, and she fell upon the closed door to the other room and pushed it open. She ran to Solomon's bed, calling "Solomon! Solomon!" The little shape of the old man never moved at all, wrapped under the quilt as if it were winter still.

"Solomon!" She pulled the quilt away, but there was another one under that, and she fell on her knees beside him. He made no sound except a sigh, and then she could hear in the silence the light springy steps of Cash walking and walking in the front room, and the ticking of Solomon's silver watch, which came from the bed. Old Solomon was far away in his sleep, his face looked small, relentless, and devout, as if he were walking somewhere where she could imagine the snow falling.

Then there was a noise like a hoof pawing the floor, and the door gave a creak, and Cash appeared beside her. When she looked up, Cash's face was so black it was bright, and so bright and bare of pity that it looked sweet to her. She stood up and held up her head. Cash was so powerful that his presence gave her strength even when she did not need any.

Under their eyes Solomon slept. People's faces tell of things and places not known to the one who looks at them while they sleep, and while Solomon slept under the eyes of Livvie and Cash his face told them like a mythical story that all his life he had built, little scrap by little scrap, respect. A beetle could not have been more laborious or more ingenious in the task of its destiny. When Solomon was young, as he was in his picture overhead, it was the infinite thing with him, and he could see no end to the respect he would contrive and keep in a house. He had built a lonely house, the way he would make a cage, but it grew to be the same with him as a great monumental pyramid and sometimes in his absorption of getting it erected he was like the builder-slaves of Egypt who forgot or never knew the origin and meaning of the thing to which they gave all the strength of their bodies and used up all their days. Livvie and Cash could see that as a man might rest from a life-labor he lay in his bed, and they could hear how, wrapped in his quilt, he sighed to himself comfortably in sleep, while in his dreams he might have been an ant, a beetle, a bird, an Egyptian, assembling and carrying on his back and building with his hands, or he might have been an old man of India or a swaddled baby, about to smile and brush all away.

Then without warning old Solomon's eyes flew wide open under the hedge-like brows. He was wide awake.

And instantly Cash raised his quick arm. A radiant sweat stood on his temples. But he did not bring his arm down—it stayed in the air, as if something might have taken hold.

It was not Livvie—she did not move. As if something said "Wait," she stood waiting. Even while her eyes burned under motionless lids, her lips parted in a stiff grimace, and with her arms stiff at her sides she stood above the prone old man and the panting young one, erect and apart.

Movement when it came came in Solomon's face. It was an old and strict face, a frail face, but behind it, like a covered light, came an animation that could play hide and seek, that would dart and escape, had always escaped. The mystery flickered in him, and invited from his eyes. It was that very mystery that Cash with his quick arm would have to strike, and that Livvie could not weep for. But Cash only stood holding his arm in the air, when the gentlest flick of his great strength, almost a puff of his breath, would have been enough, if he had known how to give it, to send the old man over the obstruction that kept him away from death.

If it could not be that the tiny illumination in the fragile and ancient face caused a crisis, a mystery in the room that would not permit a blow to fall, at least it was certain that Cash, throbbing in his Easter clothes, felt a pang of shame that the vigor of a man would come to such an end that he could not be struck without warning. He took down his hand and stepped back behind Livvie, like a round-eyed schoolboy on whose unsuspecting head the dunce cap has been set.

"Young ones can't wait," said Solomon.

Livvie shuddered violently, and then in a gush of tears she stooped for a glass of water and handed it to him, but he did not see her.

"So here come the young man Livvie wait for. Was no prevention. No prevention. Now I lay eyes on young man and it come to be somebody I know all the time, and been knowing since he were born in a cotton patch, and watched grow up year to year, Cash McCord, growed to size, growed up to come in my house in the end—ragged and barefoot."

Solomon gave a cough of distaste. Then he shut his eyes vigorously, and his lips began to move like a chanter's.

"When Livvie married, her husband were already somebody. He had paid great cost for his land. He spread sycamore leaves over the ground from wagon to door, day he brought her home, so her foot would not have to touch ground. He carried her through his door. Then he growed old and could not lift her, and she were still young."

Livvie's sobs followed his words like a soft melody repeating each thing as he stated it. His lips moved for a little without sound, or she cried too fervently, and unheard he might have been telling his whole life, and then he said, "God forgive Solomon for sins great and small. God forgive Solomon for carrying away too young girl for wife and keeping her away from her people and from all the young people would clamor for her back."

Then he lifted up his right hand toward Livvie where she stood by the bed and offered her his silver watch. He dangled it before her eyes, and she hushed crying; her tears stopped. For a moment the watch could be heard ticking as it always did, precisely in his proud hand. She lifted it away. Then he took hold of the quilt; then he was dead.

Livvie left Solomon dead and went out of the room. Stealthily, nearly without noise, Cash went beside her. He was like a shadow, but his shiny shoes moved over the floor in spangles, and the green downy feather shone like a light in his hat. As they reached the front room, he seized her deftly as a long black cat and dragged her hanging by the waist round and round him, while he turned in a circle, his face bent down to hers. The first moment, she kept one arm and its hand stiff and still, the one that held Solomon's watch. Then the fingers softly let go, all of her was limp, and the watch fell somewhere on the floor. It ticked away in the still room, and all at once there began outside the full song of a bird.

They moved around and around the room and into the brightness of the open door, then he stopped and shook her once. She rested in silence in his trembling arms, unprotesting as a bird on a nest. Outside the redbirds were flying and crisscrossing, the sun was in all the bottles on the prisoned trees, and the young peach was shining in the middle of them with the bursting light of spring.

Moon Lake

From the beginning his martyred presence seriously affected them. They had a disquieting familiarity with it, hearing the spit of his despising that went into his bugle. At times they could hardly recognize what he thought he was playing. Loch Morrison, Boy Scout and Life Saver, was under the ordeal of a week's camp on Moon Lake with girls.

Half the girls were county orphans, wished on them by Mr. Nesbitt and the Men's Bible Class after Billy Sunday's visit to town; but all girls, orphans and Morgana girls alike, were the same thing to Loch; maybe he threw in the two counselors too. He was hating every day of the seven. He hardly spoke; he never spoke first. Sometimes he swung in the trees; Nina Carmichael in particular would hear him crashing in the foliage somewhere when she was lying rigid in siesta.

While they were in the lake, for the dip or the five-o'clock swimming period in the afternoon, he stood against a tree with his arms folded, jacked up one-legged, sitting on his heel, as absolutely tolerant as an old fellow waiting for the store to open, being held up by the wall. Waiting for the girls to get out, he gazed upon some undisturbed part of the water. He despised their predicaments, most of all their not being able to swim. Sometimes he would take aim and from his right cheek shoot an imaginary gun at something far out, where they never were. Then he resumed his pose. He had been roped into this by his mother.

At the hours too hot for girls he used Moon Lake. He dived high off the crosspiece nailed up in the big oak, where the American Legion dived. He went through the air rocking and jerking like an engine, splashed in, climbed out, spat, climbed up again, dived off. He wore a long bathing suit which stretched longer from Monday to Tuesday and from Tuesday to Wednesday and so on, yawning at the armholes toward infinity, and it looked black and formal as a minstrel suit as he stood skinny against the clouds as on a stage.

He came and got his food and turned his back and ate it all alone like a dog and lived in a tent by himself, apart like a nigger, and dived alone when the lake was clear of girls. That way, he seemed able to bear it; that would be his life. In early evening, in moonlight sings, the Boy Scout and Life Saver kept far away. They would sing "When all the little ships come sailing home," and he would be roaming off; they could tell about where he was. He played taps for them, invisibly then, and so beautifully they wept together, whole tentfuls some nights. Off with the whip-poor-wills and the coons and the owls and the little bobwhites—down where it all sloped away, he had pitched his tent, and slept there. Then at reveille, how he would spit into that cornet.

Reveille was his. He harangued the woods when the little minnows were trembling and running wizardlike in the water's edge. And how lovely and altered the trees were then, weighted with dew, leaning on one another's shoulders and smelling like big wet flowers. He blew his horn into their presence—trees' and girls'—and then watched the Dip.

"Good morning, Mr. Dip, Dip, Dip, with your water just as cold as ice!" sang Mrs. Gruenwald hoarsely. She took them for the dip, for Miss Moody said she couldn't, simply couldn't.

The orphans usually hung to the rear, and every

other moment stood swayback with knees locked, the
shoulders of their wash dresses ironed flat and stuck in
peaks, and stared. For swimming they owned no bathing suits and went in in their underbodies. Even in the
water they would stand swayback, each with a fist in
front of her over the rope, looking over the flat surface
as over the top of a tall mountain none of them could
ever get over. Even at this hour of the day, they seemed
to be expecting little tasks, something more immediate
—little tasks that were never given out.

Mrs. Gruenwald was from the North and said "dup."
"Good morning, Mr. Dup, Dup, Dup, with your water
just as cold as ice!" sang Mrs. Gruenwald, fatly capering and leading them all in a singing, petering-out string
down to the lake. She did a sort of little rocking dance
in her exhortation, broad in her bathrobe. From the tail
end of the line she looked like a Shredded Wheat
Biscuit box rocking on its corners.

Nina Carmichael thought, There is nobody and nothing named Mr. Dip, it is not a good morning until you
have had coffee, and the water is the temperature of a
just-cooling biscuit, thank Goodness. I hate this little
parade of us girls, Nina thought, trotting fiercely in the
center of it. It ruins the woods, all right. "Gee, we think
you're mighty nice," they sang to Mr. Dip, while the
Boy Scout, waiting at the lake, watched them go in.

"Watch out for mosquitoes," they called to one another, lyrically because warning wasn't any use anyway,
as they walked out of their kimonos and dropped them
like the petals of one big scattered flower on the bank
behind them, and exposing themselves felt in a hundred
places at once the little pangs. The orphans ripped their
dresses off over their heads and stood in their underbodies. Busily they hung and piled their dresses on a
cedar branch, obeying one of their own number, like a
whole flock of ferocious little birds with pale topknots
building themselves a nest. The orphan named Easter appeared in charge. She handed her dress wrong-side-out
to a friend, who turned it and hung it up for her, and
waited standing very still, her little fingers locked.

"Let's let the orphans go in the water first and get the

snakes stirred up, Mrs. Gruenwald," Jinny Love Stark suggested first off, in the cheerful voice she adopted toward grown people. "Then they'll be chased away by the time *we* go in."

That made the orphans scatter in their pantie-waists, outwards from Easter; the little gauzes of gnats they ran through made them beat their hands at the air. They ran back together again, to Easter, and stood excitedly, almost hopping.

"I think we'll all go in in one big bunch," Mrs. Gruenwald said. Jinny Love lamented and beat against Mrs. Gruenwald, Mrs. Gruenwald's solid, rope-draped stomach all but returning her blows. "All take hands—march! Into the water! *Don't* let the stobs and cypress roots break your legs! *Do* your best! Kick! Stay on top if you can and hold the rope if necessary!"

Mrs. Gruenwald abruptly walked away from Jinny Love, out of the bathrobe, and entered the lake with a vast displacing. She left them on the bank with her Yankee advice.

The Morgana girls might never have gone in if the orphans hadn't balked. Easter came to a dead stop at Moon Lake and looked at it squinting as though it floated really on the Moon. And mightn't it be on the Moon?—it was a strange place, Nina thought, unlikely —and three miles from Morgana, Mississippi, all the time. The Morgana girls pulled the orphans' hands and dragged them in, or pushed suddenly from behind, and finally the orphans took hold of one another and waded forward in a body, singing "Good Morning" with their stiff, chip-like lips. None of them could or would swim, ever, and they just stood waist-deep and waited for the dip to be over. A few of them reached out and caught the struggling Morgana girls by the legs as they splashed from one barky post to another, to see how hard it really was to stay up.

"Mrs. Gruenwald, look, they want to drown us."

But Mrs. Gruenwald all this time was rising and sinking like a whale, she was in a sea of her own waves and perhaps of self-generated cold, out in the middle of the lake. She cared little that Morgana girls who learned to swim were getting a dollar from home. She had deserted them, no, she had never really been with them. Not only orphans had she deserted. In the water she kept so much to the profile that her single pushing-out eyeball looked like a little bottle of something. It was said she believed in evolution.

While the Boy Scout in the rosy light under the green trees twirled his horn so that it glittered and ran a puzzle in the sun, and emptied the spit out of it, he yawned, snappingly—as if he would bite the day, as quickly as Easter had bitten Deacon Nesbitt's hand on Opening Day.

"Gee, we think you're mighty nice," they sang to Mr. Dip, gasping, pounding their legs in him. If they let their feet go down, the invisible bottom of the lake felt like soft, knee-deep fur. The sharp hard knobs came up where least expected. The Morgana girls of course wore bathing slippers, and the mud loved to suck them off. The alligators had been beaten out of this lake, but it was said that water snakes—pilots—were swimming here and there; they would bite you but not kill you; and one cottonmouth moccasin was still getting away from the niggers—if the niggers were still going after him; he would kill you. These were the chances of getting sucked under, of being bitten, and of dying three miles away from home.

The brown water cutting her off at the chest, Easter looked directly before her, wide awake, unsmiling. Before she could hold a stare like that, she would have had to swallow something big—so Nina felt. It would have been something so big that it didn't matter to her what the inside of a snake's mouth was lined with. At the other end of her gaze the life saver grew almost insignificant. Her gaze moved like a little switch or wand, and the life saver scratched himself with his bugle, raked himself, as if that eased him. Yet the flick of a blue-bottle fly made Easter jump.

They swam and held to the rope, hungry and waiting. But they had to keep waiting till Loch Morrison blew his horn before they could come out of Moon Lake. Mrs. Gruenwald, who capered before breakfast, believed in evolution, and put her face in the water, was quarter of a mile out. If she said anything, they couldn't hear her for the frogs.

II

Nina and Jinny Love, with the soles of their feet shocked from the walk, found Easter ahead of them down at the spring.

For the orphans, from the first, sniffed out the way to the spring by themselves, and they could get there without stops to hold up their feet and pull out thorns and stickers, and could run through the sandy bottoms and never look down where they were going, and could grab hold with their toes on the sharp rutted path up the pine ridge and down. They clearly could never get enough of skimming over the silk-slick needles and setting prints of their feet in the bed of the spring to see them dissolve away under their eyes. What was it to them if the spring was muddied by the time Jinny Love Stark got there?

The one named Easter could fall flat as a boy, elbows cocked, and drink from the cup of her hand with her face in the spring. Jinny Love prodded Nina, and while they looked on Easter's drawers, Nina was opening the drinking cup she had brought with her, then collapsing it, feeling like a lady with a fan. That way, she was going over a thought, a fact: Half the people out here with me are orphans. Orphans. Orphans. She yearned for her heart to twist. But it didn't, not in time. Easter was through drinking—wiping her mouth and flinging her hand as if to break the bones, to get rid of the drops, and it was Nina's turn with her drinking cup.

Nina stood and bent over from the waist. Calmly, she held her cup in the spring and watched it fill. They could all see how it spangled like a cold star in the curling water. The water tasted the silver cool of the rim it went over running to her lips, and at moments the cup gave her teeth a pang. Nina heard her own throat swallowing. She paused and threw a smile about her. After she had drunk she wiped the cup on her tie and collapsed it, and put the little top on, and its ring over her finger. With that, Easter, one arm tilted, charged against the green bank and mounted it. Nina felt her surveying the spring and all from above. Jinny Love was down drinking like a chicken, kissing the water only.

Easter was dominant among the orphans. It was not that she was so bad. The one called Geneva stole, for example, but Easter was dominant for what she was in herself—for the way she held still, sometimes. All orphans were at once wondering and stoic—at one moment loving everything too much, the next folding back from it, tightly as hard green buds growing in the wrong direction, closing as they go. But it was as if Easter signaled them. Now she just stood up there, watching the spring, with the name Easter—tacky name, as Jinny Love Stark was the first to say. She was medium size, but her hair seemed to fly up at the temples, being cropped and wiry, and this crest made her nearly as tall as Jinny Love Stark. The rest of the orphans had hair paler than their tanned foreheads—straight and tow, the greenish yellow of cornsilk that dimmed black at the roots and shadows, with burnt-out-looking bangs like young boys' and old men's hair; that was from picking in the fields. Easter's hair was a withstanding gold. Around the back of her neck beneath the hair was a dark band on her skin like the mark a gold bracelet leaves on the arm. It came to the Morgana girls with a feeling of elation: the ring was pure dirt. They liked to look at it, or to remember, too late, what it was—as now, when Easter had already lain down for a drink and left the spring. They liked to walk behind her and see her back, which seemed spectacular from crested gold head to hard, tough heel. Mr. Nesbitt, from the Bible Class, took Easter by the wrist and turned her around to him and looked just as hard at her front. She had started her breasts. What Easter did was to bite his right hand, his collection hand. It was wonderful to have with them someone dangerous but not, so far, or provenly, bad. When Nina's little lead-mold umbrella, the size of a clover, a Crackerjack prize, was stolen the first night of camp, that was Geneva, Easter's friend.

Jinny Love, after wiping her face with a hand-made handkerchief, pulled out a deck of cards she had secretly brought in her middy pocket. She dropped them down, bright blue, on a sandy place by the spring. "Let's play cassino. Do they call you *Easter?*"

Down Easter jumped, from the height of the bank. She came back to them. "Cassino, what's that?"

"All right, what do *you* want to play?"

"All right, I'll play you mumblety-peg."

"I don't know how you play that!" cried Nina.

"Who would ever want to know?" asked Jinny Love, closing the circle.

Easter flipped out a jack-knife and with her sawed fingernail shot out three blades.

"Do you carry that in the orphan asylum?" Jinny Love asked with some respect.

Easter dropped to her scarred and coral-colored knees. They saw the dirt. "Get down if you want to play me mumblety-peg," was all she said, "and watch out for your hands and faces."

They huddled down on the piney sand. The vivid, hurrying ants were everywhere. To the squinted eye they looked like angry, orange ponies as they rode the pine needles. There was Geneva, skirting behind a tree, but she never came close or tried to get in the game. She pretended to be catching doodlebugs. The knife leaped and quivered in the sandy arena smoothed by Easter's hand.

"I may not know how to play, but I bet I win," Jinny Love said.

Easter's eyes, lifting up, were neither brown nor green nor cat; they had something of metal, flat ancient metal, so that you could not see into them. Nina's grandfather had possessed a box of coins from Greece and Rome. Easter's eyes could have come from Greece or Rome that day. Jinny Love stopped short of apprehending this, and only took care to watch herself when Easter pitched the knife. The color in Easter's eyes could have been found somewhere, away—away, under lost leaves—strange as the painted color of the ants.

Instead of round black holes in the center of her eyes, there might have been women's heads, ancient.

Easter, who had played so often, won. She nodded and accepted Jinny Love's barrette and from Nina a blue jay feather which she transferred to her own ear.

"I wouldn't be surprised if you cheated, and don't know what you had to lose if you lost," said Jinny Love thoughtfully but with an admiration almost fantastic in her.

Victory with a remark attached did not crush Easter at all, or she scarcely listened. Her indifference made Nina fall back and listen to the spring running with an endless sound and see how the July light like purple and yellow birds kept flickering under the trees when the wind blew. Easter turned her head and the new feather on her head shone changeably. A black funnel of bees passed through the air, throwing a funneled shadow, like a visitor from nowhere, another planet.

"We have to play again to see whose the drinking cup will be," Easter said, swaying forward on her knees.

Nina jumped to her feet and did a cartwheel. Against the spinning green and blue her heart pounded as heavily as she touched lightly.

"You ruined the game," Jinny Love informed Easter. "You don't know Nina." She gathered up her cards. "You'd think it was made of fourteen-carat gold, and didn't come out of the pocket of an old suitcase, that cup."

"I'm sorry," said Nina sincerely.

As the three were winding around the lake, a bird flying above the opposite shore kept uttering a cry and then diving deep, plunging into the trees there, and soaring to cry again.

"Hear him?" one of the niggers said, fishing on the bank; it was Elberta's sister Twosie, who spoke as if a long, long conversation had been going on, into which she would intrude only the mildest words. "Know why? Know why, in de sky, he say 'Spirit? Spirit?' And den he dive *boom* and say 'GHOST'?"

"Why does he?" said Jinny Love, in a voice of objection.

"Yawl knows. *I* don't know," said Twosie, in her little high, helpless voice, and she shut her eyes. They couldn't seem to get on by her. On fine days there is danger of some sad meeting, the positive danger of it. "*I* don't know what he say dat for." Twosie spoke pitifully, as though accused. She sighed. "Yawl sho ain't got yo' eyes opem good, yawl. Yawl don't know what's out here in woods wid you."

"Well, what?"

"Yawl walk right by mans wid great big gun, could jump out at yawl. Yawl don't eem smellim."

"You mean Mr. Holifield? That's a flashlight he's got." Nina looked at Jinny Love for confirmation. Mr. Holifield was their handy man, or rather simply "the man to be sure and have around the camp." He could be found by beating for a long time on the porch of the American Legion boat house—he slept heavily. "He hasn't got a gun to jump out with."

"I know who you mean. I hear those boys. Just some big boys, like the MacLain twins or somebody, and who cares about them?" Jinny Love with her switch indented the thick mat of hair on Twosie's head and prodded and stirred it gently. She pretended to fish in Twosie's woolly head. "Why ain't *you* scared, then?"

"I is."

Twosie's eyelids fluttered. Already she seemed to be fishing in her night's sleep. While they gazed at her crouched, devoted figure, from which the long pole hung, so steady and beggarlike and ordained an appendage, all their passions flew home again and went huddled and soft to roost.

Back at the camp, Jinny Love told Miss Moody about the great big jack-knife. Easter gave it up.

"I didn't mean you couldn't *drink* out of my cup," Nina said, waiting for her. "Only you have to hold it carefully, it leaks. It's engraved."

Easter wouldn't even try it, though Nina dangled it on its ring right under her eyes. She didn't say anything,

not even "It's pretty." Was she even thinking of it? Or if
not, what did she think about?

"Sometimes orphans act like deaf-and-dumbs," said
Jinny Love.

III

"Nina!" Jinny Love whispered across the tent, during
siesta. "What do you think you're reading?"

Nina closed *The Re-Creation of Brian Kent*. Jinny
Love was already coming directly across the almost-
touching cots to Nina's, walking on her knees and bearing down over Gertrude, Etoile, and now Geneva.

With Jinny Love upon her, Geneva sighed. Her sleeping face looked as if she didn't want to. She slept as she
swam, in her pantie-waist, she was in running position
and her ribs went up and down frantically—a little box
in her chest that expanded and shut without a second's
rest between. Her cheek was pearly with afternoon mois-
ture and her kitten-like teeth pearlier still. As Jinny
Love hid her and went over, Nina seemed to see her
still; even her vaccination mark looked too big for her.

Nobody woke up from being walked over, but after
Jinny Love had fallen in bed with Nina, Easter gave a
belated, dreaming sound. She had not even been in the
line of march; she slept on the cot by the door, curved
shell-like, both arms forward over her head. It was an
inward sound she gave—now it came again—of such
wholehearted and fateful concurrence with the thing
dreamed, that Nina and Jinny Love took hands and
made wry faces at each other.

Beyond Easter's cot the corona of afternoon flared
and lifted in an intensity that came through the eyelids.
There was nothing but light out there. True, the black
Negroes inhabited it. Elberta moved slowly through it,
as if she rocked a baby with her hips, carrying a bucket
of scraps to throw in the lake—to get hail Columbia for
it later. Her straw hat spiraled rings of orange and
violet, like a top. Far, far down a vista of intolerable
light, a tiny daub of black cotton, Twosie had stationed
herself at the edge of things, and slept and fished.

Eventually there was Exum wandering with his fish

pole—he could dance on a dime, Elberta said, he used to work for a blind man. Exum was smart for twelve years old; too smart. He found that hat he wore—not a sign of the owner. He had a hat like new, filled out a little with peanut shells inside the band to correct the size, and he like a little black peanut in it. It stood up and away from his head all around, and seemed only following him—on runners, perhaps, like those cartridges for change in Spights' store.

Easter's sighs and her prolonged or half-uttered words now filled the tent, just as the heat filled it. Her words fell in threes, Nina observed, like the mourning-dove's call in the woods.

Nina and Jinny Love lay speechless, doubling for themselves the already strong odor of Sweet Dreams Mosquito Oil, in a trance of endurance through the hour's siesta. Entwined, they stared—orphan-like themselves—past Easter's cot and through the tent opening as down a long telescope turned on an incandescent star, and saw the spiral of Elberta's hat return, and saw Exum jump over a stick and on the other side do a little dance in a puff of dust. They could hear the intermittent crash, splash of Loch Morrison using their lake, and Easter's voice calling again in her sleep, her unintelligible words.

But however Nina and Jinny Love made faces at they knew not what, Easter concurred; she thoroughly agreed.

The bugle blew for swimming. Geneva jumped so hard she fell off her cot. Nina and Jinny Love were indented with each other, like pressed leaves, and jumped free. When Easter, who had to be shaken, sat up drugged and stupid on her cot, Nina ran over to her.

"Listen. Wake up. Look, you can go in in my bathing shoes today."

She felt her eyes glaze with this plan of kindness as she stretched out her limp red shoes that hung down like bananas under Easter's gaze. But Easter dropped back on the cot and stretched her legs.

"Never mind your shoes. I don't have to go in the lake if I don't want to."

"You do. I never heard of that. Who picked you out? You do," they said, all gathering.

"You make me."

Easter yawned. She fluttered her eyes and rolled them back—she loved doing that. Miss Moody passed by and beamed in at them hovered around Easter's passive and mutinous form. All along she'd been afraid of some challenge to her counselorship, from the way she hurried by now, almost too daintily.

"Well, *I* know," Jinny Love said, sidling up. "I know as much as you know, Easter." She made a chant, which drove her hopping around the tent pole in an Indian step. "You don't have to go, if you don't want to go. And if it ain't so, you still don't have to go, if you don't want to go." She kissed her hand to them.

Easter was silent—but if she groaned when she waked, she'd only be imitating herself.

Jinny Love pulled on her bathing cap, which gave way and came down over her eyes. Even in blindness, she cried, "So you needn't think you're the only one, Easter, not always. What do you say to that?"

"I should worry, I should cry," said Easter, lying still, spread-eagled.

"Let's us run away from basket weaving," Jinny Love said in Nina's ear, a little later in the week.

"Just as soon."

"Grand. They'll think we're drowned."

They went out the back end of the tent, barefooted; their feet were as tough as anybody's by this time. Down in the hammock, Miss Moody was reading *The Re-Creation of Brian Kent* now. (Nobody knew whose book that was, it had been found here, the covers curled up like side combs. Perhaps anybody at Moon Lake who tried to read it felt cheated by the title, as applying to camp life, as Nina did, and laid it down for the next person.) Cat, the niggers' cat, was sunning on a post and when they approached jumped to the ground like something poured out of a bottle, and went with them, in front.

They trudged down the slope past Loch Morrison's

tent and took the track into the swamp. There they moved single file between two walls; by lifting their arms they could have touched one or the other pressing side of the swamp. Their toes exploded the dust that felt like the powder clerks pump into new kid gloves, as Jinny Love said twice. They were eye to eye with the finger-shaped leaves of the castor bean plants, put out like those gypsy hands that part the curtains at the back of rolling wagons, and wrinkled and coated over like the fortune-teller's face.

Mosquitoes struck at them; Sweet Dreams didn't last. The whining lifted like a voice, saying "I don't want . . ." At the girls' shoulders Queen Anne's lace and elderberry and blackberry thickets, loaded heavily with flower and fruit and smelling with the melony smell of snake, overhung the ditch to touch them. The ditches had dried green or blue bottoms, cracked and glazed—like a dropped vase. "I hope we don't meet any nigger men," Jinny Love said cheerfully.

Sweet bay and cypress and sweetgum and live oak and swamp maple closing tight made the wall dense, and yet there was somewhere still for the other wall of vine; it gathered itself on the ground and stacked and tilted itself in the trees; and like a table in the tree the mistletoe hung up there black in the zenith. Buzzards floated from one side of the swamp to the other, as if choice existed for them—raggedly crossing the sky and shadowing the track, and shouldering one another on the solitary limb of a moon-white sycamore. Closer to the ear than lips could begin words came the swamp sounds—closer to the ear and nearer to the dreaming mind. They were a song of hilarity to Jinny Love, who began to skip. Periods of silence seemed hoarse, or the suffering from hoarseness, otherwise inexplicable, as though the world could stop. Cat was stalking something at the black edge of the ditch. The briars didn't trouble Cat at all, it was they that seemed to give way beneath that long, boatlike belly.

The track serpentined again, and walking ahead was Easter. Geneva and Etoile were playing at her side, edging each other out of her shadow, but when they saw who was coming up behind them, they turned and ran tearing back towards camp, running at angles, like pullets, leaving a cloud of dust as they passed by.

"Wouldn't you know!" said Jinny Love.

Easter was going unconcernedly on, her dress stained green behind; she ate something out of her hand as she went.

"We'll soon catch up—don't hurry."

The reason orphans were the way they were lay first in nobody's watching them, Nina thought, for she felt obscurely like a trespasser. They, they were not answerable. Even on being watched, Easter remained not answerable to a soul on earth. Nobody cared! And so, in this beatific state, something came out of *her*.

"Where are you going?"

"Can we go with you, Easter?"

Easter, her lips stained with blackberries, replied, "It ain't my road."

They walked along, one on each side of her. Though they automatically stuck their tongues out at her, they ran their arms around her waist. She tolerated the closeness for a little while; she smelled of orphan-starch, but she had a strange pure smell of sweat, like a sleeping baby, and in her temple, so close then to their eyes, the skin was transparent enough for a little vein to be seen pounding under it. She seemed very tender and very small in the waist to be trudging along so doggedly, when they had her like that.

Vines, a magnificent and steamy green, covered more and more of the trees, played over them like fountains. There were stretches of water below them, blue-black, netted over with half-closed waterlilies. The horizontal limbs of cypresses grew a short, pale green scruff like bird feathers.

They came to a tiny farm down here, the last one possible before the muck sucked it in—a patch of cotton in flower, a house whitewashed in front, a clean-swept yard with a little iron pump standing in the middle of it like a black rooster. These were white people—an old woman in a sunbonnet came out of the house with a galvanized bucket, and pumped it full in the dooryard. That was an excuse to see people go by.

Easter, easing out of the others' clasp, lifted her arm halfway and turning for an instant, gave two waves of the hand. But the old woman was prouder than she.

Jinny Love said, "How would you all like to live there?"

Cat edged the woods onward, and at moments vanished into a tunnel in the briars. Emerging from other tunnels, he—or she—glanced up at them with a face more mask-like than ever.

"There's a short-cut to the lake." Easter, breaking and darting ahead, suddenly went down on her knees and slid under a certain place in the barbed wire fence. Rising, she took a step inward, sinking down as she went. Nina untwined her arm from Jinny Love's and went after her.

"I might have known you'd want us to go through a barbed wire fence." Jinny Love sat down where she was, on the side of the ditch, just as she would take her seat on a needlepoint stool. She jumped up once, and sat back. "Fools, fools!" she called. "Now I think you've made me turn my ankle. Even if I wanted to track through the mud, I couldn't!"

Nina and Easter, dipping under a second, unexpected fence, went on, swaying and feeling their feet pulled down, reaching to the trees. Jinny Love was left behind in the heartless way people and incidents alike are thrown off in the course of a dream, like the gratuitous flowers scattered from a float—rather in celebration. The swamp was now all-enveloping, dark and at the same time vivid, alarming—it was like being inside the chest of something that breathed and might turn over.

Then there was Moon Lake, a different aspect altogether. Easter climbed the slight rise ahead and reached the pink, grassy rim and the innocent open. Here it was quiet, until, fatefully, there was one soft splash.

"You see the snake drop off in the water?" asked Easter.

"Snake?"

"Out of that tree."

"You can have him."

"There he is: coming up!" Easter pointed.

"That's probably a different one," Nina objected in the voice of Jinny Love.

Easter looked both ways, chose, and walked on the pink sandy rim with its purpled lip, her blue shadow lolling over it. She went around a bend, and straight to an old gray boat. Did she know it would be there? It was in some reeds, looking mysterious to come upon and yet in place, as an old boat will. Easter stepped into it and hopped to the far seat that was over the water, and dropping to it lay back with her toes hooked up. She looked falling over backwards. One arm lifted, curved over her head, and hung till her finger touched the water.

The shadows of the willow leaves moved gently on the sand, deep blue and narrow, long crescents. The water was quiet, the color of pewter, marked with purple stobs, although where the sun shone right on it the lake seemed to be in violent agitation, almost boiling. Surely a little chip would turn around and around in it. Nina dropped down on the flecked sandbar. She fluttered her eyelids, half closed them, and the world looked struck by moonlight.

"Here I come," came Jinny Love's voice. It hadn't been long. She came twitching over their tracks along the sandbar, her long soft hair blowing up like a skirt in a play of the breeze in the open. "But I don't choose to sit myself in a leaky boat," she was calling ahead. "I choose the land."

She took her seat on the very place where Nina was writing her name. Nina moved her finger away, drawing a long arrow to a new place. The sand was coarse like beads and full of minute shells, some shaped exactly like bugles.

"Want to hear about my ankle?" Jinny Love asked. "It wasn't as bad as I thought. I must say you picked a queer place, I saw an *owl*. It smells like the school basement to me—peepee and old erasers." Then she stopped with her mouth a little open, and was quiet, as though something had been turned off inside her. Her eyes were soft, her gaze stretched to Easter, to the boat, the lake—her long oval face went vacant.

Easter was lying rocked in the gentle motion of the boat, her head turned on its cheek. She had not said hello to Jinny Love anew. Did she see the drop of water clinging to her lifted finger? Did it make a rainbow? Not to Easter: her eyes were rolled back, Nina felt. Her own hand was writing in the sand. Nina, Nina, Nina. Writing, she could dream that her self might get away from her—that here in this faraway place she could tell her self, by name, to go or to stay. Jinny Love had begun building a sand castle over her foot. In the sky clouds moved no more perceptibly than grazing animals. Yet with a passing breeze, the boat gave a knock, lifted and fell. Easter sat up.

"Why aren't we out in the boat?" Nina, taking a strange and heady initiative, rose to her feet. "Out there!" A picture in her mind, as if already furnished from an eventual and appreciative distance, showed the boat floating where she pointed, far out in Moon Lake with three girls sitting in the three spaces. "We're coming, Easter!"

"Just as I make a castle. *I'm* not coming," said Jinny Love. "Anyway, there's stobs in the lake. We'd be upset, ha ha."

"What do I care, I can swim!" Nina cried at the water's edge.

"You can just swim from the first post to the second post. And that's in front of camp, not here."

Firming her feet in the sucking, minnowy mud, Nina put her weight against the boat. Soon her legs were half hidden, the mud like some awful kiss pulled at her toes, and all over she tautened and felt the sweat start out of her body. Roots laced her feet, knotty and streaming. Under water, the boat was caught too, but Nina was determined to free it. She saw that there was muddy water in the boat too, which Easter's legs, now bright pink, were straddling. Suddenly all seemed easy.

"It's coming loose!"

At the last minute, Jinny Love, who had extracted

her foot from the castle with success, hurried over and climbed to the middle seat of the boat, screaming. Easter sat up swaying with the dip of the boat; the energy seemed all to have gone out of her. Her lolling head looked pale and featureless as a pear beyond the laughing face of Jinny Love. She had not said whether she wanted to go or not—yet surely she did; she had been in the boat all along, she had discovered the boat.

For a moment, with her powerful hands, Nina held the boat back. Again she thought of a pear—not the everyday gritty kind that hung on the tree in the backyard, but the fine kind sold on trains and at high prices, each pear with a paper cone wrapping it alone—beautiful, symmetrical, clean pears with thin skins, with snow-white flesh so juicy and tender that to eat one baptized the whole face, and so delicate that while you urgently ate the first half, the second half was already beginning to turn brown. To all fruits, and especially to those fine pears, something happened—the process was so swift, you were never in time for them. It's not the flowers that are fleeting, Nina thought, it's the fruits—it's the time when things are ready that they don't stay. She even went through the rhyme, "Pear tree by the garden gate, How much longer must I wait?"—thinking it was the pears that asked it, not the picker.

Then she climbed in herself, and they were rocking out sideways on the water.

"Now what?" said Jinny Love.

"This is all right for me," said Nina.

"Without oars?—Ha ha."

"Why didn't you tell me, then!— But I don't care now."

"You never are as smart as you think."

"Wait till you find out where we get to."

"I guess you know Easter can't swim. She won't even touch water with her foot."

"What do you think a *boat's* for?"

But a soft tug had already stopped their drifting. Nina with a dark frown turned and looked down.

"A chain! An old mean chain!"

"That's how smart you are."

Nina pulled the boat in again—of course nobody helped her!—burning her hands on the chain, and kneeling outward tried to free the other end. She could see now through the reeds that it was wound around and around an old stump, which had almost grown over it in places. The boat had been chained to the bank since maybe last summer.

"No use hitting it," said Jinny Love.

A dragonfly flew about their heads. Easter only waited in her end of the boat, not seeming to care about the disappointment either. If this was their ship, she was their figurehead, turned on its back, sky-facing. She wouldn't be their passenger.

"You thought we'd all be out in the middle of Moon Lake by now, didn't you?" Jinny Love said, from her lady's seat. "Well, look where we are."

"Oh, Easter! Easter! I wish you still had your knife!"

"—But let's don't go back yet," Jinny Love said on shore. "I don't think they've missed us." She started a sand castle over her other foot.

"You make me sick," said Easter suddenly.

"Nina, let's pretend Easter's not with us."

"But that's what *she* was pretending."

Nina dug into the sand with a little stick, printing "Nina" and then "Easter."

Jinny Love seemed stunned, she let sand run out of both fists. "But how could you ever know what Easter was pretending?"

Easter's hand came down and wiped her name clean; she also wiped out "Nina." She took the stick out of Nina's hand and with a formal gesture, as if she would otherwise seem to reveal too much, wrote for herself. In clear, high-waisted letters the word "Esther" cut into the sand. Then she jumped up.

"Who's that?" Nina asked.

Easter laid her thumb between her breasts, and walked about.

"Why, I call that 'Esther.' "

"Call it 'Esther' if you want to, I call it 'Easter.' "

"Well, sit down. . . ."

"And I named myself."

"How could you? Who let you?"

"I let myself name myself."

"Easter, I believe you," said Nina. "But I just want you to spell it right. Look—E-A-S—"

"I should worry, I should cry."

Jinny Love leaned her chin on the roof of her castle to say, "I was named for my maternal grandmother, so my name's Jinny Love. It couldn't be anything else. Or anything better. You see? Easter's just not a real name. It doesn't matter how she spells it, Nina, nobody ever had it. Not around here." She rested on her chin.

"I have it."

"Just see how it looks spelled right." Nina lifted the stick from Easter's fingers and began to print, but had to throw herself bodily over the name to keep Easter from it. "Spell it right and it's real!" she cried.

"But right or wrong, it's tacky," said Jinny Love. "You can't get me mad over it. All I can concentrate on out here is missing the figs at home."

" 'Easter' is real beautiful!" Nina said distractedly. She suddenly threw the stick into the lake, before Easter could grab it, and it trotted up and down in a crucible of sun-filled water. "I thought it was the day you were found on a doorstep," she said sullenly—even distrustfully.

Easter sat down at last and with slow, careful movements of her palms rubbed down the old bites on her legs. Her crest of hair dipped downward and she rocked a little, up and down, side to side, in a rhythm. Easter never did intend to explain anything unless she had to— or to force your explanations. She just had hopes. She hoped never to be sorry. Or did she?

"I haven't got no father. I never had, he ran away. I've got a mother. When I could walk, then my mother took me by the hand and turned me in, and I remember it. I'm going to be a singer."

It was Jinny Love, starting to clear her throat, who released Nina. It was Jinny Love, escaping, burrowing her finger into her castle, who was now kind, pretending Easter had never spoken. Nina banged Jinny Love on the head with her fist. How good and hot her hair was! Like hot glass. She broke the castle from her tender foot. She wondered if Jinny Love's head would break. Not at all. You couldn't learn anything through the head.

"Ha, ha, ha!" yelled Jinny Love, hitting back.

They were fighting and hitting for a moment. Then they lay quiet, tilted together against the crumbled hill of sand, stretched out and looking at the sky where now a white tower of cloud was climbing.

Someone moved; Easter lifted to her lips a piece of cross-vine cut back in the days of her good knife. She brought up a kitchen match from her pocket, lighted up, and smoked.

They sat up and gazed at her.

"If you count much on being a singer, that's not a very good way to start," said Jinny Love. "Even boys, it stunts their growth."

Easter once more looked the same as asleep in the dancing shadows, except for what came out of her mouth, more mysterious, almost, than words.

"Have some?" she asked, and they accepted. But theirs went out.

Jinny Love's gaze was fastened on Easter, and she dreamed and dreamed of telling on her for smoking, while the sun, even through leaves, was burning her pale skin pink, and she looked the most beautiful of all: she felt temptation. But what she said was, "Even after all this is over, Easter, I'll always remember you."

Off in the thick of the woods came a fairy sound, followed by a tremulous silence, a holding apart of the air.

"What's that?" cried Easter sharply. Her throat quivered, the little vein in her temple jumped.

"That's Mister Loch Morrison. Didn't you know he had a horn?"

There was another fairy sound, and the pried-apart, gentle silence. The woods seemed to be moving after it, running—the world pellmell. Nina could see the boy in the distance, too, and the golden horn tilted up. A few

minutes back her gaze had fled the present and this
scene; now she put the horn blower into his visionary
place.

"Don't blow that!" Jinny Love cried out this time,
jumping to her feet and stopping up her ears, stamping
on the shore of Moon Lake. "You shut up! We can
hear!—Come on," she added prosaically to the other
two. "It's time to go. I reckon they've worried enough."
She smiled. "Here comes Cat."

Cat always caught something; something was in his—
or her—mouth, a couple of little feet or claws bouncing
under the lifted whiskers. Cat didn't look especially
triumphant; just through with it.

They marched on away from their little boat.

IV

One clear night the campers built a fire up above the
spring, cooked supper on sticks around it, and after
stunts, a recitation of "How They Brought the Good
News from Ghent to Aix" by Gertrude Bowles, and the
ghost story about the bone, they stood up on the ridge
and poured a last song into the woods—"Little Sir
Echo."

The fire was put out and there was no bright point to
look into, no circle. The presence of night was beside
them—a beast in gossamer, with no shine of outline,
only of ornament—rings, earrings. . . .

"March!" cried Mrs. Gruenwald, and stamped down
the trail for them to follow. They went single file on the
still-warm pine needles, soundlessly now. Not far away
there were crackings of twigs, small, regretted crashes;
Loch Morrison, supperless for all they knew, was
wandering around by himself, sulking, alone.

Nobody needed light. The night sky was pale as a
green grape, transparent like grape flesh over each tree.
Every girl saw moths—the beautiful ones like ladies,
with long legs that were wings—and the little ones,
mere bits of bark. And once against the night, just before Little Sister Spights' eyes, making her cry out, hung
suspended a spider—a body no less mysterious than the
grape of the air, different only a little.

All around swam the fireflies. Clouds of them, trees of them, islands of them floating, a lower order of brightness—one could even get into a tent by mistake. The stars barely showed their places in the pale sky— small and far from this bright world. And the world would be bright as long as these girls held awake, and could keep their eyes from closing. And the moon itself shone—taken for granted.

Moon Lake came in like a flood below the ridge; they trailed downward. Out there Miss Moody would some- times go in a boat; sometimes she had a late date from town, "Rudy" Spights or "Rudy" Loomis, and then they could be seen drifting there after the moon was up, far out on the smooth bright surface. ("And she lets him hug her out there," Jinny Love had instructed them. "Like this." She had seized, of all people, Etoile, whose name rhymed with tinfoil. "Hands off," said Etoile.) Twice Nina had herself seen the silhouette of the canoe on the bright water, with the figures at each end, like a dark butterfly with wings spread open and still. Not to- night!

Tonight, it was only the niggers, fishing. But their boat must be full of silver fish! Nina wondered if it was the slowness and near-fixity of boats out on the water that made them so magical. Their little boat in the reeds that day had not been far from this one's wonder, after all. The turning of water and sky, of the moon, or the sun, always proceeded, and there was this magical hesita- tion in their midst, of a boat. And in the boat, it was not so much that they drifted, as that in the presence of a boat the world drifted, forgot. The dreamed-about changed places with the dreamer.

Home from the wild moonlit woods, the file of little girls wormed into the tents, which were hot as cloth pockets. The candles were lighted by Miss Moody, date- less tonight, on whose shelf in the flare of nightly reve- lation stood her toothbrush in the glass, her hand- painted celluloid powder box, her Honey and Almond cream, her rouge and eyebrow tweezers, and at the end of the line the bottle of Compound, containing true and false unicorn and the life root plant.

Miss Moody, with a fervent frown which precluded interruption, sang in soft tremolo as she rubbed the lined-up children with "Sweet Dreams."

> "Forgive me
> O please forgive me
> I didn't mean to make
> You cry!
> I love you and I need you—"

They crooked and bent themselves and lifted night-gowns to her silently while she sang. Then when she faced them to her they could look into the deep tangled rats of her puffed hair and at her eyebrows which seemed fixed for ever in that elevated line of adult pleading.

> "Do anything but don't say good-bye!"

And automatically they almost said, "Good-bye!" Her hands rubbed and cuffed them while she sang, pulling to her girls all just alike, as if girlhood itself were an infinity, but a commodity. ("I'm ticklish," Jinny Love informed her every night.) Her look of pleading seemed infinitely perilous to them. Her voice had the sway of an acrialist crossing the high wire, even while she sang out of the nightgown coming down over her head.

There were kisses, prayers. Easter, as though she could be cold tonight, got into bed with Geneva. Geneva like a little June bug hooked onto her back. The candles were blown. Miss Moody ostentatiously went right to sleep. Jinny Love cried into her pillow for her mother, or perhaps for the figs. Just outside their tent, Citronella burned in a saucer in the weeds—Citronella, like a girl's name.

Luminous of course but hidden from them, Moon Lake streamed out in the night. By moonlight sometimes it seemed to run like a river. Beyond the cry of the frogs there were the sounds of a boat moored somewhere, of its vague, clumsy reaching at the shore, those sounds that are recognized as being made by something sightless. When did boats have eyes—once? Nothing watched that their little part of the lake stayed roped off and protected; was it there now, the rope stretched frail-like between posts that swayed in mud? That rope was to mark how far the girls could swim. Beyond lay the deep part, some bottomless parts, said Moody. Here and there was the quicksand that stirred your footprint and kissed your heel. All snakes, harmless and harmful, were freely playing now; they put a trailing, moony division between weed and weed—bright, turning, bright and turning.

Nina still lay dreamily, or she had waked in the night. She heard Gertrude Bowles gasp in a dream, beginning to get her stomach ache, and Etoile begin, slowly, her snore. She thought: Now I can think, in between them. She could not even feel Miss Moody fretting.

The orphan! she thought exultantly. The other way to live. There were secret ways. She thought, Time's really short, I've been only thinking like the others. It's only interesting, only worthy, to try for the fiercest secrets. To slip into them all—to change. To change for a moment into Gertrude, into Mrs. Gruenwald, into Twosie —into a boy. To *have been* an orphan.

Nina sat up on the cot and stared passionately before her at the night—the pale dark roaring night with its secret step, the Indian night. She felt the forehead, the beaded stars, look in thoughtfully at her.

The pondering night stood rude at the tent door, the opening fold would let it stoop in—it, him—he had risen up inside. Long-armed, or long-winged, he stood in the center there where the pole went up. Nina lay back, drawn quietly from him. But the night knew about Easter. All about her. Geneva had pushed her to the very edge of the cot. Easter's hand hung down, opened outward. Come here, night, Easter might say, tender to a giant, to such a dark thing. And the night, obedient and graceful, would kneel to her. Easter's cal-loused hand hung open there to the night that had got wholly into the tent.

Nina let her own arm stretch forward opposite Easter's. Her hand too opened, of itself. She lay there a long time motionless, under the night's gaze, its black cheek, looking immovably at her hand, the only part of her now which was not asleep. Its gesture was like Easter's, but Easter's hand slept and her own hand knew—shrank and knew, yet offered still.

"Instead . . . me instead. . . ."

In the cup of her hand, in her filling skin, in the fingers' bursting weight and stillness, Nina felt it: compassion and a kind of competing that were all one, a single ecstasy, a single longing.'For the night was not impartial. No, the night loved some more than others, served some more than others. Nina's hand lay open there for a long time, as if its fingers would be its eyes. Then it too slept. She dreamed her hand was helpless to the tearing teeth of wild beasts. At reveille she woke up lying on it. She could not move it. She hit it and bit it until like a cluster of bees it stung back and came to life.

V

They had seen, without any idea of what he would do—and yet it was just like him—little old Exum toiling up the rough barky ladder and dreaming it up, clinging there monkeylike among the leaves, all eyes and wrinkled forehead.

Exum was apart too, boy and nigger to boot; he constantly moved along an even further fringe of the landscape than Loch, wearing the man's stiff straw hat brilliant as a snowflake. They would see Exum in the hat bobbing along the rim of the swamp like a fisherman's cork, elevated just a bit by the miasma and illusion of the landscape he moved in. It was Exum persistent as a little bug, inching along the foot of the swamp wall, carrying around a fishing cane and minnow can, fishing around the bend from their side of the lake, catching all kinds of things. Things, things. He claimed all he caught, gloating—dangled it and loved it, clasped it with suspicious glee—wouldn't a soul dispute him that? The Boy Scout asked him if he could catch an electric eel and Exum promised it readily—a gift; the challenge was a siesta-long back-and-forth across the water.

Now all rolling eyes, he hung on the ladder, too little to count as looking—too everything-he-was to count as anything.

Beyond him on the diving-board, Easter was standing —high above the others at their swimming lesson. She was motionless, barefooted, and tall with her outgrown, printed dress on her and the sky under her. She had not answered when they called things up to her. They splashed noisily under her calloused, coral-colored foot that hung over.

"How are you going to get down, Easter!" shouted Gertrude Bowles.

Miss Moody smiled understandingly up at Easter. How far, in the water, could Miss Parnell Moody be transformed from a schoolteacher? They had wondered. She wore a canary yellow bathing cap lumpy over her hair, with a rubber butterfly on the front. She wore a brassiere and bloomers under her bathing suit because, said Jinny Love, that was exactly how good she was. She scarcely looked for trouble, immediate trouble— though this was the last day at Moon Lake.

Exum's little wilted black fingers struck at his lips as if playing a tune on them. He put out a foolishly long arm. He held a green willow switch. Later they every one said they saw him—but too late. He gave Easter's heel the tenderest, obscurest little brush, with something of nigger persuasion about it.

She dropped like one hit in the head by a stone from a sling. In their retrospect, her body, never turning, seemed to languish upright for a moment, then descend. It went to meet and was received by blue air. It dropped as if handed down all the way and was let into the brown water almost on Miss Moody's crown, and went out of sight at once. There was something so positive about its disappearance that only the instinct of caution made them give it a moment to come up again; it didn't come up. Then Exum let loose a girlish howl and clung to the ladder as though a fire had been lighted under it.

Nobody called for Loch Morrison. On shore, he studiously hung his bugle on the tree. He was enormously barefooted. He took a frog dive and when he went through the air they noticed that the powdered-on dirt gave him lavender soles. Now he swam destructively into the water, cut through the girls, and began to hunt Easter where all the fingers began to point.

They cried while he hunted, their chins dropping into the brown buggy stuff and their mouths sometimes swallowing it. He didn't give a glance their way. He stayed under as though the lake came down a lid on him, at each dive. Sometimes, open-mouthed, he appeared with something awful in his hands, showing not them, but the world, or himself—long ribbons of green and terrible stuff, shapeless black matter, nobody's shoe. Then he would up-end and go down, hunting her again. Each dive was a call on Exum to scream again.

"Shut up! Get out of the way! You stir up the lake!" Loch Morrison yelled once—blaming them. They looked at one another and after one loud cry all stopped crying. Standing in the brown that cut them off where they waited, ankle-deep, waist-deep, knee-deep, chin-deep, they made a little V., with Miss Moody in front and partly obscuring their vision with her jerky butterfly cap. They felt his insult. They stood so still as to be almost carried away, in the pictureless warm body of lake around them, until they felt the weight of the currentless water pulling anyhow. Their shadows only, like the curled back edges of a split drum, showed where they each protruded out of Moon Lake.

Up above, Exum howled, and further up, some fulsome, vague clouds with uneasy hearts blew peony-like. Exum howled up, down, and all around. He brought Elberta, mad, from the cook tent, and surely Mrs. Gruenwald was dead to the world—asleep or reading— or she would be coming too, by now, capering down her favorite trail. It was Jinny Love, they realized, who had capered down, and now stood strangely signaling from shore. The painstaking work of Miss Moody, white bandages covered her arms and legs; poison ivy had appeared that morning. Like Easter, Jinny Love had no intention of going in the lake.

"Ahhhhh!" everybody said, long and drawn out, just as he found her.

Of course he found her, there was her arm sliding through his hand. They saw him snatch the hair of Easter's head, the way a boy will snatch anything he wants, as if he won't have invisible opponents snatching first. Under the water he joined himself to her. He spouted, and with engine-like jerks brought her in.

There came Mrs. Gruenwald. With something like a skip, she came to a stop on the bank and waved her hands. Her middy blouse flew up, showing her loosened corset. It was red. They treasured that up. But her voice was pre-emptory.

"This minute! Out of the lake! Out of the lake, out-out! Parnell! Discipline! March them out."

"One's drowned!" shrieked poor Miss Moody.

Loch stood over Easter. He sat her up, folding, on the shore, wheeled her arm over, and by that dragged her clear of the water before he dropped her, a wrapped bundle in the glare. He shook himself in the sun like a dog, blew his nose, spat, and shook his ears, all in a kind of leisurely trance that kept Mrs. Gruenwald off—as though he had no notion that he was interrupting things at all. Exum could now be heard shrieking for Miss Marybelle Steptoe, the lady who had had the camp last year and was now married and living in the Delta.

Miss Moody and all her girls now came out of the lake. Tardy, drooping, their hair heavy-wet and their rubber shoes making wincing sounds, they edged the shore.

Loch returned to Easter, spread her out, and then they could all get at her, but they watched the water lake in her lap. The sun like a weight fell on them. Miss Moody wildly ran and caught up Easter's ankle and pushed on her, like a lady with a wheelbarrow. The Boy Scout looped Easter's arms like sashes on top of her and took up his end, the shoulders. They carried her, looking for shade. One arm fell, touching ground. Jinny Love, in the dazzling bandages, ran up and scooped Easter's arm in both of hers. They proceeded, zigzag, Jinny Love turning her head toward the rest of them, running low, bearing the arm.

They put her down in the only shade on earth, after

all, the table under the tree. It was where they ate. The table was itself still mostly tree, as the ladder and diving board were half tree too; a camp table had to be round and barky on the underside, and odorous of having been chopped down. They knew that splintery surface, and the ants that crawled on it. Mrs. Gruenwald, with her strong cheeks, blew on the table, but she might have put a cloth down. She stood between table and girls; her tennis shoes, like lesser corsets, tied her feet solid there; and they did not go any closer, but only to where they could see.

"I got her, please ma'am."

In the water, the life saver's face had held his whole impatience; now it was washed pure, blank. He pulled Easter his way, away from Miss Moody—who, however, had got Easter's sash ends wrung out—and then, with a turn, hid her from Mrs. Gruenwald. Holding her folded up to him, he got her clear, and the next moment, with a spread of his hand, had her lying there before him on the table top.

They were silent. Easter lay in a mold of wetness from Moon Lake, on her side; sharp as a flatiron her hipbone pointed up. She was arm to arm and leg to leg in a long fold, wrong-colored and pressed together as unopen leaves are. Her breasts, too, faced together. Out of the water Easter's hair was darkened, and lay over her face in long fern shapes. Miss Moody laid it back.

"You can tell she's not breathing," said Jinny Love.

Easter's nostrils were pinched-looking like an old country woman's. Her side fell slack as a dead rabbit's in the woods, with the flowers of her orphan dress all running together in some antic of their own, some belated mix-up of the event. The Boy Scout had only let her go to leap onto the table with her. He stood over her, put his hands on her, and rolled her over; they heard the distant-like knock of her forehead on the solid table, and the knocking of her hip and knee.

Exum was heard being whipped in the willow clump; then they remembered Elberta was his mother. "You little black son-a-bitch!" they heard her yelling, and he howled through the woods.

Astride Easter the Boy Scout lifted her up between his legs and dropped her. He did it again, and she fell on one arm. He nodded—not to them.

There was a sigh, a Morgana sigh, not an orphans'. The orphans did not press forward, or claim to own or protect Easter any more. They did nothing except mill a little, and yet their group was delicately changed. In Nina's head, where the world was still partly leisurely, came a recollected scene: birds on a roof under a cherry tree; they were drunk.

The Boy Scout, nodding, took Easter's hair and turned her head. He left her face looking at them. Her eyes were neither open nor altogether shut but as if her ears heard a great noise, back from the time she fell; the whites showed under the lids pale and slick as watermelon seeds. Her lips were parted to the same degree; her teeth could be seen smeared with black mud.

The Boy Scout reached in and gouged out her mouth with his hand, an unbelievable act. She did not alter. He lifted up, screwed his toes, and with a groan of his own fell upon her and drove up and down upon her, into her, gouging the heels of his hands into her ribs again and again. She did not alter except that she let a thin stream of water out of her mouth, a dark stain down the fixed cheek. The children drew together. Life-saving was much worse than they had dreamed. Worse still was the carelessness of Easter's body.

Jinny Love volunteered once more. She would wave a towel over things to drive the mosquitoes, at least, away. She chose a white towel. Her unspotted arms lifted and criss-crossed. She faced them now; her expression quietened and became ceremonious.

Easter's body lay up on the table to receive anything that was done to it. If *he* was brutal, her self, her body, the withheld life, was brutal too. While the Boy Scout as if he rode a runaway horse clung momently to her and arched himself off her back, dug his knees and fists into her and was flung back careening by his own tactics, she lay there.

Let him try and try!

*

The next thing Nina knew was a scent of home, an adult's thumb in her shoulder, and a cry, "Now what?" Miss Lizzie Stark pushed in front of her, where her hips and black purse swung to a full stop, blotting out everything. She was Jinny Love's mother and had arrived on her daily visit to see how the camp was running.

They never heard the electric car coming, but usually they saw it, watched for it in the landscape, as out of place as a piano rocking over the holes and taking the bumps, making a high wall of dust.

Nobody dared tell Miss Lizzie; only Loch Morrison's grunts could be heard.

"Some orphan get too much of it?" Then she said more loudly, "But what's he doing to her? Stop that."

The Morgana girls all ran to her and clung to her skirt.

"Get off me," she said. "Now look here, everybody. I've got a weak heart. You all know that.—Is that *Jinny Love?*"

"Leave me alone, Mama," said Jinny Love, waving the towel.

Miss Lizzie, whose hands were on Nina's shoulders, shook Nina. "Jinny Love Stark, come here to me, Loch Morrison, get off that table and shame on you."

Miss Moody was the one brought to tears. She walked up to Miss Lizzie holding a towel in front of her breast and weeping. "He's our life saver, Miss Lizzie. Remember? Our Boy Scout. Oh, mercy, I'm thankful you've come, he's been doing that a long time. Stand in the shade, Miss Lizzie."

"Boy Scout? Why, he ought to be—he ought to be—I can't stand it, Parnell Moody."

"Can't any of us help it, Miss Lizzie. Can't any of us. It's what he came for." She wept.

"That's Easter," Geneva said. "That is."

"He ought to be put out of business," Miss Lizzie Stark said. She stood in the center of them all, squeezing Nina uncomfortably for Jinny Love, who flouted her up in front, and Nina could look up at her. The white rice powder which she used on the very front of her face twinkled on her faint mustache. She smelled of red pepper and lemon juice—she had been making them some mayonnaise. She was valiantly trying to make up for all the Boy Scout was doing by what she was thinking of him: that he was odious. Miss Lizzie's carelessly flung word to him on sight—the first day—had been, "You little rascal, I bet you run down and pollute the spring, don't you?" "Nome," the Boy Scout had said, showing the first evidence of his gloom.

"Tears won't help, Parnell," Miss Lizzie said. "Though some don't know what tears are." She glanced at Mrs. Gruenwald, who glanced back from another level; she had brought herself out a chair. "And our last afternoon. I'd thought we'd have a treat."

They looked around as here came Marvin, Miss Lizzie's yard boy, holding two watermelons like a mother with twins. He came toward the table and just stood there.

"Marvin. You can put those melons down, don't you see the table's got somebody on it?" Miss Lizzie said. "Put 'em down and wait."

Her presence made this whole happening seem more in the nature of things. They were glad Miss Lizzie had come! It was somehow for this that they had given those yells for Miss Lizzie as Camp Mother. Under her gaze the Boy Scout's actions seemed to lose a good deal of significance. He was reduced almost to a nuisance—a mosquito, with a mosquito's proboscis. "Get him off her," Miss Lizzie repeated, in her rich and yet careless, almost humorous voice, knowing it was no good. "Ah, get him off her." She stood hugging the other little girls, several of them, warmly. Her gaze only hardened on Jinny Love; they hugged her all the more.

She loved them. It seemed the harder it was to get out here and the harder a time she found them having, the better she appreciated them. They remembered now —while the Boy Scout still drove up and down on Easter's muddy back—how they were always getting ready for Miss Lizzie; the tents even now were straight and the ground picked up and raked for her, and the tea for supper was already made and sitting in a tub in the lake; and sure enough, the niggers' dog had barked at the car just as always, and now here she was. She could have stopped everything; and she hadn't stopped it. Even her opening protests seemed now like part of things—what she was supposed to say. Several of the little girls looked up at Miss Lizzie instead of at what was on the table. Her powdered lips flickered, her eyelids hooded her gaze, but she was there.

On the table, the Boy Scout spat, and took a fresh appraisal of Easter. He reached for a hold on her hair and pulled her head back. No longer were her lips faintly parted—her mouth was open. It gaped. So did his. He dropped her, the head with its suddenness bowed again on its cheek, and he started again.

"Easter's dead! Easter's d—" cried Gertrude Bowles in a rowdy voice, and she was slapped rowdily across the mouth to cut off the word, by Miss Lizzie's hand.

Jinny Love, with a persistence they had not dreamed of, deployed the towel. Could it be owing to Jinny Love's always being on the right side that Easter mustn't dare die and bring all this to a stop? Nina thought, It's I that's thinking. Easter's not thinking at all. And while not thinking, she is not dead, but unconscious, which is even harder to be. Easter had come among them and had held herself untouchable and intact. Of course, for one little touch could smirch her, make her fall so far, so deep.—Except that by that time they were all saying the nigger deliberately poked her off in the water, meant her to drown.

"Don't touch her," they said tenderly to one another.

"Give up! Give up! Give up!" screamed Miss Moody —she who had rubbed them all the same, as if she rubbed chickens for the frying pan. Miss Lizzie without hesitation slapped her too.

"Don't touch her."

For they were crowding closer to the table all the time.

"If Easter's dead, I get her coat for winter, all right," said Geneva.

"Hush, orphan."

"Is she then?"

"You shut up." The Boy Scout looked around and panted at Geneva. "You can ast *me* when I ast you to ast me."

The niggers' dog was barking again, had been barking.

"Now who?"

"A big boy. It's old Ran MacLain and he's coming."

"He would."

He came right up, wearing a cap.

"Get away from me, Ran MacLain," Miss Lizzie called toward him. "You and dogs and guns, keep away. We've already got all we can put up with out here."

She put her foot down on his asking any questions, getting up on the table, or leaving, now that he'd come. Under his cap bill, Ran MacLain set his gaze—he was twenty-three, his seasoned gaze—on Loch and Easter on the table. He could not be prevented from considering them all. He moved under the tree. He held his gun under his arm. He let two dogs run loose, and almost imperceptibly, he chewed gum. Only Miss Moody did not move away from him.

And pressing closer to the table, Nina almost walked into Easter's arm flung out over the edge. The arm was turned at the elbow so that the hand opened upward. It held there the same as it had held when the night came in and stood in the tent, when it had come to Easter and not to Nina. It was the one hand, and it seemed the one moment.

"Don't touch her."

Nina fainted. She woke up to the cut-onion odor of Elberta's under-arm. She was up on the table with Easter, foot to head. There was so much she loved at home, but there was only time to remember the front yard. The silver, sweet-smelling paths strewed themselves behind the lawn mower, the four-o'clocks blazed. Then Elberta raised her up, she got down from the table, and was back with the others.

"Keep away. Keep away, I told you you better keep away. Leave me alone," Loch Morrison was saying with short breaths. "I dove for her, didn't I?"

They hated him, Nina most of all. Almost, they hated Easter.

They looked at Easter's mouth and at the eyes where they were contemplating without sense the back side of the light. Though she had bullied and repulsed them earlier, they began to speculate in another kind of allurement: was there danger that Easter, turned in on herself, might call out to them after all, from the other, worse, side of it? Her secret voice, if soundless then possibly visible, might work out of her terrible mouth like a vine, preening and sprung with flowers. Or a snake would come out.

The Boy Scout crushed in her body and blood came out of her mouth. For them all, it was like being spoken to.

"Nina, you! Come stand right here in my skirt," Miss Lizzie called. Nina went and stood under the big bosom that started down, at the neck of her dress, like a big cloven white hide.

Jinny Love was catching her mother's eye. Of course she had stolen brief rests, but now her white arms lifted the white towel and whipped it bravely. She looked at them until she caught their eye—as if in the end the party was for *her*.

Marvin had gone back to the car and brought two more melons, which he stood holding.

"Marvin. We aren't ready for our watermelon. I told you."

"Oh, Ran. How could you? Oh, Ran."

That was Miss Moody in still a third manifestation.

By now the Boy Scout seemed for ever part of Easter and she part of him, he in motion on the up-and-down and she stretched across. He was dripping, while her skirt dried on the table; so in a manner they had changed places too. Was time moving? Endlessly, Ran MacLain's dogs frisked and played, with the niggers' dog between.

Time was moving because in the beginning Easter's face—the curve of her brow, the soft upper lip and the milky eyes—partook of the swoon of her fall—the al-

207

most forgotten fall that bathed her so purely in blue for that long moment. The face was set now, and ugly with that rainy color of seedling petunias, the kind nobody wants. Her mouth surely by now had been open long enough, as long as any gape, bite, cry, hunger, satisfaction lasts, any one person's grief, or even protest.

Not all the children watched, and their heads all were beginning to hang, to nod. Everybody had forgotten about crying. Nina had spotted three little shells in the sand she wanted to pick up when she could. And suddenly this seemed to her one of those moments out of the future, just as she had found one small brief one out of the past; this was far, far ahead of her—picking up the shells, one, another, another, without time moving any more, and Easter abandoned on a little edifice, beyond dying and beyond being remembered about.

"I'm so tired!" Gertrude Bowles said. "And hot. Ain't you tired of Easter, laying up there on that table?"

"My arms are about to break, you all," and Jinny Love stood and hugged them to her.

"I'm so tired of Easter," Gertrude said.

"Wish she'd go ahead and die and get it over with," said Little Sister Spights, who had been thumb-sucking all afternoon without a reprimand.

"I give up," said Jinny Love.

Miss Lizzie beckoned, and she came. "I and Nina and Easter all went out in the woods, and I was the only one that came back with poison ivy," she said, kissing her mother.

Miss Lizzie sank her fingers critically into the arms of the girls at her skirt. They all rose on tiptoe. Was Easter dead then?

Looking out for an instant from precarious holds, they took in sharply for memory's sake that berated figure, the mask formed and set on the face, one hand displayed, one jealously clawed under the waist, as if a secret handful had been groveled for, the spread and spotted legs. It was a betrayed figure, the betrayal was over, it was a memory. And then as the blows, automatic now, swung down again, the figure itself gasped.

"Get back. Get back." Loch Morrison spoke between cruel, gritted teeth to them, and crouched over.

And when they got back, her toes webbed outward. Her belly arched and drew up from the board under her. She fell, but she kicked the Boy Scout.

Ridiculously, he tumbled backwards off the table. He fell almost into Miss Lizzie's skirt; she halved herself on the instant, and sat on the ground with her lap spread out before her like some magnificent hat that has just got crushed. Ran MacLain hurried politely over to pick her up, but she fought him off.

"Why don't you go home—now!" she said.

Before their eyes, Easter got to her knees, sat up, and drew her legs up to her. She rested her head on her knees and looked out at them, while she slowly pulled her ruined dress downward.

The sun was setting. They felt it directly behind them, the warmth flat as a hand. Easter leaned slightly over the table's edge, as if to gaze down at what might move, and blew her nose; she accomplished that with the aid of her finger, like people from away in the country. Then she sat looking out again; in another moment her legs dropped and hung down. The girls looked back at her, through the yellow and violet streams of dust—just now reaching them from Ran MacLain's flivver—the air coarse as sacking let down from the tree branches. Easter lifted one arm and shaded her eyes, but the arm fell in her lap like a clod.

There was a sighing sound from them. For the first time they noticed there was an old basket on the table. It held their knives, forks, tin cups and plates.

"Carry me." Easter's words had no inflection. Again, "Carry me."

She held out her arms to them, stupidly.

Then Ran MacLain whistled to his dogs.

The girls ran forward all together. Mrs. Gruenwald's fists rose in the air as if she lifted—no, rather had lowered—a curtain and she began with a bleating sound, "Pa-a-ack—"

"—up your troubles in your old kit bag
And smile, smile, smile!"

The Negroes were making a glorious commotion, all of them came up now, and then Exum escaped them all and ran waving away to the woods, dainty as a loosened rabbit.

"Who was he, that big boy?" Etoile was asking Jinny Love.

"Ran MacLain, slow-poke."

"What did he want?"

"He's just waiting on the camp. *They're* coming out tomorrow, hunting. I heard all he said to Miss Moody."

"Did Miss Moody *know* him?"

"Anybody knows him, and his twin brother too."

Nina, running up in the front line with the others, sighed—the sigh she gave when she turned in her examination papers at school. Then with each step she felt a defiance of her own. She screamed, "Easter!"

In that passionate instant, when they reached Easter and took her up, many feelings returned to Nina, some joining and some conflicting. At least what had happened to Easter was out in the world, like the table itself. There it remained—mystery, if only for being hard and cruel and, by something Nina felt inside her body, murderous.

Now they had Easter and carried her up to the tent, Mrs. Gruenwald still capering backwards and leading on,

"—in your old kit bag!
Smile, girls-instead-of-boys, that's the style!"

Miss Lizzie towered along darkly, groaning. She grabbed hold of Little Sister Spights, and said, "Can *you* brush me off!" She would be taking charge soon, but for now she asked for a place to sit down and a glass of cold water. She did not speak to Marvin yet; he was shoving the watermelons up onto the table.

Their minds could hardly capture it again, the way Easter was standing free in space, then handled and turned over by the blue air itself. Some of them looked back and saw the lake, rimmed around with its wall-within-walls of woods, into which the dark had already come. There were the water wings of Little Sister Spights, floating yet, white as a bird. "I know another Moon Lake," one girl had said yesterday. "Oh, my child, Moon Lakes are all over the world," Mrs. Gruenwald had interrupted. "I know of one in Austria . . ." And into each fell a girl, they dared, now, to think.

The lake grew darker, then gleamed, like the water of a rimmed well. Easter was put to bed, they sat quietly on the ground outside the tent, and Miss Lizzie sipped water from Nina's cup. The sky's rising clouds lighted all over, like one spread-out blooming mimosa tree that could be seen from where the trunk itself should rise.

VI

Nina and Jinny Love, wandering down the lower path with arms entwined, saw the Boy Scout's tent. It was after the watermelon feast, and Miss Lizzie's departure. Miss Moody, in voile and tennis shoes, had a date with old "Rudy" Loomis, and Mrs. Gruenwald was trying to hold the girls with a sing before bedtime. Easter slept; Twosie watched her.

Nina and Jinny Love could hear the floating songs, farewell-like, the cheers and yells between. An owl hooted in a tree, closer by. The wind stirred.

On the other side of the tent wall the slats of the Boy Scout's legs shuttered open and shut like a fan when he moved back and forth. He had a lantern in there, or perhaps only a candle. He finished off his own shadow by opening the flap of his tent. Jinny Love and Nina halted on the path, quiet as old campers.

The Boy Scout, little old Loch Morrison, was undressing in his tent for the whole world to see. He took his time wrenching off each garment; then he threw it to the floor as hard as he would throw a ball; yet that seemed, in him, meditative.

His candle—for that was all it was—jumping a little now, he stood there studying and touching his case of sunburn in a Kress mirror like theirs. He was naked and there was his little tickling thing hung on him like the last drop on the pitcher's lip. He ceased or exhausted study and came to the tent opening again and stood leaning on one raised arm, with his weight on one foot —just looking out into the night, which was clamorous.

It seemed to them he had little to do!

Hadn't he surely, just before they caught him, been pounding his chest with his fists? Bragging on himself? It seemed to them they could still hear in the beating air of night the wild tattoo of pride he must have struck off. His silly, brief, overriding little show they could well imagine there in his tent of separation in the middle of the woods, in the night. Minnowy thing that matched his candle flame, naked as he was with that, he thought he shone forth too. Didn't he?

Nevertheless, standing there with the tent slanting over him and his arm knobby as it reached up and his head bent a little, he looked rather at loose ends.

"We can call like an owl," Nina suggested. But Jinny Love thought in terms of the future. "I'll tell on him, in Morgana tomorrow. He's the most conceited Boy Scout in the whole troop; and's bowlegged.

"You and I will always be old maids," she added.

Then they went up and joined the singing.

The Bride of the Innisfallen

There was something of the pavilion about one raincoat, the way—for some little time out there in the crowd—it stood flowing in its salmony-pink and yellow stripes down toward the wet floor of the platform, expanding as it went. In the Paddington gloom it was a little dim, but it was parading through now, and once inside the compartment it looked rainbow-bright.

In it a middle-aged lady climbed on like a sheltered girl—a boost up from behind she pretended not to need or notice. She was big-boned and taller than the man who followed her inside bringing the suitcase—he came up round and with a doll's smile, his black suit wet; she turned a look on him; this was farewell. The train to Fishguard to catch the Cork boat was leaving in fifteen minutes—at a black four o'clock in the afternoon of that spring that refused to flower. She, so clearly, was the one going.

There was nobody to share the compartment yet but one girl, and she not Irish.

Over a stronghold of a face, the blue hat of the lady in the raincoat was settled on like an Indian bonnet, or, rather, like an old hat, which it was. The hair that had been pulled out of its confines was flirtatious and went into two auburn-and-gray pomegranates along her cheeks. Her gaze was almost forgiving, if unsettled; it held its shine so long. Even yet, somewhere, sometime, the owner of those eyes might expect to rise to a tragic occasion. When the round man put the suitcase up in the rack, she sank down under it as if something were now done that could not be undone, and with tender glances brushed the soot and raindrops off herself, somewhat onto him. He perched beside her—it was his legs that were short—and then, as her hands dropped into her bright-stained lap, they both stared straight ahead, as if waiting for a metamorphosis.

The American girl sitting opposite could not have taken in anything they said as long as she kept feeling it necessary, herself, to subside. As long as the train stood in the station, her whole predicament seemed betrayed by her earliness. She was leaving London without her husband's knowledge. She was wearing rather worn American clothes and thin shoes, and, sitting up very straight, kept pulling her coat collar about her ears and throat. In the strange, diminished light of the station people seemed to stand and move on some dark stage; by now platform and train must be almost entirely Irish in their gathered population.

A fourth person suddenly came inside the compartment, a small, passionate-looking man. He was with them as suddenly as a gift—as if an arm had thrust in a bunch of roses or a telegram. There seemed something in him about to explode, but—he pushed off his wet coat, threw it down, threw it up overhead, flung himself into the seat—he was going to be a good boy.

"What's the time?" The round man spoke softly, as if perhaps the new man had brought it.

The lady bowed her head and looked up at him: *she* had it: "Six minutes to four." She wore an accurate-looking wristwatch.

The round man's black eyes flared, he looked out at the rain, and asked the American if she, too, were going to Cork—a question she did not at first understand; his voice was very musical.

"Yes—that is—"

"Four minutes to four," the lady in the raincoat said, those fours sounding fated.

"You don't need to get out of the carriage till you get to Fishguard," the round man told her, murmuring it softly, as if he'd told her before and would tell her again. "Straight through to Fishguard, then you book a berth. You're in Cork in the morning."

She looked fondly as though she had never heard of Cork, wouldn't believe it, and opened and shut her great white heavy eyelids. When he crossed his knees she stole her arm through his and seesawed him on the seat. Holding his rows of little black-rimmed fingers together like a modest accordion, he said, "Two ladies going to Cork."

"Two minutes to four," she said, rolling her eyes.

"You'll go through the customs when you get to Fishguard," he told her. "They'll open your case and see what there is to detect. They'll be wanting to discover if you are bringing anything wrongly and improperly into the country." He eyed the lady, above their linked arms, as if she had been a stranger inquiring into the uses and purposes of customs inspection in the world. By ceasing to smile he appeared to anchor himself; he said solidly, "Following that, you go on board."

"Where you won't be able to buy drink for three miles out!" cried the new passenger. Up to now he had been simply drawing quick breaths. He had a neat, short, tender, slightly alarmed profile—dark, straight hair cut not ten minutes ago, a slight cut over the ear. But this still-bleeding customer, a Connemara man as he was now announcing himself, always did everything last-minute, because that was the way he was made.

There was a feel of the train's being about to leave. Then the guard was shouting.

The round man and the lady in the raincoat rose and moved in step to the door together, all four hands enjoined. She bent her head. Hers was a hat of drapes and shapes. There in the rainy light it showed a chaos of blue veil falling behind, and when it sadly turned, shining directly over the eyes was a gold pin in the shape of

a pair of links, like those you are supposed to separate in
amateur-magician sets. Her raincoat gave off a pepper-
mint smell that might have been stored up for this moment.

"You won't need to get out of the carriage at all," he
said. She put her head on one side. Their cheeks glittered as did their eyes. They embraced, parted; the man
from Connemara watched him out the door. Then the
pair clasped hands through the window. She might have
been standing in a tower and he elevated to her level as
far as possible by ladder or rope, in the rain.

There was a great rush of people. At the very last
minute four of them stormed this compartment. A little
boy flung in over his own bags, whistling wildly, paying
no attention to being seen off, no attention to feet
inside, consenting to let a young woman who had followed him in put a small bag of his in the rack and save
him a seat. She was being pelted with thanks for this by
young men and girls crowding at the door; she smiled
calmly back at them; even in this she was showing preg-
nancy, as she showed it under her calm blue coat. A
pair of lovers slid in last of all, like a shadow, and filled
two seats by the corridor door, trapping into the middle
the man from Connemara and somewhat crowding the
American girl into her corner. They were just not twin-
ing, touching, just not angry, just not too late. Without
the ghost of impatience or struggle, without shifting
about once, they were settled in speechlessness—two
profiles, his dark and cleared of temper, hers young,
with straight cut hair.

"Four o'clock."

The lady in the raincoat made the announcement in a
hollow tone; everybody in the compartment hushed as
though almost taken by surprise. She and the wistful
round man still clasped hands through the window and
continued to shine in the face like lighthouses smiling.
The outside doors were banged shut in a long retreat in
both directions, and the train moved. Those outside appeared running beside the train, then waving handkerchiefs, the young men shouting questions and envious
things, the girls—they were certainly all Irish, wildly

pretty—wildly retreating, their hair whipped forward in long bright and dark pennants by the sucking of the train. The round little man was there one moment and, panting, vanished the next.

The lady, still standing, was all at once very noticeable. Her body might have solidified to the floor under that buttoned cover. (What she had on under her raincoat was her own business and remained so.) The next moment she put out her tongue, at everything just left behind.

"*Oh* my God!" The man from Connemara did explode; it sounded like relief.

Then they were underway fast; the lady, having seated herself, smoothed down the raincoat with rattles like the reckless slamming of bureau drawers, and took from her purse a box of Players. She extracted a cigarette already partly burned down, and requested a light. The lover was so quick he almost anticipated her. When the butt glowed, her hand dropped like a shot bird from the flame he rather blindly stuck out. Between draws she held her cigarette below her knees and turned inward to her palm—her hand making a cauldron into which the little boy stared.

The American girl opened a book, but closed it. Every time the lady in the raincoat walked out over their feet—she immediately, after her cigarette, made several excursions—she would fling them a look. It was like "Don't say a word, start anything, fall into each other's arms, read, or fight, until I get back to you." She might both inspire and tantalize them with her glare. And she was so unpretty she ought to be funny, like somebody on the stage; perhaps she would be funny later.

The little boy whistled *"Funiculi, Funicula"* in notes almost too high for the ear to hear. On the windows it poured, poured rain. The black of London swam like a cinder in the eye and did not go away. The young wife, leaning back and letting her eyes fall a little while on the child, gave him dim, languorous looks, not quite shaking her head at him. He stopped whistling, but at the same time it could be felt how she was not his mother; her face showed degrees of maternity as other faces show degrees of love or anger; she was only acting his mother for the journey.

It was nice of her then to begin to sing *"Funiculi, Funicula,"* and the others joined, the little boy very seriously, as if he now hated the song. Then they sang something more Irish, about the sea and coming back. But the throb of the rails made the song oddly Spanish and hopelessly desirous; they were near the end of the car, where the beat was single and strong.

After the lady in the raincoat undid her top button and suggested "Wild Colonial Boy," her hatted head kept time, started to lead them—perhaps she kept a pub. The little boy, giving the ladies a meeting look, brought out a fiercely shining harmonica, as he would a pistol, and almost drowned them out. The American girl looked as if she did not know the words, but the lovers now sang, with faces strangely brave.

At some small, forgotten station a schoolgirl got on, took the vacant seat in this compartment, and opened a novel to page 1. They quieted. By the look of her it seemed they must be in Wales. They had scarcely got a word at the child before she began reading. She sat by the young wife; especially from her, the school hat hid the bent head like a candle snuffer; of her features only the little mouth, slightly open and working, stayed visible. Even her upper lip was darkly freckled, even the finger that lifted and turned the page.

The little boy sped his breath up the harmonica scale; the young wife said "Victor!" and they all felt sorry for him and had his name.

"Air," she suddenly said, as if she felt their look. The man from Connemara hurled himself at the window and slid the pane, then at the corridor door, and opened it wide onto a woman passing with an eight- or nine-months-old baby. It was a red-haired boy with queenly jowls, squinting in at the world as if to say, "Will what has just been said be very kindly repeated?"

"Oh, isn't he *beautiful!*" the young wife cried reproachfully through the door. She would have put out her hands.

There was no response. On they went.

"An English nurse traveling with an Irish child, look at that, he's so grand, and such style, that dress, that petticoat, do you think she's kidnaped the lad?" suggested the lady in the raincoat, puffing.

"*Oh* my God," said the man from Connemara.

For a moment the schoolgirl made the only sounds— catching her breath and sobbing over her book.

"Kidnaping's farfetched," said the man from Connemara. "Maybe the woman's deaf and dumb."

"I couldn't sleep this night thinking such wickedness was traveling on the train and on the boat with me." The young wife's skin flooded to her temples.

"It's not *your* fault."

The schoolgirl bent lower still and, still reading, opened a canvas satchel at her feet, in which—all looked—were a thermos, a lunchbox under lock and key, a banana, and a Bible. She selected the banana by feel, and brought it up and ate it as she read.

"If it's kidnaping, it'll be in the Cork paper Sunday morning," said the lady in the raincoat with confidence. "Railway trains are great systems for goings on of all kinds. You'll never take me by surprise."

"But this is *our* train," said the young wife. "Women alone, sometimes exceptions, but often on the long journey alone or with children."

"There's evil where you'd least expect it," the man from Connemara said, somehow as if he didn't care for children. "There's one thing and another, so forth and so on, run your finger down the alphabet and see where it stops."

"I'll never see the Cork paper," replied the young wife. "But oh, I tell you I would rather do without air to breathe than see that poor baby pass again and put out his little arms to me."

"Ah, then. Shut the door," the man from Connemara said, and pointed it out to the lover, who after all sat nearer.

"Excuse me," the young man whispered to the girl,

and shut the door at her knee and near where her small open hand rested.

"But why would she be kidnaping the baby *into* Ireland?" cried the young wife suddenly.

"Yes—you've been riding backwards: if we were going the other way, 'twould be a different story." And the lady in the raincoat looked at her wisely.

The train was grinding to a stop at a large station in Wales. The schoolgirl, after one paralyzed moment, rose and got off through the corridor in a dream; the book she closed was seen to be *Black Stallion of the Downs.* A big tall man climbed on and took her place. It was this station, it was felt, where they actually ceased leaving a place and from now on were arriving at one.

The tall Welshman drove into the compartment through any remarks that were going on and with great strength like a curse heaved his bag on top of several of theirs in the rack, where it had been thought there was no more room, and took the one seat without question. With serious sets of his shoulders he settled down in the middle of them, between Victor and the lady in the raincoat, facing the man from Connemara. His hair was in two corner bushes, and he had a full eye—like that of the horse in the storm in old chromos in the West of America—the kind of eye supposed to attract lightning. In the silence of the dreary stop, he slapped all his pockets—not having forgotten anything, only making sure. His hands were powdered over with something fairly black.

"Well! How far do *you* go?" he put to the man from Connemara and then to them in turn, and each time the answer came, "Ireland." He seemed unduly astonished.

He lighted a pipe, and pointed it toward the little boy. "What have you been doing in England, eh?"

Victor writhed forward and set his teeth into the strap of the outer door.

"He's been to a wedding," said the young wife, as though she and Victor were saying the same thing in two different ways, and smiled on him fully for the first time.

"Who got married?"

"Me brother," Victor said in a strangled voice, still holding on recklessly while the train, starting with a jerk, rocked him to the side.

"Big wedding?"

Two greyhounds in plaid blankets, like dangerously ecstatic old ladies hoping no one would see them, rushed into, out of, then past the corridor door which the incoming Welshman had failed to shut behind him. The glare in the eye of the man who followed, with his belt flying about him as he pulled back on the dogs, was wild, too.

"Big wedding?"

"Me family was all over the place if that's what you mean." Victor wildly chewed; there was a smell of leather.

"Ah, it has driven his poor mother to her bed, it was that grand a wedding," said the young wife. "That's why she's in England, and Victor here on his own."

"You must have missed school. What school do you go to—you *go* to school?" By the power of his eye, the Welshman got Victor to let go the strap and answer yes or no.

"School, yes."

"You study French and so on?"

"Ah, them languages is no good. What good is Irish?" said Victor passionately, and somebody said, "Now what does your mother tell you?"

"What ails your mother?" said the Welshman.

"Ah, it's her old trouble. Ask *her*. But there's two of me brothers at one end and five at the other."

"You're divided."

The young wife let Victor stand on the seat and haul her paper parcel off the rack so she could give him an orange. She drew out as well a piece of needlepoint, square and tarnished, which she spread over her pretty arm and hung before their eyes.

"Beautiful!"

" 'A Wee Cottage' is the name it has."

"I see the cottage. 'Tis very wee, and so's every bit about it."

" 'Twould blind you: 'tis a work of art."

"The little rabbit peeping out!"

"Makes you wish you had your gun," said the Welsh-man to Victor.

The young wife said, "Me grandmother. At eighty she died, very sudden, on a visit to England. God rest her soul. Now I'm bringing this masterpiece home to Ireland."

"Who could blame you."

"Well you should bring it away, all those little stitches she put in."

She wrapped it away, just as anyone could see her— as she might for the moment see herself—folding a blanket down into the crib and tucking the ends. Victor, now stained and fragrant with orange, leapt like a tiger to pop the parcel back overhead.

"No, I shouldn't think learning Irish would do you much good," said the Welshman. "No real language."

"Why not?" said the lady in the raincoat instantly. "I've a brother who is a very fluent Irish speaker and a popular man. You cannot doubt yourself that when the English hear you speaking a tongue they cannot follow, in the course of time they are due to start holding respect for you."

"From London you are." The Welshman bit down on his pipe and smoked.

"*Oh* my God." The man from Connemara struck his head. "I have an English wife. How would she like that, I wouldn't like to know? If all at once I begun on her in Irish! How would you like it if your husband would only speak to you in Irish? Or Welsh, my God?" He searched the eyes of all the women, and last of the young Irish sweetheart—who did not seem to grasp the question. "Aha ha ha!" he cried urgently and despair-ingly at her, asking her only to laugh with him.

But the young man's arm was thrust along the seat and she was sitting under its arch as if it were the entrance to a cave, which surely they all must see.

"Will you eat a biscuit now?" the young wife gently asked the man from Connemara. He took one wordlessly; for the moment he had no English or Irish. So she broke open another paper parcel beside her. "I have oceans," she said.

"Oh, *you wait*," said the lady in the raincoat, rising. And *she* opened a parcel as big as a barrel and it was full of everything to eat that anybody could come out of England with alive.

She offered candy, jam roll, biscuits, bananas, nuts, sections of bursting orange, and bread and butter, and they all in the flush of the hospitality and heat sat eating. Everybody partook but the Welshman, who had presumably had a dinner in Wales. It was more than ever like a little party, all the finer somehow, sadly enough, for the nose against the windowpane. They poured out tea from a couple of steaming thermoses; the black windows—for the sun was down now, never having been out of the fogs and rains all day—coated warmly over between them and what flew by out there.

"Could you tell me the name of a place to stay in Cork?" The American girl spoke up to the man from Connemara as he gave her a biscuit.

"In Cork? Ah, but you don't want to be stopping in Cork. Killarney is where you would do well to go, if you're wanting to see the wonders of Ireland. The lakes and the hills! Blue as blue skies, the lakes. That's where you want to go, Killarney."

"She wants to climb the Hill of Tara, you mean," said the guard, who with a burst of cold wind had entered to punch their tickets again. "All the way up, and into the raths, too, to lay her eyes by the light of candles on something she's never seen before; if that's what she's after. Have you never climbed the Hill and never crept into those, lady? Maybe 'twould take a little boost from behind, I don't know your size; but I think 'twould not be difficult getting you through." He gave her ticket its punch, with a keen blue glance at her, and banged out.

"Well, *I'm* going to the sitting in the dining car now." The lady in the raincoat stood up under the dim little lights in the ceiling that shone on her shoulders. Then down her long nose she suggested to them each to come, too. Did she really mean to eat still, and after all that largess? They laughed, as if to urge her by their shock to go on, and the American girl witlessly murmured, "No, I have a letter to write."

Off she went, that long coat shimmering and rattling. The little boy looked after her, the first sea wind blew in at the opened door, and his cowlick nodded like a dark flower.

"Very grand," said the Connemara man. "Very high and mighty she is, indeed."

Out there, nuns, swept by untoward blasts of wind, shrieked soundlessly as in nightmares in the corridors. It must be like the Tunnel of Love for them—the thought drifted into the young sweetheart's head.

She was so stiff! She struggled up, staggered a little as she left the compartment. All alone she stood in the corridor. A young man went past, soft fair mustache, soft fair hair, combing the hair—oh, delicious. Here came a hat like old Cromwell's on a lady, who had also a fur cape, a stick, flat turning-out shoes, and a heavy book with a pencil in it. The old lady beat her stick on the floor and made a sweet old man in gaiters and ribbon-tied hat back up into a doorway to let her by. All these people were going into the dining cars. She hung her head out the open corridor window into the Welsh night, which, seen from inside itself—her head in its mouth—could look not black but pale. Wales was formidable, barrier-like. What contours which she could not see were raised out there, dense and heraldic? Once there was a gleam from their lights on the walls of a tunnel, from the everlasting springs that the tunnelers had cut. Should they ever have started, those tunnelers? Sometimes there were sparks. She hung out into the wounded night a minute: let him wish her back.

"What do you do with yourself in England, keep busy?" said the man from Wales, pointing the stem of his pipe at the man from Connemara.

"I do, I raise birds in Sussex, if you're asking my hobby."

"A terrific din, I daresay. Birds keep you awake all night?"

"On the contrary. Never notice it for a minute. Of course there are the birds that engage in conversation rather than sing. I might be listening to the conversation."

"Parrots, you mean. You have parrots? You teach them to talk?"

"Budgies, man. Oh, I did have one that was a lovely talker, but curious, very strange and curious, in his habits of feeding."

"What was it he ate? How much would you ask for a bird like that?"

"Like what?"

"Parrot that could talk but didn't eat well, that you were just mentioning you had."

"That bird was an exception. Not for sale."

"Are you responsible for your birds?"

They all sat waiting while a tunnel banged.

"What do you mean responsible?"

"Responsible: you sell me a bird. Presently he doesn't talk or sing. Can I bring it back?"

"You cannot. That's God-given, lads."

"How old is the bird now? Good health?"

"Owing to conditions in England I could not get him the specialties he liked, and came in one morning to find the bird stiff. Still it's a nice hobby. Very interesting."

"Would you have got five pounds for this bird if you had found a customer for her? What was it the bird craved so?"

" 'Twas a male, not on the market, and if there had been another man, that would sell him to you, 'twould have cost you eight pounds."

"Ah. He ate inappropriate food?"

"You might say he *could not get* inappropriate food. He was destroyed by a mortal appetite for food you'd call it unlikely for a bird to desire at all. Myself, I never raised a bird that thrived so, learned faster, and had more to say."

"You never tried to sell him."

"For one thing I could not afford to turn him loose in

Sussex. I told my wife not to be dusting his cage without due caution, not to be talking to him so much herself, the way she did."

The Welshman looked at him. He said, "Well, he died."

"Pass by my house!" cried the man from Connemara. "And look in the window, as you'll likely do, and you'll see the bird—stuffed. You'll think he's alive at first. Open beak! Talking up to the last, like you or I that have souls to be saved."

"Souls: Is the leading church in Ireland Catholic, would you call Ireland a Catholic country?" The Welshman settled himself anew.

"I would, yes."

"Is there a Catholic church where you live, in your town?"

"There is."

"And you go?"

"I do."

"Suppose you miss. If you miss going to church, does the priest fine you for it?"

"Of course he does not! Father Lavery! What do you mean?"

"Suppose it's Sunday—tomorrow's Sunday—and you don't go to church. Would you have to pay a fine to the priest?"

The man from Connemara lowered his dark head; he glared at the lovers—for she had returned to her place. "Of course I would not!" Still he looked at the girl.

"Ah, in the windows black as they are, we do look almost like ghosts riding by," she breathed, looking past him.

He said at once, "A castle I know, you see them on the wall."

"What castle?" said the sweetheart.

"You mean what ghosts. First she comes, then he comes."

"In Connemara?"

"Ah, you've never been there. Late tomorrow night I'll be there. She comes first because she's mad, and he slow—got the dagger stuck in him, you see? Destroyed by her. She walks along, carries herself grand, not shy. Then he comes, unwilling, not touching with his feet— pulled through the air. By the dagger, you might say, like a hooked fish. Because they're a pair, himself and herself, sure as they was joined together—and while you look go leaping in the bright air, moonlight as may be, and sailing off together cozy as a couple of kites to start it again."

That girl's straight hair, cut like a little train to a point at the nape of her neck, her little pointed nose that came down in the one unindented line which began at her hair, her swimming, imagining eyes, held them all, like her lover, perfectly still. Love was amazement now. The lovers did not touch, for a thousand reasons, but that was one.

"Start what again?" said the Welshman. "Have you personally seen them?"

"I have, I'm no exception."

"Can you say who they might be?"

"Visit the neighborhood for yourself and there'll be those who can acquaint you with the gory details. Myself I'm acquainted with only the general idea of their character and disposition, formed after putting two and two together. Have you never seen a ghost, then?"

The Welshman gave a look as if he'd been unfairly struck, as if a question coming at him now in here was carrying things too far. But he only said, "Heard them."

"Ah, do keep it to yourself then, for the duration of the journey, and not go bragging, will you?" the young wife cried at him. "Irish ghosts are enough for some of us for the one night without mixing them up with the Welsh and them shrieking things, and just before all of us are going on the water except yourself."

"You don't mind the Lord and Lady Beagle now, do you? They shouldn't frighten you, they're lovely and married. Married still. Why, their names just come to me, did you hear that? Lord and Lady Beagle—like they sent in a card. Ha! Ha!" Again the man from Connemara tried to bring that singing laugh out of the frightened sweetheart, from whom he had not yet taken his glances away.

"Don't," the young wife begged him, forcing her eyes to his salver-like palm. "Those are wild, crazy names for ghosts."

"Well, what kind of ghosts do you think they ever are!" Their glances met through their laughter and remorse. She tossed her head.

"There ain't no ghosts," said Victor.

"Now suck this good orange," she whispered to him, as if he were being jealous.

"Here comes the bride," announced the Welshman.

"*Oh* my God." But what business was she of the Welshman's?

In came the lady in the raincoat beaming from her dinner, but he talked right around her hip. "Do you have to confess?" he said. "Regularly? Suppose you make a confession—swear words, lewd thoughts, or the like: *then* does the priest make you pay a fine?"

"Confession's free, why not?" remarked the lady, stepping over all their feet.

"You're a Catholic, too?" he said, as she hung above his knee.

And as they all closed their eyes she fell into his lap, right down on top of him. Even the dogs, now rushing along in the other direction, hung on the air a moment, their tongues out. Then one dog was inside with them. This greyhound flung herself forward, back, down to the floor, her tail slapped out like a dragon's. Her eyes gazed toward the confusion, and little bubbles of boredom and suspicion played under the skin of her jowls, puff, puff, puff, while wrinkles of various memories and agitations came and went on her forehead like little forks of lightning.

"Well, look what's with us," said the lover. "Here, lad, here, lad."

"That's Telephone Girl," said the lady in the raincoat, now on her feet and straightening herself with distant sweepings of both hands. "I was just in conversation with the keeper of those. Don't be getting her stirred up. She's a winner, he has it." She let herself down into the seat and spread a look on all of them as if she had always been too womanly for the place. Her mooning face turned slowly and met the Welshman's stern, strong glance: *he* appeared to be expecting some apology from some source.

" 'Tisn't everybody runs so fast and gets nothing for it in the end herself, either," said the lady. Telephone Girl shuddered, ate some crumbs, coughed.

"I'm ashamed to hear you saying that, she gets the glory," said the man from Connemara. "How many human beings of your acquaintance get half a dog's chance at glory?"

"You don't like dogs." The lady looked at him, bowing her head.

"They're not my element. That's not the way I'm made, no."

The man in charge rushed in, and out he and the dog shot together. Somebody closed the door; it was the Welshman.

"Now: what time of the night do you get to Cork?" he asked.

The lover spoke, unexpectedly. "Tomorrow morning." The girl let out a long breath after him.

"What time of the morning?"

"Nine!" shouted everybody but the American.

"Travel all night," he said.

"Book a berth in Fishguard!"

The mincing woman with the red-haired baby boy passed—the baby with his same fat, enchanted squint looked through the glass at them.

"Oh, I always get seasick!" cried the young wife in fatalistic enthusiastic tones, only distantly watching the baby, who, although he stretched his little hand against the glass, was not being kidnaped now. She leaned over to tell the young girl, "Let me only step off the train at Fishguard and I'm dying already."

"What do you usually do for an attack of seasickness when you're on the Cork boat?"

"*I* just stay in one place and never move, that's what *I* do!" she cried, the smile that had never left her sad, sweet lips turned upon them all. "I don't try to move at all and I die all the way." Victor edged a little away from her.

"The boat rocks," suggested the Welshman. Victor edged away from him.

"The *Innisfallen?* Of course she rocks, there's a far, wide sea, very deep and treacherous, and very historic." The man from Connemara folded his arms.

"It takes six weeks, don't you think?" The young wife appealed to them all. "To get over the journey. I tell me husband, a fortnight is never enough. Me husband is English, though. I've never liked England. I have six aunts all living there, too. Me mother's sisters." She smiled. "They all are hating it. Me grandmother died while she was in England."

His cheeks sunk on his fists, Victor leaned forward over his knees. His hair, blue-black, whorled around the cowlick like a spinning gramophone record; he seemed to dream of being down on the ground, and fighting somebody on it.

"God rest her soul," said the lady in the raincoat, as if she might have passed through the goods car and seen where Grandmother was riding with them, to her grave in Ireland; but in that case the young wife would have been with the dead, and not playing at mother with Victor.

"Then how much does the passage cost you? Fishguard to Cork, Cork back to Fishguard? I may decide to try it on holiday sometime."

"Where are you leaving us this night?" asked the young wife, still in the voice in which she had spoken of her grandmother and her mother's sisters.

He gave out a name to make her look more commiserating, and repeated, "What is the fare from Fishguard to Cork?"

They stopped just then at a dark station and a paper boy's voice called his papers into the train.

"*Oh* my God. Where are we!"

The Welshman put up his finger and called for a paper, and one was brought inside to him by a strange, dark child.

At the sight of the man opening his newspaper, the lady in the raincoat spoke promptly and with her lips wooden, like an actress. "How did the race come out?"

"What's that? Race? What race would that be?" He gave her that look he gave her the time she sat down on him. He stretched and rattled his paper without exposing it too widely to anybody.

She tilted her head. "Little Boy Blue, yes," she murmured over his shoulder.

A discussion of Little Boy Blue arose while he kept on reading.

"How much money at a time do you bet on the races?" the Welshman asked suddenly, coming out from behind the paper. Then as suddenly he retreated, taking back the question entirely.

"Now the second race," murmured the lady in the raincoat. Everybody wreathed in the Welshman. He was in the middle of the Welsh news, silent as the dead.

The man from Connemara put up a hand as the page might have been turned, "Long Gone the favorite! You were long gone yourself," he added politely to the lady in the raincoat. Possibly she had been punished enough for going out to eat and coming in to fall down all over a man.

"Yes I was," she said, lifting her chin; she brought out a Player and lighted it herself. She puffed. " 'Twas a long way, twelve cars. 'Twas a lovely dinner—chicken. One man rose up in the aisle when it was put before him and gave a cry, 'It's rabbit!' "

They were pleased. The man from Connemara gave his high, free laugh. The lovers were strung like bows in silent laughter, but the lady blew a ring of smoke, at which Victor aimed an imaginary weapon.

"A lovely, long dinner. A man left us but returned to the car to say that while we were eating they shifted the carriages about and he had gone up the train, down the train, and could not find himself at all." Her voice was so moody and remote now it might be some wandering of long ago she spoke to them about.

The Welshman said, over his paper, "Shifted the carriages?"

All laughed the harder.

"He said his carriage was gone, yes. From where he had left it: he hoped to find it yet, but I don't think he has. He came back the second time to the dining car and spoke about it. He laid his hand on the guard's arm. 'While I was sitting at the table and eating my dinner, the carriages have been shifted about,' he said. 'I wandered through the cars with the dogs running and cars with boxes in them, and through cars with human beings sitting in them I never laid eyes on in the journey —one party going on among some young people that would altogether block the traffic in the corridor.'"

"All Irish," said the young wife, and smoothed Victor's head; he looked big-eyed into space.

"The guard was busy and spoke to a third party, a gentleman eating. Yes, they were, all Irish. 'Will you mercifully take and show this gentleman where he is traveling, when you can, since he's lost?' 'Not lost,' he said, 'distracted,' and went through his system of argument. The gentleman said he could jolly well find his own carriage. The man opposite him rose up and that was when he declared the chicken was rabbit. The gentleman put down his knife and said man lost or not, carriage shifted or not, the stew rabbit or not, the man could just the same fight back to where he had come from, as he himself jolly well intended to do when he could finish the dinner on his plate in peace." She opened her purse, and passed licorice drops around.

"He sounds vulgar," said the man from Connemara.

"'Twas a lovely dinner."

"*You* weren't lost, I take it?" said the Welshman, accepting a licorice drop. "Traveled much?"

"Oh dear Heaven, traveled? Well, I have. Yes, no end to it."

"*Oh* my God."

"No, *I'm* never lost."

"Let's drop the subject," said the Welshman.

The lovers settled back into the cushions. They were the one subject nobody was going to discuss.

"Look," the young girl said in a low voice, from within the square of the young man's arm, but not to him. "I see a face that keeps going past, looking through the window. A man, plying up and down, could he be the one so unfortunate?"

"Not him, he's leading greyhounds, didn't we see him come in?" The young man spoke eagerly, to them all. "Leading, or they leading him."

" 'Tis a long train," the lady murmured to the Welshman. "The longest, most populated train leaving England, I would suppose, the one going over to catch the *Innisfallen*."

"Is that the name of the boat? You were glad to leave England?"

"It is and I was—pleased to be starting my journey, pleased to have it over." She gave a look at him—then at the others, the compartment, the tumbled baggage, everything. Outside, dim Wales clapped strongly at the window, like some accompanying bird. "I'll just lower the shade, will I?" she said.

She pulled at the window shade and fastened it down, and pulled down the door shade after it. The minute she did that, the window shade flew up, with a noise like a turkey.

They shouted for joy—they knew it! She *was* funny.

The train stopped and waited a long time in the dark, out from nowhere. They sat awhile, swung their feet; the man from Connemara whistled for a minute marvelously, Victor had his third orange.

"Suppose we're late!" shouted the man from Connemara. The mountains could hear him; they had opened the window to look out hoping to see the trouble, but could not. "And the *Innisfallen* sails without us! And we don't reach the other side in this night!"

"Then you'll all have to spend the night in Fishguard," said the Welshman.

"Oh, what a scene there'll be in Cork, when we don't arrive!" cried the young wife merrily. "When the boat sails in without us, oh poor souls."

Victor laughed harshly. He had made a pattern with his orange peel on the window ledge, which he now swept away.

"There's none too much room for the traveler in the town of Fishguard," said the Welshman over his pipe. "You'll do best to keep dry in the station."

"Won't they *die* of it in Cork?" The young wife cocked her head.

"Me five brothers will stand ready to give me a beating!" Victor said, then looked proud.

"I daresay it won't be the first occasion you've put in the night homeless in Fishguard."

"In Fishguard?" warningly cried the man from Connemara. A scowl lit up his face and his eyes opened wide with innocence. "Didn't you know this was the boat train you're riding, man?"

"Oh, is that what you call it?" said the Welshman in equal innocence.

"They *hold* the boat for us. I feel it's safe to say that every soul on board this train saving yourself is riding to catch the boat."

"Hold the *Innisfallen* at Fishguard Harbor? For how long?"

"If need be till doomsday, but we are generally sailing at midnight."

"No sir, we'll never be left helpless in Fishguard, this or any other night," said the lady in the raincoat.

"Or!" cried the man from Connemara. "Or! We could take the other boat if we're as late as that, to Rosslare, oh my God! And spend the Sunday bringing ourselves back to Cork!"

"You're going to Connemara to see your mother," the young wife said psychically.

"I'm sure as God's truth staying the one night in Cork first!" he shouted across at her, and banged himself on the knees, as if they were trying to take Cork away from him.

The Welshman asked, "What is the longest on record they have ever held the boat?"

"Who knows?" said the lady in the raincoat. "Maybe 'twill be tonight."

"Only can I get out now and see where we've stopped?" asked Victor.

"*Oh* my God—we've started! *Oh* that Cork City!"

"When you travel to Cork, do the lot of you generally get seasick?" inquired the Welshman. swaying among them as they got under way.

The lady in the raincoat made him a grand gesture with one hand, and rose and pulled down her suitcase. She opened it and fetched out from beneath the hot water bottle in pink flannel a little pasteboard box.

"What's that going to be—pills for seasickness?" he said.

She lifted the lid and passed the box under his eyes and then under their eyes, although too fast to be quite offering anything. " 'Tis a present," she said. "A present of seasick pills, given me for the journey."

The lovers smiled simultaneously, as they would at the thought of any present.

The train stopped again, started; stopped, started. Here on the outer edge of Wales it advanced and hesitated as rhythmically and as interminably as a needle in a hem. The wheels had taken on that defenseless sound peculiar to running near the open sea. Oil lamps burned in their little boxes at the halts; there was a pull at the heart from the feeling of the trees all being bent the same way.

"*Now* where?" They had stopped again.

A sigh escaped the lovers, who had drawn a breath of the sea. A single lamp stared in at their window, like the eye of a dragon lifted out of the lid of sleep.

"It's my station!" The Welshman suddenly addressed himself. He reared up, banged down the bushes on his head under a black hat, collected his suitcase and overcoat, and almost swept away with it the parcel with the "Wee Cottage" in it, belonging to the young wife. He got past them, dragging his suitcase with a great heave of the shoulder—God knew what was inside. He wrenched open the door, turned and looked at the lot of them, and then gently backed down into the outdoors.

Only to reappear. He had mistaken the station after all. But he simply held his ground there in the doorway, brazening it out as the train darted on.

"I may decide on raising my own birds some day," he said in a somewhat louder voice. "What did you begin with, a cock and a hen?"

On the index finger which the man from Connemara raised before he answered was a black fingernail, like

the mark of a hammer blow; it might have been a
reminder not to do something or other before he got
home to Ireland.

"I would advise you to begin with a cock and two
hens. Don't go into it without getting advice."

"What did you start with?"

"Six cocks—"

Another dark station, and down the Welshman
dropped.

"And six hens!"

It was almost too much that his face rose there *again*.
He wasn't embarrassed at himself, any more than he
was by how black and all impenetrable it was outside in
Wales, and asked, "Do you have to produce a passport
to go into Ireland?"

"Certainly, a passport or a travel card. *Oh* my God."

"What do you mean by a travel card? Let me see
yours. Every one of you carry one with you?"

Travel cards and passports were produced and
handed up to him.

"Oh, how beautiful your mother is!" cried the young
wife to Victor, over his shoulder. "Is that a wee straw-
berry mark she has there on her cheek?"

" 'Tis!" he cried in agony.

The Welshman was holding the American's different-
looking passport open in his hand; she looked startled,
herself, that she had given it up and at once, as if this
were required and he had waked her up in the night. He
read out her name, nationality, age, her husband's
name, nationality. It was not that he read it officially—
worse: as if it were a poem in the paper, only with the
last verse missing.

"My husband is a photographer. We've made a little
darkroom in our flat," she told him.

But he all at once turned back and asked the man
from Connemara, "And you give it as your opinion
your prize bird died of longings for food from far
away."

"There've been times when I've dreamed a certain
person may have had more to do with it!" the man from

Connemara cried in crescendo. "That I've never mentioned till now. But women are jealous and uncertain creatures, I've been thinking as we came this long way along tonight."

"Of *birds!*" cried the young wife, her fingers going to her shoulders.

"Name your poison."

"Why birds?"

"Why not?"

"Because it talked?"

"Name your poison."

Another lantern, another halt of the train.

"It'll be raining over the water," the Welshman called as he swung open his door. From the step he looked back and said, "What do you take the seasick pills in, have you drink to take them in?"

"I have."

He said out of the windy night, "Can you buy drink on board the ship? Or is it not too late for that?"

"Three miles out 'tis only the sea and glory," shouted the man from Connemara.

"Be good," the Welshman tossed back at him, and quite lightly he dropped away. He disappeared for the third time into the Welsh black, this time for keeps. It was as though a big thumb had snuffed him out.

They smoothed and straightened themselves behind him, all but the young lovers spreading out in the seats; she rubbed her arm, up and down. Not a soul had inquired of that poor vanquished man what he did, if he had wife and children living—he might have only had an auntie. They never let him tell what he was doing with himself in either end of Wales, or why he had to come on this very night, or even what in the world he was carrying in that heavy case.

As they talked, the American girl laid her head back, a faint smile on her face.

"Just one word of advice," said the man from Connemara in her ear, putting her passport, warm from his hand, into hers. "Be careful in future who you ask questions of. You were safe when you spoke to me, I'm a married man. I was pleased to tell you what I could—

go to Killarney and so forth and so on, see the marvelous beauty of the lakes. But next time ask a guard."

Victor's head tumbled against the watchful side of the young wife, his right hand was flung in her lap, a fist floating away. In Fishguard, they had to shake him awake and pull him out into the rain.

No traveler out of that compartment was, actually, booked for a berth on the *Innisfallen* except the lady in the raincoat, who marched straight off. Most third-class train passengers spent the night third-class in the *Innisfallen* lounge. The man from Connemara was the first one stretched, a starfish of exhaustion, on a cretonne-covered couch. The American girl stared at a page of her book, then closed it until they were under way. The lovers disappeared. In the deeps of night that bright room reached some vortex of quiet, like a room where all brains are at work and great decisions are on the brink. Occasionally there was a tapping, as of drumming fingernails—that meant to closed or hypnotized eyes that dogs were being sped through. The random, gentle old men who were walking the corridors in their tweeds and seemed lost as Jesus's lambs, were waiting perhaps for the bar to open. The young wife, as desperate as she'd feared, saw nothing, forgot everything, and even abandoned Victor, as if there could never be any time or place in the world but this of her suffering. She spoke to the child as if she had never seen him before and would never see him again. Victor took the last little paper of biscuits she had given him away to a corner and slowly emptied it, making a mountain of the crumbs; then he bent his head over his travel card with its new stamp, on which presently he rolled his cheek and floated unconscious.

Once the man from Connemara sat up out of his sleep and stared at the American girl pinned to her chair across the room, as if he saw somebody desperate who had left her husband once, endangered herself among strangers, been turned back, and was here for the second go-round, asking again for a place to stay in

Cork. She stared back motionless, until he was a starfish again.

Then it was morning—a world of sky coursing above, streaming light. The *Innisfallen* had entered the Lee. Almost at arm's reach were the buff, pink, gray, salmon fronts of houses, trees shining like bird wings, and bells that jumped toward sound as the ship, all silent, flowed past. The Sunday, the hour, too, were encroaching-real. Each lawn had a flag-like purity that braved and invited all the morning senses, even smell, as snow can—as if snow had fallen in the night, and this sun and this ship had come to trace it and melt it.

It was that passing, short, yet inviolate distance between ship and land on both sides that made an arrow-like question in the heart. Someone cried at random, "What town is this?" Any of them should have known, but the senses waked back home can fill too full, until black lines and framework vanish like names, leaving only shapes of light and color without knowledge or memory to inform them.

To wake up to the river, no longer the sea! There was more than one little town, that in their silent going they saluted while not touching or deviating to it at all. After the length of the ship had passed a ringing steeple, and the hands had glinted gold at them from the clockface, an older, harsher, more distant bell rang from an inland time: *now*.

Now sea gulls paced city lawns. *They* moved through the hedges, the ship in the garden. A thrush could be heard singing, and there he sang—so clear and so early it all was. On deck a little girl clapped her hands. "Why do you do that!" her brother lovingly encouraged her.

On shore a city street appeared, and now cars were following the ship along; passengers inside blew auto horns and waved handkerchiefs up and down. There was a sidewise sound of a harmonica, frantic, tiny and bold. Victor was up where he ought not to be on deck, handing out black frowns and tunes to the docks sliding into sight. Now he had to look out for his brothers.

Perhaps deep in the lounge his guardian was now sleeping at last, white and exhausted, inhumanly smiling in her sleep.

The lovers stood on the lower, more shaded deck—two backs. A line of sun was between them like a thread that could be picked off. One ought not yet to look into their faces, watching water. How far, how deep was this day to cut into their hearts? From now on everything would cut deeper than yesterday. Her wintry boots stiff from their London wet looked big on the ship, pricked with ears, at that brink of light they hung over. And suddenly she changed position—one shoe tapped, pointing, back of the other. She poised there. The boat whistle thundered like a hundred organ notes, but she did not quake—now as used to boat whistles as one of the sea gulls; or as far away.

"There's a bride on board!" called somebody. "Look at her, look!"

Sure enough, a girl who had not yet showed herself in public now appeared by the rail in a white spring hat and, over her hands, a little old-fashioned white bunny muff. She stood there all ready to be met, now come out in her own sweet time. Delight gathered all around, singing began on board, bells could by now be heard ringing urgently in the town. Surely that color beating in their eyes came from flags hung out up the looming shore. The bride smiled but did not look up; she was looking down at her dazzling little fur muff.

They were in, the water held still about them. The gulls converged; just under the surface a newspaper slowly went down with its drowned news.

In the crowd of the dock, the lady in the raincoat was being confronted with a flock of beautiful children—red flags in their cheeks, caps on their heads, little black boots like pipes—and by a man bigger than she was. He stood smoking while the children hurled themselves up against her. As people hurried around her carrying their bundles and bags in the windy bright of the Cork dock, she stood camouflaged like a sportsman in his own polychrome fields, a hand on her striped hip. Vague, luminous, smiling, her big white face held a moment and bent down for its kiss. The man from Connemara strode by, looking down on her as if now her head were in the basket. His cap set at a fairly desperate angle, he went leaping into the streets of Cork City.

Victor was shouting at the top of his lungs, "Here I am!" The young wife, coming forth old but still alive, was met by old women in cloaks, three young men to embrace her, and a donkey and cart to ride her home, once she had put Victor with his brothers.

Perhaps regardless of the joy or release of an arrival, or because of it, there is always for someone a last-minute, finger-like touch, a reminder, a promise of confusion. Behind shut lids the American girl saw the customs' chalk mark just now scrawled on the wall of her suitcase. Like a gypsy's sign found on her own front door, it stared at her from the sensitized optic dark, and she felt exposed—as if, in spite of herself, when she didn't know it, something had been told on her. "A rabbit ran over my grave," she thought. She left her suitcase in the parcel room and walked out into Cork.

When it rained late in that afternoon, the American girl was still in Cork, and stood sheltering in the doorway of a pub. She was listening to the pub sounds and the alley sounds as she might to a garden's and a fountain's.

She had had her day, her walk, that began at the red, ferny, echo-hung rock against which the lowest houses were set, where the ocean-river sent up signals of mirrored light. She had walked the hill and crossed the swan-bright bridges, her way wound in among people busy at encounters, meetings, it seemed to her reunions. After church in the streets of Cork dozens of little girls in confirmation dresses, squared off by their veils into animated paper snowflakes, raced and danced out of control and into charmed traffic—like miniature and more conscious brides. The trees had almost rushed with light and blossom; they nearly had sound, as the bells did. Boughs that rocked on the hill were tipped and weighted as if with birds, which were really their own bursting and almost-bursting leaves. In all Cork today every willow stood with gold-red hair springing and falling about it, like Venus alive. Rhododendrons swam in light, leaves and flowers alike; only a shadow could separate them into colors. She had felt no lonelier than that little bride herself, who had come off the boat. Yes, somewhere in the crowd at the dock there must have been a young man holding flowers: he had been taken for granted.

In the future would the light, that had jumped like the man from Connemara into the world, be a memory, like that of a meeting, or must there be mere faith that it had been like that?

Shielding the telegraph-form from her fellow writers at the post-office table, she printed out to her husband in England, "England was a mistake." At once she scratched that out, and took back the blame but without words.

Love with the joy being drawn out of it like anything else that aches—that was loneliness; not this. *I* was nearly destroyed, she thought, and again was threatened with a light head, a rush of laughter, as when the Welshman had come so far with them and then let them off.

If she could never tell her husband her secret, perhaps she would never tell it at all. You must never betray pure joy—the kind you were born and began with—either by hiding it or by parading it in front of people's eyes; they didn't want to be shown it. And still you must tell it. Is there no way? she thought—for here I am, this far. I see Cork's streets take off from the waterside and rise lifting their houses and towers like note above note on a page of music, with arpeggios running over it of green and galleries and belvederes, and the bright sun raining at the top. Out of the joy I hide for fear it is promiscuous, I may walk for ever at the fall of evening by the river, and find this river street by the red rock, this first, last house, that's perhaps a boarding house now, standing full-face to the tide, and look up to that window—that upper window, from which the mystery will never go. The curtains dyed so many times over are still pulled back and the window looks out open to the evening, the river, the hills, and the sea.

For a moment someone—she thought it was a woman—came and stood at the window, then hurled a cigarette with its live coal down into the extinguishing garden. But it was not the impatient tenant, it was the window itself that could tell her all she had come here to know—or all she could bear this evening to know, and that was light and rain, light and rain, dark, light, and rain.

"Don't expect me back yet" was all she need say tonight in the telegram. What was always her trouble? "You hope for too much," he said.

When early this morning the bride smiled, it might almost have been for her photograph; but she still did not look up—as though if even her picture were taken, she would vanish. And now she had vanished.

Walking on through the rainy dusk, the girl again took shelter in the warm doorway of the pub, holding her message, unfinished and unsent.

"Ah, it's a heresy, I told him," a man inside was shouting, out of the middle of his story. A barmaid glimmered through the passage in her frill, a glad cry went up at her entrance, as if she were the heresy herself, and when they all called out something fresh it was like the signal for a song.

The girl let her message go into the stream of the street, and opening the door walked into the lovely room full of strangers.